# The Knight
# Before Christmas

## MARILYN BRANT

Twelfth Night
Publishing

The Knight Before Christmas
Copyright © 2019 Marilyn B. Weigel
Twelfth Night Publishing

All rights reserved.

Editor - Hamilton Editing
Proofreader - Kimberly Dawn
ISBN-13: 978-0-9983964-9-1

# DEDICATION & THANKS

*Thanks, as always, to my family and my wonderful readers. Extra-special love and appreciation to my early reviewers & my book club friends—you're the best. This story is for YOU!*

# OTHER BOOKS BY MARILYN BRANT

According to Jane

Friday Mornings at Nine

A Summer in Europe

The Sweet Temptations Collection
~On Any Given Sundae
~Double Dipping
~Holiday Man

The Perfect Pair
~Pride, Prejudice and the Perfect Match
~Pride, Prejudice and the Perfect Bet

The Road to You
The Road and Beyond (expanded edition)

All About Us (novella)

The Mirabelle Harbor Series
~Take a Chance on Me
~The One That I Want
~You Give Love a Bad Name
~Stranger on the Shore
~One Night Love Affair
~Coming Home
~Going For It

Wanderlust in Suburbia (nonfiction essays)

# Prologue

## *Twenty Years Ago ~ Crystal Corners, Minnesota*

Six-year-old Emma Westwood watched the TV screen with breathless anticipation as the man in shining silver armor galloped on horseback across the English countryside. A beautiful woman came into view at the edge of the forest, and the knight locked eyes with his lady.

Without a word, he rode straight to her, seemingly oblivious to the sounds of swords clanking around him and warring men shouting in the distance. He held his strong hand out to her, and when she grasped it, he effortlessly tugged her closer, cinched her waist, and lifted her up onto his white steed, setting her down protectively in front of him.

"You're safe now, milady," he whispered, holding her tight. "To the castle we go."

"Thank you, sir," she said, leaning back against him, and despite all the metal he was wearing, somehow she made their embrace look comfortable.

1

Emma sighed happily, her young heart flooded with pure joy at this final scene. It was just *so* romantic! Knights. Castles. Damsels in distress. Golden goblets. Silver swords. Strong horses. What could be cooler?

As the ending credits rolled, she smoothed out the velvet ruffles on her new Christmas dress, snapped off her bedroom TV, and prepared to join her parents and family guests downstairs for the delicious Christmas Eve dinner that awaited them.

As an only child, and the youngest of the cousins by far, Emma had grown quite used to being indulged and having her whims and hobbies honored. She had huge posters of magnificent horses decorating her bedroom, a model castle that she'd received for her last birthday, which took up a sizable portion of the downstairs playroom, and shelves of stunningly illustrated storybooks in their family library about the adventures of Sir Lancelot and Lady Guinevere in the land of King Arthur and his brave men.

Her parents had even given her an exquisite princess gown that she'd worn for Halloween a couple of months ago, along with a pointy pale-pink hat with white tulle and lacy ribbons flowing out of the top. She was a lucky girl, and she knew it.

But there was something she didn't yet have, and truth be told, even as a first grader, Emma knew she'd never be completely happy until she got it.

She flounced to her desk, pulled out a sheet of her finest stationery—the cream-colored ones that her Auntie Barbara had ordered for her with her name embossed in fancy gold script at the top—and reached for her faux quill pen.

*Dear Santa,* she began in her best penmanship.

*I know Christmas is tomorrow, and I'm sorry for the last-minute request, but I think you already know what I want. Please bring me a knight. Soon.*

*Thanks!*

*Love, Emma*

The next morning, Emma awoke to a snowy Christmas Day, and she raced downstairs to open her presents.

There were at least a dozen new packages of various shapes and sizes, in addition to all of the gifts she'd already received. Her entire immediate and extended family could afford to be generous, and without fail, they were.

There were also several large presents from Santa Claus. But, despite Emma's disappointment in not finding Sir Lancelot himself sitting under the tree with a red bow on his head, there was one inconspicuous box hidden behind the other gifts that just looked...well, a little different from the rest.

She saved it for last. The tag simply read: *TO EMMA FROM SANTA.*

And when, finally, she pulled back the holly-print wrapping paper and curly green ribbons, lifted the lid on the box, and unearthed the heavy item from the mass of white tissue paper, she was rewarded with the loveliest gift she'd ever seen. A metal statuette—wonderfully crafted and filling both of her palms with beauty. The figurine featured a handsome knight on horseback brandishing a silver sword.

*Her* knight.

She turned the object every which way, examining the man and his steed from each possible angle. So gorgeous! She clasped the statuette to her chest. "Thank you, Santa," she whispered.

One day, though, she wanted a real-life knight.

And with the certainty of someone well accustomed to getting what she desired, young Emma Westwood figured it was only a matter of time until her fantasy became a reality.

# One

**Present Day ~ Two Weeks to Christmas**

Clearly, chivalry was a lost art in this world.

Emma narrowed her blue eyes at the broad-shouldered, dark-haired man a few feet away in the produce aisle. The one who'd just stolen her shopping cart.

The cart in question didn't exactly have her name etched on it, but it was the *last* one left by the rack, and he'd nabbed it a mere five seconds before she could get to it. Now she'd have to make do with a tiny plastic basket to carry her purchases or, worse, struggle to hold everything she needed *herself* until she got to the register.

She huffed, crossed her arms, and stared at the man even harder, but he didn't meet her gaze, let alone give up the cart. How ill-mannered of him!

She nearly stamped her foot. Would that get his attention? (Probably not.)

The First Street Market, the only grocery store in Crystal Corners, Minnesota, had many advantages, but their major drawback was that they tended to have more customers than carts, especially during the busy holiday season.

Until today, however, this had never been a problem for Emma personally. She'd always scored a cart and was patently unused to being unnoticed—especially by men.

Perhaps she'd never been overcome to the point of swooning by the etiquette of the guys of her acquaintance, but the vast majority of them at least *tried* to be gentlemanly when they saw her. If they were, for instance, to spot her desperately scanning the grocery store for a cart to hold the numerous items she was planning to buy for the community center food drive, they always offered her theirs.

Who was this heathen?

She tilted her head and stared even more carefully at the stranger. Admittedly, there was something sort of familiar about him, but she hadn't gotten a clear view of his face. After snatching her cart, he'd rudely turned his back on her, so she actually had to approach him—circumnavigating her way around an enticing pyramid of New Zealand pears—in order to get a closer look.

"Emma?" a friendly female voice called to her from somewhere in the vicinity of the arugula and red leaf lettuce.

Emma turned. Ah, Bethany Jane Knightley—now Jefferson. A newlywed, just a couple of years younger than Emma, Bethany had returned to Crystal Corners from her nursing internship in Chicago last year with a degree and a fiancé, Dr. Reggie Jefferson. They'd just gotten married over Thanksgiving.

Emma waved at her, but when she glanced back at cart-stealing heathen, he was making a beeline toward the clementines. And still ignoring her.

She took a purposeful step toward him but Bethany, carrying a clear plastic bag of romaine and another bag of organic broccoli, reached the guy first. She put the produce in the heathen's cart and grinned at Emma. "It's so good to see you." She pointed between Emma and the cart-stealer. "You remember my brother Austin, right?"

Emma blinked as the dark-haired man finally turned to face her. Austin Knightley, back in town again after nearly a decade away? "Um, yeah," she murmured. "Hi."

He nodded briefly in her direction, not appearing entirely pleased by this reintroduction. "Hi." Then he leveled a look at his kid sister. "I'm gonna grab some milk. See you at checkout."

"Five minutes," Bethany said. "I'll meet you there."

He disappeared with the cart into another aisle, his sister smiling proudly at his retreating form. "I'll grant you, he's not always the most social man in the room," Bethany said with a laugh, "but Austin's done amazing work in the Twin Cities. Who would've thought that my dorky older brother would turn out to be such a respected builder and businessman?"

Emma smiled at the younger woman, but something clenched at her throat, making it hard for her to speak all of a sudden. Thanks to the trust fund her parents had set up for her and a four-year degree at a selective liberal arts college, Emma was both well-educated and independently wealthy at the age of twenty-six. Nothing had ever made her feel inadequate or remotely "old."

Until now.

The reappearance of Austin, however, seemed to scratch a bit at an unexpected insecurity. He was only a year older than Emma, and while the Knightley family was hardly impoverished, they weren't as well-to-do as her family. Yet, he'd managed to become very successful in his time away from Crystal Corners, establishing himself in his big-city life with nary a second glance. (Emma, by contrast, couldn't wait to get back to their hometown and be a larger fish in a smaller pond again.) And Bethany, at twenty-four, not only had a good degree but was already married and probably on the verge of motherhood. For the first time ever, Emma felt almost behind, or at least not at the head of the pack.

It was an uncomfortable and unwelcome sensation.

"How, um, long is your brother planning to stay in town? Just for Christmas and New Year's, right?"

Bethany leaned in and lowered her voice. "This is still a secret—so don't tell anyone yet—but Austin's company is doing so well that he's begun branching out into other cities. He's already hired managers to run two of the branches and is working on getting someone in place to manage the original site he started in Minneapolis/St. Paul. If all that goes well, he'll be able to oversee all of the operations from anywhere he wants to live, including Crystal Corners!"

"So, you're saying he might be moving back here...permanently?"

"Yes!" Bethany all but shrieked.

Oh, dear.

"Wow," Emma murmured. "That's terrific. And, uh, really impressive."

"I know, isn't it?" his sister gushed. "It'll be amazing to have the whole family back together again all year long, not just during the holidays. Our parents are beside themselves with excitement. Connor, of course, has his own place at the edge of town. Reggie and I just bought a condo here together. And our baby brother, David, is planning to return home after he finishes up at the university in the spring. So, to get Austin back into the nest will make our family dinners complete and even more fun."

"Sounds like it," Emma said. As an only child, she could only imagine the chaos of living in a family with four siblings. Mr. and Mrs. Knightley—Ned and Pam—had named their children alphabetically in the order of their birth: Austin, then Bethany, then Connor, who ran a landscaping business for the three milder seasons and a snow-removal service during the winter months and, finally, David, a marketing major at a college in Duluth. Emma didn't know the younger Knightley men very well, but she knew they were as gregarious as their sister. In fact, the entire family, parents included, were extroverted and had a penchant for oversharing—except for Austin, who'd been the brooding type even as a grade-schooler. "I can see how you'd love that," Emma added with sincerity.

Bethany nodded happily. "It's so nice for Reggie, too, to get to know all of my brothers. He's bonding with them and becoming one of the guys," she remarked, clearly still in the glow of that newlywed state. "And he loves his work at the hospital, too."

Emma had met the nice doctor a few times and had been charmed by his friendliness, intelligence, and fine manners. Reggie grew up in New Orleans before coming up to the Midwest for med school and his Chicago residency. His African-American and Creole heritage was culturally interesting, and his natural sense of humor made him a delightful conversationalist. A pleasant addition to their little town. Although it was unfortunate, in Emma's opinion, that the majority of new men who moved to Crystal Corners, like Reggie, weren't single.

Once again, Emma felt an uninvited twinge of matronliness. She liked to see good romantic matches happen and did her best to engineer them herself whenever possible. She'd set up several friends and acquaintances in town that led to successful couples in recent years.

There was Mack and Lila, who were now dating steadily. All the more of a triumph because Mack had been one of Emma's boyfriends last year, but she felt Lila was a much more suitable match for him. Naturally, she was right.

Sonja and Ben (another of Emma's former boyfriends) were now engaged.

Jason and Kent, both townies who'd gotten to know

each other through Emma, moved in together back in October.

And her greatest matchmaking success to date—Vera and Steve—who'd been married for almost two years and were expecting their first baby in February. (Rumor had it that if the happy couple had a girl, they were going to name her after Emma...of course!)

"Is there a special someone in Austin's life?" Emma asked, figuring she ought to pump his sister for a little information on her brother while she could.

Bethany shook her head. She got as far as saying, "Not right now, but there was this one uppity girlfriend he had in Minneapolis who—" before Austin himself called out his sister's name from halfway across the store.

He was glowering at them from the nearest checkout lane, almost as if he knew he was the subject of their discussion.

"Coming!" Bethany called back with a laugh.

And just as Emma was following her and, perhaps, finally going to purloin their no-longer-needed cart, Austin set their groceries on the conveyor belt and very graciously said, "Would you like this cart?"

Emma grinned and began to nod. Better late than never. But before she could voice her acceptance, she realized he wasn't talking to her.

He was, in fact, addressing an older townswoman— Mrs. Harriet Smithwick—who was juggling a few handfuls of bagged produce and who'd just managed to spill a sack full of red potatoes, which were currently rolling around the aisle and creating an unexpected obstacle course for one toddler and several adults. Austin jumped to Harriet's aid immediately.

Emma found herself torn between being impressed by his kindness to the elderly lady and miffed that none of his helpful impulses were directed at *her*. Why did he persist in ignoring her?

Behind her, Emma heard a crotchety middle-aged couple, the Eltons, sniping about people in their typical disagreeable manner. This time, the subject of their criticism was Harriet.

"That Smithwick woman is always making a spectacle of herself in public," Myra Elton commented.

"So messy," William, her mean-spirited husband, replied. "One of those people who always needs someone to come to their rescue."

"Sometimes," Myra hissed, "a woman has to be willing to help herself, not just rely on others."

This from a woman who, along with her miserly husband, were known throughout Crystal Corners for being two of the very few stingy and spiteful residents in town. Ugh.

Emma narrowed her eyes at them. And Bethany, overhearing these vicious remarks, glanced at Emma, shook her head in irritation, and proceeded to help her brother pick up a few of Harriet's wayward potatoes. Emma quickened her step and grabbed several of them, too.

Austin, upon their arrival, smiled gently at the older woman and sent her on her way with the retrieved produce and the cart, but despite his sister's chirpiness, he'd turned silent and uncommunicative again in Emma's presence.

"Well, I suppose I should finish my shopping," Emma told them. Bethany expressed a desire to chat again soon, but her taciturn brother only glanced at her with an air of disinterest bordering on disapproval.

The second he was done paying for their groceries, he grabbed the bags and tersely told his sister, "Let's go," with only the coolest of nods in Emma's direction. How incredibly rude!

Bethany, seemingly oblivious to this blatant slight toward Emma, hugged her quickly and then scampered after her boorish brother.

No one—especially no man!—had *ever* treated her like

this. However sweet Bethany might be, Emma had no intention of stopping to talk with her in town again if that discourteous brother of hers was tagging along.

# *Two*

"Seriously, sis, did you have to spill my entire life story to that rich and snotty gossipmonger?" Austin Knightley spit out to his chatty little sister once they were in the privacy of his truck—with the doors closed and locked, and all the windows rolled up so they couldn't be overheard—and safely on the road to their parents' house.

*Emma Westwood.* After all these years.

Still as cute as a baby bunny in the snow, but she had a mouth on her as big as a crocodile's. He should know. He'd grown up hearing it every day for years on the school bus. It was always talk, talk, talk. Or, as she'd probably say, socialize, socialize, socialize.

Bethany laughed. "Emma is rich, yes, but she's not snotty. A little high-maintenance, maybe—"

"A *little?*"

"—and she's hardly more gossipy than most of the other ladies in town. Plus, she's very charitable and has good intentions."

Austin wasn't buying it, at least not entirely. The perfectly put together blonde he remembered from his childhood may not have been intentionally mean-spirited, but she was practically cataloging every word that everyone in the store had said aloud, likely for the purpose of being able to recite it to somebody else later.

He didn't appreciate being a topic of conversation for the idle folks in town who had nothing better to do than prattle on about each other and meddle in the business of their neighbors. It was for reasons like these, and all the other fish bowl experiences he'd had growing up, that he'd bolted out of Crystal Corners the summer after high school graduation and had only come back for vacations, national holidays, and important family events.

Well, until now.

But the situation was different these days. For one thing, he could afford to come back in style, which made a difference. And for another, his parents were getting older, and all of their children needed to pitch in to help them when possible. That included him.

Still, he'd better make his limits clear to Bethany right away, or these little social nightmares would be never-ending.

"I'd just as soon you left me out of future conversations like that, sis," he said firmly. "I mean it. Or I might be back in the Twin Cities sooner rather than later."

Bethany shot him a sour look, but she was too good-natured to argue with him or call him out for being a grump. And he was definitely being a grump. There was just something about seeing Emma again that got under his skin. He'd been way too attracted to that type of woman for way too long, and he didn't like that any part of that feeling was still there.

His sister flipped on the car radio and scanned for stations until she came to the Z-104's All Christmas, All the Time playlist, which had been pumping a steady stream of holiday hits since the day after Thanksgiving. "Maybe 'Have a Holly Jolly Christmas' is what you need," she said.

He rolled his eyes. "Yeah, maybe." Then, because what he desperately needed was a change of subject, he asked, "Is Reggie meeting us at the folks' house tonight?"

"Should be." She clicked on her phone to check her messages. "He's seeing patients at the hospital for another hour, but he says he'll be at the house in time to help us put the finishing touches on dinner."

"I hope you hid the spices." It was a running joke in their family that Reggie went a little too heavy on the chili powder, the curry, the Cajun seasonings, the crushed red pepper flakes, and pretty much any kind of hot sauce he could get his hands on.

His sister laughed. "Mom and Dad don't have anything too dangerous in their pantry, except for maybe the garlic. As long as he doesn't bring a jar of that ghost pepper powder from our place, we should be okay."

Austin grinned. Reggie Jefferson had proven himself to be a good guy, and Bethany very much adored him. Austin loved seeing her so happy, and her new husband appeared to be doing everything in his power to keep her that way. "Alrighty then. So, do you need a sous chef or something for this healthy masterpiece?" He pointed behind them, in the general direction of the grocery bags.

She nodded vigorously. "Yes, please. I've got the chicken for the stew already marinating in Mom and Dad's fridge, but the veggies all need to be chopped up—for both the stew and the salad. David should be there to help us, too, but I'm not sure yet when Connor will show up." She side-punched him affectionately in the bicep. "I'm so glad you're back home!"

"Me, too, sis," he said, and he meant it—annoying distractions like Emma Westwood aside. He wasn't planning on voicing this aloud just yet, but he'd missed evenings like this when he was in the Twin Cities. He missed talking face to face with his family. Cooking with his family. Just being in the presence of his family, period.

14

Not to say that he hadn't loved his independence in Minneapolis. He'd worked hard to make a name for himself and had built a terrific team with many wonderful associates. But work colleagues and employees weren't always the same as *friends*, and he could get pretty lonely there, too.

Especially once things with his ex-girlfriend, Taylor, went south.

Not that he wanted her back—*oh, no, never again!*—but he did miss having someone special to share the seasons with and the holidays in particular. For now, however, nothing could top being with his parents and siblings at Christmas.

When they arrived at their parents' house, twilight had just descended on the sprawling five-bedroom ranch. The warm lights from inside the family room cast a cozy glow, like one of those beautiful Thomas Kinkade paintings where the house seemed lit from within. And outside, the holiday decorations and strings of Christmas lights twinkled into the night sky and created a kaleidoscope of color on the snow-covered lawn.

He smiled. Home sweet home.

He'd been staying here for the past few days since his return to Crystal Corners, getting reacclimated to being back in town and enjoying the sentimental feelings that being home for the holidays inspired. Something about sleeping in his childhood bedroom always made him feel youthful, like he was a kid again and not practically thirty.

"You two back from the store already?" Mom called to them when he and Bethany walked through the front door, grocery bags in tow.

"We are, Mom," he called back. "And Chef Beth is gonna cook us up a feast."

"I'll wash my hands, and I can help," Mom said.

He and his sister exchanged a quick look. Mom's arthritis had become a bigger issue lately. Between that and

15

her old carpal tunnel problems, washing and chopping fruits and veggies for a large crowd—even with the help of a food processor—was too much for her.

"Maybe you can set the table while Austin and I cook," Bethany suggested. "Big brother here volunteered to be my sous chef, and I don't want him squirming out of it. We need to put this big-city boy back to work before he becomes a hometown slacker again."

Their mom laughed, and Austin gave his sister an approving wink. *Well played, Bethany.*

"And where's David hiding out?" he asked. "I thought he was done with finals for the semester and going to be here tonight."

"He is. He's with your father," Mom said. She pointed toward an empty spot on the carpet near the family room's front window. "They went to get the Christmas tree. Connor is meeting them at the lot and then the three of them will bring it back home, so we can all string the lights tonight. Together. Won't that be nice?" She beamed as she said that, her eyes glistening with a brightness that only came from unshed tears, although Austin knew they were happy ones.

He set down the bags and gave her a quick hug and a peck on both cheeks. "Yeah, it will. It'll be fun, Mom," he whispered to her.

She nodded as a few tears escaped. He pretended not to notice when she swiped them away and just trailed his sister into the large kitchen.

While Bethany ordered him around and set him up at the island countertop, chopping a mountain of stew and salad veggies, he felt a couple of tears prick the corners of his eyes as well. The past several months had been an emotional roller coaster for them all, not just because of Bethany and Reggie's wedding—which had been a joyful occasion—but because their dad had needed emergency bypass surgery just a couple of months before that. Though

Dad was older than their mom by eight years, he'd barely turned seventy before his heart operation, and it was a wake-up call to them all that life was short and unpredictable.

That was when Austin started putting into motion his plan to return home for longer than a weekend...and one of the reasons why his sister and her new husband had chosen Crystal Corners as their residence, when both of them could have easily found jobs in larger cities.

Having the two of them nearby and in the medical field was a godsend. Connor, who'd never left town for longer than a couple of weeks, had always helped out their parents with trimming bushes, mowing the lawn, and other yard-related tasks, but he'd stepped it up even more this winter. The folks' driveway was always meticulously plowed and salted, and he checked in on them multiple times per week. Austin knew that Connor must have jumped to meet Dad and David at the Christmas tree lot to avoid their father having to lift even the lighter side of the tree.

Austin was well aware that he couldn't turn back the clock and make their parents young and pain-free again, but he could be there to ease their burden a bit. Not only in the kitchen, with his rudimentary but serviceable cooking skills, but as a businessman, who could help them automate their finances a bit more. Also, as a builder, he could construct some of the home adaptations they would certainly be needing in the years ahead. Mom's arthritis was degenerative, her doctors had told them, affecting the joints in her spine, neck, knees, and hips, as well as her hands. Austin could foresee home modifications where ramps or lifts could be installed in place of stairs, or areas where it would be preferable for the shelving to be lowered to make items more easily reachable. That would be helpful for Dad, as well as for Mom.

Most importantly, though, he could just spend time with them. He knew they needed that above all.

Within twenty minutes, Mom had beautifully set the table for all seven of them and had gone into her bedroom to change clothes. Austin and Bethany had prepared the salad and gotten the chicken and veggie stew well underway. He was in the middle of slicing a long loaf of crusty French bread to accompany the meal when his kid brothers—Connor and David—burst through the door with the freshly cut tree.

"This is heavier than I thought," David said, grunting.

"Dude, I thought you said you've been working out at that college of yours." Connor snorted. "Or have you been going to the gym just to watch the *ladies* exercising?"

"Hey, I lift at least—"

"Be careful of your mom's hall table!" their father bellowed, interrupting them.

There was a small crash.

"Oops," Connor muttered.

Austin and his sister exchanged a look.

"You'd better go out there and help," Bethany suggested. "I can handle things in here."

He set down the bread knife and sprinted out of the kitchen.

Their dad, giving Austin's brothers directions like an Army sergeant, managed to steer them toward the open spot by the living room's picture window, but not without a few near misses with Mom's delicate Christmas decorations and the breaking of one small ceramic vase. Fortunately, Austin knew it wasn't one of their mother's favorites.

While brushing up the pieces of the vase and straightening the other items on the hall table, Austin had to laugh at the disaster that was now the front room. With his brothers and their dad clomping around, there was snow scattered everywhere, not to mention a few muddy footprints and several stray pine needles.

"Did you guys at least get the Christmas tree stand

ready before you left?" Austin asked. "Or do I have to hunt for it in the garage?"

"Over there." David pointed toward a box near their dad's black recliner. "And hi to you, too, big brother. Way to welcome me home and start my very first night of vacation by being all judging and overbearing," he said with a smirk.

Austin laughed, grabbed the tree stand, and helped his brothers set it up so the tree would be upright and fully secured. Then he pulled his snarky twenty-one-year-old brother into a bear hug. "Missed ya, Davey-boy."

"Missed ya, too," David whispered, squeezing hard.

"Ow, my poor ribs," Austin faux moaned. "Connor's wrong. You *have* been working out."

Dad and Austin's brothers all laughed.

"So, where's *my* hug?" Connor replied in his trademark mocking tone, holding out his arms like a little toddler instead of a twenty-three-year-old man. "The middle brother is always ignored and—"

Both Austin and David flanked him, sandwiching Connor in a massive hug that was more like an attack than a sign of affection.

"FYI, you two. The snow outside is, like, *perfect* for packing," David hinted, and Austin didn't need to be told twice.

"Snowball fight!" he cried.

Connor let out a whoop, breaking free from the other two. "Get your jacket on," he demanded, punching Austin in the chest and motioning between him and David. "I'm gonna beat you both to a pulp. Just. Like. Always."

"Not a chance," Austin called, grabbing for his winter coat.

"Them are fightin' words," David called at the same time, retying one of his boots.

Their mom walked in just as the three of them were racing to the front door. "What about dinner?" she asked.

Bethany peeked her head out from the kitchen. "We're still waiting on Reggie. He should be here in the next ten or fifteen minutes," she informed them. "But then, if these knuckleheads don't come inside and settle down like civilized humans, I'll go out and get them. And. They'll. Be. Sorry."

"Ooooooh!" Austin and his brothers cooed together, reacting to their sister's threat in the same way as they had when they were kids. Really, aside from a decade or two having zipped by, nothing much had changed in their sibling relationships.

"You've been warned," Bethany shouted after them, but they could barely hear her when their feet hit the snowy front lawn.

Austin, Connor, and David spent their first minute or two outside subdividing the yard into three territories and building up their individual stashes of snowballs. A colossal pummeling followed. The trio sent snow flying toward each other at speeds that would have made their junior high gym teachers very proud.

"You're gonna be blasted clear into Wisconsin," Connor shouted as he pitched a fast snowball at their baby brother.

David got smacked in the chest but retaliated by whipping a curveball right back.

Austin released three snowballs in rapid succession, hitting Connor, David, and then Connor again.

Their neighbor, Mr. Parsons, pulled into his driveway next door and stopped for a minute to watch the battle. He caught Austin's eye and called out a greeting.

"Nice to see you boys having fun," Mr. Parsons added.

Austin raised his hand to wave and got immediately snow-bombed by both of his brothers.

"That's what you get for being distracted," Connor shouted.

And David, pausing only to say, "Happy Holidays, Mr.

Parsons!" wasn't fast enough to escape Austin's latest pitch. He got whacked right on his open mouth.

Mom and Dad, both watching from the front window, laughed at the antics of their three sons. And although his fingers were quickly turning into icicles and he was covered in snow, Austin couldn't remember when he'd had a better time.

A sturdy dark-green sedan pulled into their driveway a few minutes later. Reggie.

"Hey, don't shoot!" he cried. "I come bearing apple pie and red wine."

"Yo, there!" Connor called out as Reggie made his way to the porch. "The doctor is in the house."

Bethany appeared at the front door just as Reggie said, "Where's my beautiful wife?"

He handed off the pie and the bottle of wine to their parents and then, pulling a sprig of mistletoe out of his jacket pocket, he drew Bethany to him, held the mistletoe above their heads, and planted a ginormous kiss on her lips.

"Whoo-hoo!" Connor yelled.

David wolf whistled.

And Austin, who couldn't have admired his new brother-in-law more, pelted Reggie with an enormous snowball. "Take it inside, you lovebirds," he taunted.

Reggie spun around. "Which one of you crazy fools hit me?"

Connor and David both pointed at Austin. Reggie cackled maniacally. "Aw, man, you're gonna pay!"

"Bring it on, Reg. Let's see what you got," he called back, rubbing his palms together and preparing for the next round of the snow wars.

Reggie whispered something in Bethany's ear as her three brothers looked on. Austin couldn't help but feel a stab of envy at their loving, easygoing relationship. Reg fit in with the Knightley clan like a hand in a custom-made glove. Austin had hoped for something similar with Taylor, but it was a futile wish. She couldn't relax and let down her guard to save her life, not even for one lone evening with his wacky family. The woman was even more intense than Emma Westwood, and that was saying something.

Their sister surveyed all of them for a long moment, looking half amused, half exasperated. "What did I tell you boys? You've got five minutes, and *only* five. If you're not in the house, ready for dinner then, I'm coming out after you."

"She's just sayin' that," David bellowed, egging her on.

"What'd you say, Davey? Are you trash talkin' my sweet wife?" cried Reggie, packing his first snowball and sending it smashing right into David's forehead.

Connor let out a battle cry, and soon, all four of them were so covered in snow that they looked like a set of Sasquatch quadruplets.

Reggie was the first to give up and stumble inside. "Your sister said five minutes. I'm not taking any chances," he joked, disappearing into the warm house.

Austin and his brothers, however, elected to ignore Bethany's warning. They were enjoying themselves way too much.

It wasn't until he got pelted hard in the back of the neck when Austin remembered—too late—that Bethany had a better throwing arm than any of them. She'd been an all-star softball player throughout high school and had even played on her college team for her first two years of undergrad. Their cunning sister, in a sneak attack from the west side of the house, appeared with an entire *bucketful* of extremely well-packed snowballs and unfurled every single one of them at his, Connor's, and David's heads. She had excellent aim.

"Ow!" David cried.

"I think you blinded me," Connor grumbled.

But even then, his brothers tried to keep the battle going. The three of them ganged up on her, despite the fact that she was beating them soundly all by herself.

Finally, Reggie appeared at the front door—a large soup ladle in his fist and a curious expression on his face. "Guess who put me in charge of the stew?" he said, breaking into an evil grin.

Connor was the first to catch on. "You left him *alone* with the spices?" He froze in place and glared accusingly at their sister.

Bethany burst out laughing. "Oooh, serves you guys right." She dropped her now-empty bucket and brushed the caked-on flecks of snow from her mittens. "If you three don't come in for dinner right this second, you'd better make yourselves some snow cones to cool your burning tongues. I told Reggie to add a tablespoon of hot chili pepper for every minute you keep us waiting."

Austin, David, and Connor glanced at each other—jaws dropping, eyes popping—and then they all rushed inside.

# *Three*

The brisk December air, filled with tiny but powerful snowflakes, swirled around Emma like a swarm of angry insects, albeit icy ones.

She tugged her winter cloak tighter around her body and wished her pretty paisley scarf were a bit thicker. It was, like much of her wardrobe, slightly more on the fashionable than functional side, but she had a personal dress code to adhere to and a schedule to keep.

As she walked down Main Street, she thought through her mental checklist of required stops on this blistery Thursday morning. Adele's Bakery, The Jubilee Christmas Store, and Gift-Wrapping Central were already behind her, as the packages she carried in both hands could attest. However, she had at least five other businesses or organizations where she needed to put in an appearance before noon.

"Morning, Emma!" Mrs. McBride called out to her.

"Lovely seeing you today," she called back to the sweet lady who owned Crystal Corners Coffeehouse. "I just sent a few visitors over to your shop," she confided. "Told them you had the best orange-cranberry scones and hazelnut coffee anywhere in the Midwest."

"Oh, thank you, sweetie," Mrs. McBride replied, a grin stretching wide. "I think you've single-handedly doubled my revenue this year alone with all of your recommendations."

Emma smiled and accepted the compliment with pride. As the face of Westwood International, the charitable foundation her parents created, as well as its full-time manager in their absence, Emma had significant duties to juggle behind the scenes. To the outside world, she appeared to mostly socialize under the guise of shopping, but the cornerstone of her career was really networking and making the kind of strong connections and associations that enabled her to get things done. Both in their community and out of it.

It could get rather tedious, of course, going door to door (or store to store) like a congresswoman on the campaign trail or an insatiable bargain hunter, but Emma relished her place at the center of Crystal Corners society. And, furthermore, no matter what anyone thought of her or her well-connected family, she knew she was good at her job.

She pushed through the revolving door of the post office, preparing to mail several holiday packages to charities supported by her family's foundation.

Mr. Parsons, their local postmaster, greeted her with a cheery, "Good day to you, Miss Westwood. And how are you on this fine morning?"

"A bit chilled, to be honest," Emma replied, "but I'm glad to be in your toasty warm post office." She set down the first parcel that needed to be sent overseas. Then a second one. Then four domestic packages, all ready to be shipped. And, finally, one wrapped but unboxed gift.

Mr. Parsons pointed to it. "Do you need packaging supplies for that?"

Emma shook her head and smiled as the postmaster

stamped and put sticky labels on her boxes. "This one is for you and the staff," she said. "Just a little something I picked up from Adele's Bakery as a thank you from my parents and me for all the things you do for us throughout the year. Merry Christmas."

The older gentleman placed his hand over his heart. "Oh, that's so kind of you. Everything Adele makes is delicious, so I know we'll all enjoy it. Thank you."

"My pleasure." She paid for the parcels to be mailed and then bundled herself up tightly again in anticipation of heading back outdoors. "Only snowmen would love this weather," she joked.

"Or people who love snowball fights." Mr. Parsons laughed. "The Knightley kids were having quite a battle in their yard yesterday."

Emma paused and took a step back toward the counter. She'd forgotten that Mr. Parsons lived next door to Austin and Bethany's parents. "You mean *all* the kids?"

"Oh, yeah. Every one of 'em, including Bethany's new husband. I wouldn't be surprised if the lot of them ended up with frostbite today, but they looked like they were having a blast last night."

Of course they were. Austin may have been cold and snippy to *her*, but he clearly wasn't averse to being nice to *other* people.

"Yes, well," she said quickly, not at all in the mood to talk about Austin or any of the Knightleys. "Have a lovely day."

She pushed through the revolving door and reentered the winterfest outside. But if she thought she was going to escape either the persistent snowflakes or conversation about Austin, her next several stops in town proved otherwise.

There was Mrs. Reed, the local piano and guitar teacher, who was gushing about how wonderful it was to see David, Austin's youngest brother, back in town. That

26

he'd visited her this morning and told her he'd kept practicing piano at college, even though he wasn't a music major. "Such a talented family," she said with a happy sigh. "And his big brother is back home now, too."

"Yes," Emma murmured. "I'm aware of that."

At the local gym, where she'd stopped to pick up a few free six-month memberships they were donating to the community gift chest, she ran into her friends Jason and Kent. Jason ran the theater and Kent was a finance guy, but they were both heavily into fitness and worked out daily. They were one of Emma's (many!) matchmaking successes, and it always made her happy to chat with them.

Jason threw his arms around her in a dramatic greeting. "Darling, Em! So good to see you."

She kissed both his cheeks and did the same to Kent, who ruffled the top of her head and said, "What brings you to the gym? Getting a jump on those New Year's fitness resolutions?"

Jason rolled his eyes. "It's going to be a nightmare finding an open machine in January. Seriously, the place is pretty dead right now, but from January second until, like, Valentine's Day, it's crazy."

"Yeah," Kent agreed. "So get started early. Or let us know when you're coming in, and we can snag a treadmill or an elliptical for you."

She laughed. Emma would not, of course, brag about this, but her parents had a home gym, and it was outfitted with all the exercise equipment she could ever want—from weights to an array of cardio machines to a small sauna. But she simply said, "Thanks so much for the offer, guys. If I decide to join, you two will be the first to know." She then explained about how she was collecting Christmas donations for the Crystal Corners Community Center and needed to get the gift membership vouchers from the gym director.

"Oh! Drop by the theater this week, and I'll throw in a

few pairs of tickets to the holiday show and maybe even a season pass or two," Jason said.

"And I'll fund a couple of gift cards for free tax service and financial planning," Kent offered. "April will be here before we know it."

"You guys are the best," Emma said, meaning it. She loved her friends and their generosity.

"You should definitely hit up Austin Knightley for a donation," Kent suggested. "He's been batting it out of the park with his business this year. His dad's been raving about him almost every day."

"You talk to his dad almost every day?" Emma asked. Sure, Crystal Corners was a small town, but she didn't think that Ned Knightley and Kent ran in the same circles, and certainly not so frequently.

"Oh, yeah, he's always here for exercise and PT," Kent replied. "A good cardiac rehab program after heart surgery is important."

And Jason said, "Usually his wife brings him, but Austin did the honors this morning. Chatted with us for a while, too."

"Oh...oh, yeah?" Emma knew, of course, through the town's grapevine, that Austin's dad had undergone heart surgery in the fall, but that was a few months ago, and she hadn't really connected Austin's reappearance with his father's health. Bethany had hinted that Austin might be back to stay. But maybe his reasons for wanting to return were more personal than professional.

"Yeah," Jason said. "Once you get to know him, Austin's a friendly guy."

Right. To everyone but her, it seemed. But Emma didn't point this out, however sorely she was tempted. She just bid her friends farewell and continued on her way, eventually ending up at the community center, which was her last stop of the morning.

Ginger Mae Jones was waiting for her.

"Girlie, ya ready to help me with this stash of packages? My old bones can't move things the way I used to," Ginger Mae said. She was ninety-one, a longtime widow, and a transplant from southern Kentucky. Never mind that she'd lived in Minnesota for four decades, her southern accent had only deepened with the passing years.

"Absolutely," Emma said at once, pulling off her cloak, scarf, and gloves and preparing to work.

Ginger Mae had been the chair of the Goodwill Toward Men & Women Project at the community center since Emma was a little girl and, lately, she'd been entrusting Emma with various offshoots of the Project, namely the big holiday gift chest for families in need, the food drive, and the community mitten-and-winter-hat tree for anyone who didn't have enough warm outerwear this season.

Plus, there was Emma's personal pet project, which had been her brainchild about four years ago and her Christmas gift to the community every holiday season since.

Emma added her latest, newly packaged presents to the community chest collection and began following Ginger Mae's instructions on where to move the various gifts.

"I'm thinkin' we could turn this old storage room into a kind of distribution center," Ginger Mae said. "Different gifts set up on different tables by age range and type. They'll be easier to find and can then be given away by the volunteers to the families in need."

"Sounds like an excellent plan," she said.

Emma worked tirelessly for the next few hours moving each package to the location Ginger Mae specified. She had to admit, it was an efficient system for the sorting and organizing of this particular project.

But Emma had her own way and her own system for the personal project she headed herself. In fact, the thing she liked best about it was that it was for the children in town. *All* of the children, whether they came from needy families or not.

Her reasoning for deciding to give similar gifts to everyone came from a deep understanding of how kids thought about the world. How very sensitive they were to status—who among them had money and who didn't. They were keenly aware of such discrepancies, even if no one said a word.

She herself had been a girl who'd grown up with a lot of advantages and significantly more presents than she ever needed. It was tempting to want to even the score for the kids who had little or nothing at the holidays. Her parents had always encouraged her to be generous and to donate her extra gifts to toy drives and other such charitable purposes.

But what Emma realized during her early adult years was that human psychology was more complex than that. She wanted to give the neediest children what they wanted most, which went beyond a package. It was that feeling of being normal, of belonging. Being one of the crowd, not singled out—either by being given extra or not being given anything at all.

So that was the basis of her plan. That *every* child in Crystal Corners between the ages of two and twelve would receive something special. Something picked out just for them. Then they would all have something to show after the holidays. Something to talk about. A shared experience...not merely a gift.

Since her most prized Christmas present had been the knight statuette that Santa gave her when she was six, Emma spent the year finding, ordering, and amassing a collection of statuettes specific to the individual personalities and passions of the town's children. She had help, of course. She used her networking skills to get to know as many of the kids personally as she could. But she also tapped into the knowledge of their parents, coaches, and teachers, focusing on one age group per month throughout the calendar year, until she had one unique and highly personalized statuette for every single child in town. Then, she set up her display on Christmas morning and handed each gift to every child herself in the town's square. It had become her very favorite holiday tradition.

Ginger Mae sent her home with a steaming cup of hot cocoa to ward off the chill and an extra hard hug. "You go be good to yourself, girlie. You've done enough work for today. Rest up and have fun with your friends tonight, ya hear?"

Emma nodded and prepared to make her way home, but she couldn't tell the sweet older woman the truth: That she had no plans for this evening or, indeed, for any evening this week.

She had friends enough, sure, but she'd done such a stellar job of letting everyone know how busy she was during the Yuletide season that no one actually thought to ask her to their gatherings. Anything social she did in the weeks leading up to Christmas was primarily on behalf of her family's foundation or her community's volunteer services—which kept her busy for hours every day. But with her parents away this month for their anniversary celebration, she'd be spending almost all of her remaining free time alone.

She walked into the Westwood mansion, which was lit beautifully, but it echoed with emptiness. Only their housekeeper and their cook were currently in residence, and in the spirit of the season, Emma made sure to give them extra time off so they could spend more evenings with their families.

It was lonely for her, though, being in a such a big house all alone.

"I made you a nice piece of baked salmon, Miss Westwood," Jennings, their talented chef, said. "There are sides of garlic mashed potatoes and steamed asparagus spears, and a freshly baked peach cobbler for dessert."

"Oh, that sounds heavenly," Emma told him, her mouth

already beginning to water.

"Enjoy it, Miss. I'll be back in the morning early enough to make you a veggie and cheese omelet with hash browns. Eight a.m. still your preference for your Friday morning breakfast?"

"Yes, that would be perfect, Jennings. And thank you very much. Enjoy tonight with your niece and nephew."

"I will." His whole face lit up at the prospect of seeing them again. They were visiting from Argentina for just the next two weeks, and it had been over three years since he'd gotten together with them last. Emma made sure Jennings's hours were as light as possible while they were in town.

Before Darla, her parents' longtime housekeeper, left for the day, also to attend a family function, Emma asked if the delivery she'd been expecting had been put in the garage as she instructed in her notes to the company.

"I'm afraid not, Miss Westwood," Darla told her, a look of concern crossing her face. "It hasn't yet arrived."

Emma glanced at the grandfather clock in the foyer. "It was supposed to be here no later than two p.m. It's after four."

"Perhaps it's on account of the weather, Miss," Darla suggested. "Even though we didn't get a lot of new snow here, some of the other towns were hit harder. Where was the delivery truck coming from?"

"A furniture warehouse in White Bear Lake." Emma clicked on her phone to check for messages from the company and, when she didn't see any, to look up the road conditions in their area. "They did get several inches earlier today, so you may be right," she told the housekeeper. "But I'm very surprised they didn't let me know there'd be a delay. We had this delivery time and date worked out months ago."

Darla offered to stay longer to help Emma make phone inquiries, but she told the older woman not to worry about it and to enjoy the evening with her daughter, son-in-law, and new grandchild. "It's possible it'll still get here before nightfall. I'll contact them myself in the next hour, or if they're already closed for today and don't show up tonight, I'm sure I'll be able to reach them tomorrow morning."

"Very good, Miss Westwood. But please don't hesitate to let me know if I can be of help to you later."

And then Darla, too, left the house for the night.

To try to temper the depressing silence, Emma turned on some music. If there was a time for blasting cheery Christmas carols throughout her home, it was now.

Then she set about attempting to contact the furniture company, whose workers had built her new statuette display case to her ideal specifications. She'd seen the final picture just a few weeks ago, and it was absolutely perfect. Exactly what she'd ordered.

But she couldn't seem to get ahold of the owner—or any of his staff—to save her life. No one was answering the telephone, and she had no idea if someone was even there to receive the urgent email she sent from her laptop.

She sighed. She'd just have to be patient...but that really wasn't Emma's forte.

To pass the time, she turned the music up even louder and danced around the large living room to "Rockin' Around the Christmas Tree." Irony was that Emma hadn't bothered to even put up a Christmas tree this year. Her parents had left for Europe just after Thanksgiving, and it hardly seemed worth it to make the house all festive just for herself. They'd be back right before New Year's, though, so maybe she should consider decorating a little with that in mind. Champagne glasses, those annoying noisemakers, Baby New Year hats, and the like.

A ding from her laptop had her racing across the room to check her emails. But it wasn't from the furniture company.

She grinned and clicked on the message. It was a note from her parents, who were currently in Vienna.

"Have time for a video chat with your old folks?" her mom wrote.

"Of course!" Emma replied. A moment later, the call came in through the computer, and she answered. "Hi," she said into the screen, waving at them. "How are you two enjoying the latest leg of the tour?"

"Oh, it's fabulous, honey," her dad said, grinning like a schoolboy. "We're having the best time. The only thing that would have made it better is if you were here with us."

"Awww, thanks, Dad." Emma's parents were truly indulgent. It was their thirtieth wedding anniversary, and they'd offered to bring her along on their celebration grand European trip. But, much as she knew they'd meant it sincerely, there was no way she was going to intrude on her parents' month-long romantic getaway. Besides, she had the foundation to manage in their absence, a number of community center projects to run, and a Christmas gift giveaway to oversee for the children. She just wished they hadn't chosen the lengthiest guided tour in the travel brochure. A full thirty days away.

"One trip day for every year of marriage," her mom had said with a chuckle when they'd booked the vacation. "I think we deserve it."

Emma had to concede that this was true.

Right now, however, her mother was smiling but smothering a yawn.

"Hey, isn't it really late in Austria?" Emma asked. It was almost five p.m. here, and she knew they were several hours ahead.

"Closing in on midnight," her mom replied, "but we just got back to the hotel. We had a spectacular day of sightseeing and dining and evening entertainment." She proceeded to rave about the gorgeous palace they'd visited on the outskirts of the city. And her dad piped in with commentary about the Mozart concert they'd enjoyed in the orchestral hall tonight.

The two of them laughed and looked at each other like they were newlyweds. It warmed Emma's heart to see them both so carefree and happy. They'd always had a strong marriage, but she knew they needed time away every once in a while to cement their bond and to be reminded of their affection for each other.

Once again, Emma was glad she hadn't become a third wheel on their private adventure, much as she would have appreciated their company during the holidays. One of the problems with being an only child was that you got used to your parents as your companions. But Mom and Dad, while always loving, were not actually like siblings.

"We truly couldn't have asked for a better experience," her dad said. "Your mom found this 'Christmas Across Europe' tour, and our guide, Rafael, has been the best."

"He really knows these major European cities well," Mom added. "Everything we've seen so far in London, Paris, Geneva, Munich, Salzburg, and now Vienna has been spectacular. But Rafael is Italian, so we're especially looking forward to that leg of the journey, which is coming soon."

Yes, Emma had committed their itinerary to memory. Her parents would be traveling to Budapest next, but then they'd be on to Italy—Venice, Florence, Pisa, Rome—before ending their tour in Athens.

"I'm so glad to hear that," she said, fighting back a small pang of envy. "It sounds like a dream trip."

Emma had been to Europe a couple of times with her parents and always enjoyed herself, but she more than suspected it would be a vastly different experience going with a significant other. Maybe someday...but, well, probably not. It was one thing to match up couples in Crystal Corners. It was altogether another to *be* part of a couple. Romance just didn't seem to work out well for her.

"Oh! I've got some fun pictures to share with you," Mom said. "Let me upload them and email them to you before I forget. Your dad and I tried this amazing dessert at a Viennese coffeehouse this afternoon—*Sachertorte*."

"So good!" her dad interjected.

"I'm not sure what's in the original recipe—from what we were told, it's a closely guarded secret—but I've got pictures of the version we tried, *and* I found a variation online that I think sounds kind of like it," her mom said triumphantly. "Maybe Jennings can make it for us all when we get back home."

Emma laughed. "That would be wonderful." Then she caught both her parents yawning. "You two need to get some sleep. Thanks so much for calling me, though, and sharing your day." She didn't dare tell them that this conversation was the highlight of hers for fear they'd immediately guess how lonely she was and cut their trip short at the midpoint.

"Okay, but we just missed our beautiful daughter so much and were glad to catch up a bit," Mom said. "Don't do too much work, sweetheart. Take time for a little fun. And please don't feel like you have to handle everything yourself. If you need help with anything, don't be afraid to ask for it."

"Love you, baby girl," Dad called out, blowing a kiss through the screen.

After bidding them both good night and turning away from her laptop, Emma listened and danced to another two lively Christmas songs ("Jingle Bell Rock" and "Step into Christmas") before her mother's email came through with all of the promised pictures, as well as that dessert recipe.

Emma read through the ingredients for the Viennese torte, step by step. It was a kind of dense chocolate cake with apricot filling and chocolate icing. It sounded delicious. She printed it out and tacked it to her bulletin board to show to Jennings in a couple of weeks.

She knew she should be tired after the industriousness of her day. That tonight would be the perfect time to just kick back, relax, eat the delicious dinner Jennings had prepared, and watch a romantic Christmas movie on TV.

And she did.

But even after the final ending credits rolled on the screen, Emma still felt restless.

In an attempt to combat this, she answered a handful of business emails, walked for twenty minutes on the treadmill downstairs, and enjoyed a cup of hot tea on the sofa.

However, much to her annoyance, nothing seemed to keep her mind from spinning in circles and remembering tidbits of her grade school years that she hadn't thought about in ages. She blamed seeing Austin again for activating these old memories.

She found herself wandering into the playroom that housed her childhood library—all of those beautiful books on knights and castles and pretty princesses. The gorgeous illustrations made her sigh every time.

It made her think about something that had happened when she was in eighth grade and he, a whole year older, was a freshman in high school. They were on the bus, heading home from a long day of school, but Emma always enjoyed the bus rides. Unless she had an afterschool club to attend or a get-together planned with her girlfriends, her social life came to a screeching halt once she walked into the house. Her parents were loving but busy. They were adults, not peers, after all, and they had limited time for lengthy preteen discussions about cute boys or popular music or whatever movie actor had recently caught her fancy. So Emma made the most of her ride home with friends.

Austin, by contrast, never seemed to like being on the bus. He looked trapped in those vinyl seats, often pressed against the window with one of his garrulous brothers typically sitting beside him and jabbering to someone across the aisle.

There was this one day, though, when no one was sitting next to him. She'd already been seated when he walked onto the bus (junior high kids were picked up before the high schoolers) and she noticed he'd looked at her when he strode past, choosing to sit in the row directly behind her and putting his backpack next to him so he could have the whole seat to himself. It had been a dress-up day for the eighth graders, and she was wearing one of her prettiest princess gowns. Yards of royal purple—she loved it! Austin was in his usual T-shirt and jeans, but his gaze lingered on her for a long moment before he chose his seat. That he decided to sit so close was encouraging to her.

He was holding something in his hands that snagged her interest, and Emma hoped that, maybe, if she asked him about the object, it might draw him out. He looked so sweet when he smiled, but that didn't happen frequently on the way to or from school.

So, she turned in her seat and grinned at him. He looked back at her, not exactly grinning but at least not scowling.

"What did you make?" she asked.

He considered her question for a moment before exhaling and holding up a wooden plaque with very smooth edges. It was carved with the words "The Knightley Family." He cleared his throat. "Woodworking class project."

"Oh, that's really lovely!" she exclaimed and very politely asked him some interested follow-up questions about it, just like her parents had taught her to do.

His responses kept getting even shorter and more curt.

After she asked, "So, do *all* high schoolers take that class?" He merely shook his head and stared out the window.

She tried to be even more charming and amiable. "I think it would be fascinating to learn about—"

"It's an *elective*, Emma," he said brusquely. "Anyone can choose to take it or not. Even you." He set the plaque down next to his backpack and pulled out a thick novel. "Thanks for your interest, but if you don't mind, I'm gonna read now."

So she shrugged, turned back around in her seat, and started chatting with Ben Danielson in the row ahead of her, who was also in high school but not nearly so condescending about it.

It was strange that after all these years, it still rankled that she couldn't win Austin over. It was as if he'd made a judgment call against her when she was a kid and refused to reverse that verdict.

The good thing, though, was that she didn't have to deal with him most of the time. If the worst that happened was that she ran into him at the market every once in a while, that wouldn't be too terrible. As long as his sister wasn't nearby, attempting to spark a conversation between them all.

On the subject of wooden things, however, there was still no word back from the furniture company. Frustrating to be sure, but if they didn't respond tonight, they would certainly be more attentive tomorrow. With the possible exception of Austin Knightley, no one ever ignored Emma for long, and she had no doubt she'd hear from them very soon.

# *Four*

Emma checked the calendar. *Friday the thirteenth.* Oh, goody.

It was the Yuletide of course, not Halloween, but maybe the date explained why she was having her own personal nightmare before Christmas.

She'd been trying for hours to reach a woodworker, a manager, a receptionist, anybody at Don's Fine Furnishings—but no one was answering, least of all Don himself. The voice message was a standard "we're not available now but will get back to you soon" kind of thing, but they still hadn't returned her calls from yesterday, let alone her urgent inquiries today.

Her emails had also gone unanswered, which surprised her even more since everyone at the company had replied so promptly to her messages in the past.

Emma wasn't inclined toward being superstitious, but maybe the bizarre goings-on today were on account of the inauspicious date. All she needed was to cross paths with a black cat or walk under a ladder to cement her bad luck.

Of course, it was too cold outside for the average

housecat to be running around, and no one with sense would set up a ladder on an icy sidewalk. So, Emma was fairly confident she wouldn't come upon any additionally unlucky entities during her morning errands in town.

Until she ran into Austin Knightley.

Literally.

"Oooph," he said as she slid into him with a thud at the corner of Main Street and Second Avenue.

"Oh! I'm so sorry!" she exclaimed as he steadied her and then quickly stepped away from her body as if she had a virus. "I-I wasn't looking. My apologies."

Despite the cold, she could feel her cheeks heating up. How embarrassing. She'd been looking at Santa standing out in front of Nick's Toy Shoppe and returning his friendly wave when she'd rounded the corner. Of course, of *all* the people in Crystal Corners she could possibly run into, it just had to be Austin.

Friday the thirteenth strikes again.

"No worries," he said with a small smile that cracked the otherwise impervious mask of his face. "This jacket is thick enough to protect me from a boulder crashing into me. You didn't leave a dent."

Emma swallowed, unable to keep from noticing how well he wore that jacket. Dark gray suited him. "Um, good," she murmured. Then she paused, waiting for him to comment again. He was studying her strangely, and she couldn't help but feel he found her wanting somehow.

Eventually, he kind of shook his head, as if dismissing her, and simply said, "Well, have a nice day, Emma," before he stepped past her and continued on his journey.

She watched him leave and caught sight of the same store Santa waving at Austin—an extra gleam, perhaps, in the older gentleman's bright eyes.

Austin returned the wave to the man in red, but he didn't look back at her.

She let out a breath she hadn't realized she'd been

holding and tried to think through the action plan she had for the rest of the morning.

It was only eleven fifteen but, seriously, could this day get any worse?

Austin was pretty sure bad things came in threes...and that had to be triply true on Friday the thirteenth.

First, his dad had taken a spill at physical therapy this morning. He was fine, overall, but a little bruised and in need of an ice pack.

Then, the candidate Austin had been most interested in hiring to manage the Twin Cities branch of his company withdrew his application because he'd accepted a position elsewhere. That left him having to go back to the drawing board and rethink the merits of the remaining applicants.

And, finally, just when he thought the day couldn't go any further downhill, he'd run smack into Emma Westwood.

A woman who looked absolutely ridiculous on this frigid December morning.

What kind of birdbrain wore a lightweight designer cloak-like thing in the midst of a Minnesotan winter? Or a scarf that thin? (There were weird patterns on it, and he could've sworn it had *sparkles*.) Or "boots," for want of a better word, with heels that spiked and lacked any real tread? A strong gust of wind could have toppled her over or sent her flying across the road.

But, he had to confess, she made a pretty picture surrounded by the snow-covered evergreen bushes that lined the sidewalk and all of those downtown holiday decorations.

He shook his head. *Don't go there, man,* he told himself. *It's not worth it.*

He hadn't taken more than twenty steps, though, before someone called his name.

"I'd heard this nasty rumor that you were back in town, but I didn't wanna believe it until I saw you for myself."

Austin shot a glance to his right, and sure enough, there stood his old high school soccer buddy, Mack Morales, grinning at him from the doorway of Sports & Rec.

He crossed his arms and mock-glared at his longtime friend. "Can't go anywhere in this town without tripping over some doofus...from the *best* soccer team in the Mid-State Valley Region."

Both guys laughed and man-hugged right there in front of the sporting goods store.

Mack backhanded Austin across his chest. "Look at you, dude. You're lookin' fighting fit. And your brother, Connor, gave me the 4-1-1 on your company's growth. That's outstanding."

"Thank you," Austin said sincerely. He, too, had heard good things about Mack's life from Connor and proceeded to praise his friend on the success of his store. Sports & Rec had been Mack's brainchild about six or seven years ago and a staple in the downtown Crystal Corners business lineup for nearly that long.

"My mouthy brother also told me you've been getting serious with Lila Harris." Austin raised a brow. "How, exactly, did *that* unlikely event happen?"

Mack chuckled. "Well, you know I had the hugest crush on her in high school. But she moved away for about eight years. I'd just started dating someone else, and my girlfriend at the time invited Lila to this huge summer barbeque she'd organized. And, of course, I was there, too. Absolutely nothing happened between Lila and me then, but somehow my girlfriend sensed that Lila and I would make a better couple. So, not long after that, Emma set us up and we—"

"Wait. Emma...*who?*" Austin interrupted. He only

knew two females in Crystal Corners who were named Emma, and one of them was seven. "You don't mean Emma Westwood, do you?"

Mack nodded.

"You were, um, dating her?"

"For, like, a minute," Mack replied. "It wasn't serious, and obviously, it wasn't meant to be. Emma's definitely into men, but I'm not sure there's any guy in town who's a match for her. She's pretty independent."

"Huh," Austin managed. "I—um, I'm just kinda surprised."

His buddy squinted at him. "She was only a year younger than us, Austin. Didn't you ever talk to her back then? Did you maybe have a thing for her? Or—"

"No," Austin said, cutting him off. And also lying through his teeth. "I've just, uh, run into her a couple of times since I've been back."

"That's real interesting," Mack said with a sly grin. "'Cuz you've only been back, like, forty-eight hours."

This was one of the problems with small towns. People knew—and kept track of—every stinkin' detail of your life.

"Well, I'm gonna be here for a lot longer than that, so we oughta catch up soon. Over beer and football, maybe?" Austin suggested.

Mack slapped him on the back and nodded. "It's a plan. Let's just get through this Christmas craziness, and we'll get together."

Austin tipped his imaginary hat at his friend. "Looking forward to it."

But as he wound his way home, he found himself uncomfortably preoccupied with thoughts of one very particular five-foot-six blonde...who was chummy with his sister, ridiculously underdressed for winter, and had formerly dated one of his best friends.

*Don't go there, man,* he told himself again. *Really.*

Emma had heard it reported that both good things and bad things came in threes, but she'd figured that not being able to reach the furniture company and also running into a disapproving Austin was already quite enough negativity for one day.

Still, there was an impending sense of waiting for the other shoe to be dropped that dogged her throughout the afternoon.

She'd almost convinced herself that, Friday the thirteenth or no, the day would end on an uneventful note, when there was a knock at the front door.

"Adele!" she cried, pleased to see the buoyant forty-something woman who was the owner of her favorite town bakery.

Adele Garoletto stood on Emma's doorstep with a large pastry box in both hands, a legal-sized white envelope tucked underneath the box, and an impish grin on her face. "Brought you a treat, Little Miss Em. May I come in?"

Emma swung the door open and welcomed her kind neighbor inside. "What deliciousness do you have here?"

Adele set the box down on the hall table. "It's from the first batch of Lemon-Glazed Sugar Cookie Stars. I remembered how much you liked them last year."

Emma clasped her hands together. See? A very *good* thing had just happened! The day was on its way up. "Oh, thank you. I can't wait to try one. Let me make us some hot chai, and we can have that with our cookies."

Adele said, "I'll gratefully take a cup of chai, but I'd better not eat any more sweets. I've been sampling my own products like crazy this month. Put on four pounds already."

Emma laughed. It was wonderful to have company, and such a sweet—no pun intended—person, too. Whether

Adele came bearing gifts or not, Emma always enjoyed spending time with her. But this afternoon, after such a day of frustration and loneliness, her neighbor from a few doors down was even more of a welcome sight. "Please make yourself at home, and I'll be in the living room in a moment."

When Emma rejoined Adele a few minutes later, the other woman held out the large envelope to her. "I *think*—although I'll confess I'm not positive—that this is yours." Adele pointed to the address on the front of the envelope, which was written with such dreadfully scrawled handwriting that it was hardly legible. And the name of the addressee only looked vaguely like Emma's name.

"It was in my mailbox today," Adele continued, "but don't blame Mr. Parsons and his staff. I'm surprised they even figured out the correct street, based on this penmanship."

Emma glanced at the return address, which was also handwritten, but she managed to make out the city. "White Bear...um, Lake." She paused and thought. "Oh! This is where the furniture company is located."

Convinced that, indeed, the poorly addressed envelope was intended for her, she slit open the flap and pulled out a sheet of paper with the words "Don's Fine Furnishings" professionally embossed across the top.

"Is this about your pretty wooden display case?" Adele guessed, having seen the picture of it that Emma had gotten just a couple of weeks ago.

Emma began to nod but couldn't speak. Her throat went dry, and her gaze kept snagging on the terribly troubling words typed on that single sheet of paper. Words like "Sorry" and "Warehouse Fire" and "Very Unfortunate" and "Refund to Be Issued by Insurance" and "No Delivery Possible."

She blinked at the page, mute, and just handed it to Adele by way of explanation.

Adele read it and shrieked. "What? Oh, no! Emma..."

Emma was engulfed in one of her friend's ample hugs, but her arms, along with her brain, were in shock.

Her perfect display case. It rotated. It had glassed-in sections. It could hold enough statuettes for every child in town. And it was gone.

She'd planned her event for the children so carefully, not leaving any aspect un-researched or any detail left to the last minute. And, yet, here she was, less than two weeks before Christmas, and her project plan was in shambles. Or, rather, in ashes.

Her neighbor handed her a star-shaped sugar cookie frosted with a tangy lemon glaze. "Eat this," she ordered.

Adele herself stuffed half of a lemon star in her mouth and started chomping. Then she guzzled several sips of chai before finishing her first cookie and starting on another.

Emma didn't know how many star cookies she and Adele stress-ate before she managed to recover her voice, but the first thing Emma said aloud when she did was, "I've got to fix this. And no one—*no one*—is going to keep me from doing my Christmas morning event just the way I planned."

How, exactly, to fix it was the big question, of course, but she was determined. And with very few exceptions, she'd never met an obstacle persistence couldn't overcome.

Austin inhaled the distinctive scent of fried onion rings and settled deeper into the booth he and his brother were inhabiting.

Ah, Friday night at Overtime, the only true sports bar and grill in Crystal Corners. Hanging out with Connor. Kicking back and enjoying the hockey game the two of them were sort of watching on one of the big screen TVs.

He'd missed doing things like this.

Sure, they could have spent the evening at their folks' house and caught the game there, but his brother wanted to "take him out on the town," and Austin wasn't going to refuse a reasonable sibling request.

"So, let's talk women," Connor said. "What's the deal with you and Taylor?"

Austin squinted at him. "We're going to start with that?" He shook his head. "Nah, I don't think so, bro. Why don't you tell me about *you* and *your* ex-girlfriends, hmm? That's much more entertaining."

His brother laughed. "Not much to tell. Not now, anyway."

Then Connor proceeded to list a string of women—some townies and some from cities nearby—that he'd dated over the past year. It sounded like an episode of *The Bachelor: After the Final Rose*, with all of those horrifying post-mortem date analyses of drama queen behavior, hurt feelings, and disaster dates.

Austin ate a few greasy onion rings. "Look, I can't compete with any of that. You win, man. My old relationships are pretty boring by comparison."

"But why did things with Taylor crash and burn so fast?" Connor asked him. "I know she was kind of...um, intense and not really fun, but the two of you went out for almost a year. There must've been something you liked about her, wasn't there?"

He thought about this. "Yeah, sure. She was intelligent, attractive, and ambitious. But we were definitely opposites. I'm not looking for someone who's so different from me. Next time I date anyone—and that's probably going to be a long, long time from now—it'll have to be a woman who's practically my clone," he joked. "Well, hopefully, she's a lot prettier than me, but she's not going to be high-strung or some socialite type or have any qualities I totally don't understand." An image of Emma Westwood flashed in his head. *Seriously, no one like her,* he reminded himself.

"Eh, well, there are opposites, and there are *opposites*," Connor said with a shrug. "I mean, you know the saying, 'opposites attract,' right?"

Austin nodded. He loathed that saying.

"The thing is," his brother continued, waxing philosophical around a mouthful of fried food, "you can be opposite of someone in ways that are either important or unimportant. The trick is to find out which is which."

"Okay, smart guy, since you've got all the answers, why haven't you found the perfect woman yet?"

His brother burst out laughing. "Because I'm not *looking* for the perfect woman yet." He reached for another onion ring. "I'm not *you*. But if I was, I'd try to figure out which qualities are nonnegotiable ones. The values you *need* to have in common. Then you can separate them out from all the other optional stuff."

Austin inclined his head in Connor's direction. His advice wasn't bad, actually, especially considering the guy was almost four years younger than Austin. Then again, Connor had dated *a lot*.

"Did you ever go out with someone and you knew the relationship probably looked great on paper, but when you got real about it, things just didn't click deep down?" Austin asked him.

"About every other girlfriend," Connor replied.

He grinned. "Yeah, so, that was what it was like for me with some of the women I dated before Taylor. When they're too similar, I'm bored. When they're too different, I'm put off. I feel like I can't quite find the right combination."

"Maybe you're trying too hard," his brother suggested. "Maybe this next time around, you should let her come to you."

Austin pondered these words late into the night, even when he knew he should have gone to bed. He pulled out a new novel and read for an hour, hoping to get tired enough to sleep.

He'd always enjoyed fiction and read widely across multiple genres, especially sci-fi, fantasy, and mystery. This much he knew: Sometimes the heroes of these epic tales were passive, but mostly they weren't. Mostly the heroes went out into the world and made their fortunes and sought out their soul mates. Austin had achieved the fortune part already. The notion of waiting for love to appear on his doorstep didn't sit well with him, though, even if that strategy worked (at least half the time) for his more loquacious and laid-back brother.

Besides, Austin was back in Crystal Corners now, not living in a metropolitan area like Minneapolis/St. Paul. The only women who'd show up on his parents' front porch were his sister or his mom's book club friends. So, he was probably safe there.

But if he ever decided to open up his heart to love again, he'd need to do a thorough search for "the one." No way was she coming to him.

# *Five*

It may have been a mid-December weekend in a small Midwestern town, but Emma was like a military commander, undertaking a mission of grand international scope and importance. She laid out her action plan for the day and then set about making a miracle happen.

But even military leaders and miracle workers could run into major obstacles during the holidays.

Despite having canvassed all of the businesses in downtown Crystal Corners, used her substantial networking skills to get names of potential helpers, and attempted to call in long-overdue favors from numerous and sundry sources, Emma still turned up empty-handed.

Ginger Mae had a cousin in Rochester who could build furniture both beautifully and quickly, but he was booked solid until March.

Adele had a good friend who was married to a professional carpenter, only the couple was in Aruba for Christmas and wouldn't be back in Minnesota until after New Year's.

And Jason worked with a local set designer who was

neither overbooked or away on vacation, but just when Emma was about to get her hopes up, her friend explained the bad news.

"Unfortunately, Leo got injured while working on this collapsing set for a production of *The Play That Goes Wrong* in St. Paul. Broke his right hand and is out of commission for at least a month."

Kent, who was finishing his Saturday afternoon lift at the gym as Jason and Emma conversed next to him, set down his free weights and caught his breath. "I think I'm getting old," he muttered. "I only managed to do three sets of twelve reps."

Jason rolled his eyes. "Yeah, at the ripe old age of thirty-two. Stop being vain and focus here. Emma needs our help. Who can she get to build this cabinet thingy in, like, ten days or less?"

Kent fiddled with his black-and-red workout towel and patted his forehead as he considered the question. "Does the display case have to be *exactly* like the one that got destroyed in the fire? Because if you just needed shelving, then maybe a bookstore or library could let you borrow—"

"No," Emma said stubbornly. "I'd envisioned it this way for months and designed it very specifically to be what I needed. Not just lovely to look at but sturdy and safe. You remember how unstable the other display case was? It almost crushed a toddler last year. No, I'm not doing it that way again."

"But maybe you could take the whole event inside," Jason suggested thoughtfully, "rather than having it out by the town tree. Then the shelves could be secured and—"

"Definitely no," Emma snapped, her patience fraying after a long day of struggles, although she deeply appreciated her friends trying to brainstorm alternate ideas. "The point is for this to be a shared community experience for the children. We don't have an indoor venue large enough for all the local kids to gather around a tree. The

Crystal Corners Theater stage is too narrow—you know that, Jason. The Town Hall assembly room is too small. And the community center's gathering spaces are already spoken for this holiday season. I can't displace the volunteers and service groups who've already committed to—"

"Okay, okay. We get it, kiddo. You need the display case you want, and you need it just the way you'd ordered it. Let me think," Kent said, his lean, chiseled face getting all scrunchy as he concentrated. "Hey, have you talked with Austin Knightley yet about a donation to the community gift chest? Because the guy runs a construction company. He probably knows a good builder, or he might even be able to make it himself."

*Absolutely not,* Emma wanted to shout, but she knew Kent was just trying to help. So, she just shook her head and said, "I haven't yet asked him about a donation, but I really don't think he's the guy to help build this cabinet. He constructs *big* things, like ramps and sheds and stuff. Plus, I'm sure he's got his hands full with his parents and family and business and all. I don't want to bother him."

Jason raised one thin dark-blond eyebrow in obvious disbelief. "Seriously? I mean, I love ya like a sister, Em, but since when do you not want to 'bother' someone if they can help you get what you want?"

Kent smothered a laugh. "What he means to say—and far more tactfully—is just think about it, Emma. Only if you run out of other options, of course," he added quickly. "But don't rule out any viable paths just yet, all right? You might be surprised by, um, what's possible."

"I suppose if I'm desperate," she conceded, but she didn't think she'd ever reach that point.

She was wrong.

By the nightfall on Sunday, Emma had to admit that *desperate* was exactly what she felt.

She'd reached out to so many residents in town. And

almost all of them had tried their best to come to her aid. Her failure thus far wasn't for lack of effort or friendliness or desire on their parts, it was simply that what she needed right now wasn't readily available. And neither her charm nor her money could get it—at least not in the limited timeframe she had to work with.

It was dispiriting, but if she had no other choice, she'd do what she must.

So, as early on Monday morning as was reasonable, Emma showed up at the Knightley family residence and knocked at the door.

Austin's mom answered. "Why, hello, Emma. How nice to see you," Pam Knightley said, ushering her inside the house and out of the cold. "What brings you over today?"

"I—um, I had a question for Austin." She glanced around the quiet front room, featuring a beautiful fresh-cut Christmas tree adorned only with a string of colored lights, but she did not immediately spot the person she came to see. "Is he, uh, here? If not, that's totally fine." She took a few steps in the direction of the door, her courage starting to flag, which was highly unusual for her. "I can visit later or, maybe, call—"

"Don't be silly, dear," Mrs. Knightley said with a laugh. "He's just bringing in some firewood from the garage. He'll be back in a moment. Here, let me take your coat. Would you like some hot coffee? Tea? Cocoa?"

"Oh, no, thank you. That's very kind. I'm fine, though. Really, I'm not planning to stay long, I just needed to ask him—"

"Hey, Mom, I saw a car in the drive. Who's—" Austin appeared in the doorway and stopped abruptly. The friendly expression fled from his face, and Emma felt a shudder of trepidation. She may have been desperate, but she wasn't stupid. Austin Knightley disapproved of her. She wasn't quite sure why, but his reaction to seeing her standing there was as clear as a beacon, and it wasn't positive.

Immediately, she regretted coming over. If it were only about her, she would've snatched up her cloak and sped out of the house without a backwards glance.

But it *wasn't* only about her. And, apparently, this was something she had to keep reminding herself of when she was in Austin's judgmental presence.

She cleared her throat. "Hello, Austin."

He blinked at her and then walked to the stone fireplace in the corner of the room and set down an armful of logs. When he straightened up again, he nodded at her slowly. "Hi there, Emma."

And then...silence.

"She came here to talk to you," his mother said brightly. She turned toward Emma. "Are you sure I can't get you something hot to drink? It's so cold out there. I'm making myself a butter-rum latte. Hot milk, a little coffee, this delicious sweet creamer. It's my new favorite winter drink."

That did sound good, but Emma wasn't sure she could swallow anything at this point. Being around Austin and having to speak in coherent sentences was challenging enough without managing a beverage, too. She didn't remember having had this difficulty when they were in school together. Why was it happening now?

But to his mom, she just said, "No, but thanks again."

"How about you, honey?" Mrs. Knightley asked her son. "Some coffee? Tea?"

He shook his head mutely, not taking his suspicious gaze off of Emma.

"Okey-dokey, then," his mom chirped. "I'll just be going into the kitchen now to clean up. You two call out if you need anything, you hear?" And with that, the only smiling face in the room spun on her heels and walked away, leaving Emma with an inhospitable Austin.

"So, what brings you here, Emma?" he asked, his voice

polite if emotionally detached.

"Well, I had a—an unfortunate circumstance occur this past week," she began, filling him in briefly on the warehouse fire and the subsequent destruction of the pretty display case she'd ordered. She pulled out a picture of the original and held it out to him. "It looked like this, see?"

He barely glanced at it. "Yeah. I'm very sorry to hear about the fire. The owner must be reeling. I hope no one was hurt."

Emma could answer this, having read over the letter from the furniture company upwards of three thousand times since Friday night. "Thankfully, no. All humans and animals on the property at the time of the blaze were brought to safety, but my rotating cabinet was not."

He breathed a long, slow sigh before responding. "It's a very sad thing, of course, that you lost the piece of furniture you were expecting, but I really don't understand why you're coming to me with this. I'm not familiar with the company or their products."

She almost rolled her eyes. Couldn't he take a hint? Did she have to spell out *everything* to him? Most men in town weren't half this obtuse, even the ones who weren't naturally as intelligent as Austin.

"Well, I was hoping that, perhaps, you'd be willing to lend a hand in its reconstruction," Emma said carefully. "Particularly someone as talented with wood and nails and stuff as you." She sent him her most winning smile.

He scowled in return. "Wood and nails and stuff..." he repeated. Then he shook his head. "I don't think so, Emma. But, uh, thanks for thinking of me. I'm sure there are *lots* of other people you know who'd jump at the chance to assist. But I have my hands full here."

She licked her lips, which were incredibly parched. Maybe she should have taken up his mom on that hot drink offer. Then she exhaled and tried again, planning to go just a little heavier on the flattery this time. "Actually, I've spoken with quite a few townspeople and...and your name came up as the person best suited to build it. You've been very successful at constructing things, so when my other possible contacts didn't come together as quickly as I thought, I really wanted to bring up this project with you."

"You're saying I'm your last resort?"

"Oh, no, no, of course not, Austin. Just that, um, time is of the essence with this. It needs to be ready by Christmas morning for a community event." She hoped by telling him this that it would activate his charitable side, but he didn't look any closer to committing.

Instead, he surprised her by bringing up something completely unrelated. "I ran into Mack Morales the other day. He told me a really interesting story about how he and Lila Harris became a couple."

"Yes," Emma said, grinning at that particularly delightful matchmaking triumph. "They're such a perfect pair. I just knew when I suggested they go out for that first date that they'd be happy together."

"You seem well accustomed to people being amenable to your, er, suggestions," he said, narrowing his eyes at her. "Perhaps a bit too accustomed."

What was he saying? It almost sounded like he was implying that she was manipulative. Which was just plain mean. Not to mention ungrateful.

"Aren't you and Mack friends, Austin? Would you have wanted him to b-be lonely? Or un-unhappy?" she sputtered.

"Of course not," he said sharply. "But I think your 'projects' need to be contained to individuals who welcome them. I don't think I'm that person."

"I wasn't asking you to do this for free," she said. "I mean, naturally, I'll pay you for your time and work."

"I don't need your money, Emma. I'm not mercenary, and I can't be bought."

"But this isn't for *me*—it's for the community," she

insisted, once again trying to allude that he could be more gracious and sympathetic to the needs of others.

He was having none of it.

"Sorry," he said simply. "I'm not your guy."

And there was nothing left for her to do but leave—confused, frustrated, and feeling uncharacteristically misunderstood.

Why wouldn't he help? Why was he so unreceptive? Anyone would think that a man trying to reintegrate into his hometown would be anxious to want to be of service to his community. But, no. Not the high and mighty Austin Knightley.

She wrinkled her nose. That almost rhymed, and she didn't like the sound of it. At all. Besides, she fully intended to bring him down a peg or two. She just wished she didn't need his assistance quite so much.

At home, in the same former playroom that held her favorite old storybooks, she began the final inventory of the statuettes she'd collected for the children. Feeling a little like Santa herself, Emma double-checked every child's name on the official town list and made sure she had a special figurine purchased and gift-tagged for each one of them.

Some of these she'd found months earlier and smiled when she saw the boat statuette for little Aaron, who was four and loved all things nautical. Or the tower of desserts statuette for eight-year-old Janie, the daughter of one of Adele's staff members, who'd spent her summer vacation learning to make cookies and brownies at the bakery.

And then there was Tyler. She thought about him as she held the guitar figurine. He was twelve, and like Emma, he came from one of the town's more affluent families. But he was a lonely child, even though he had lots of toys and several siblings. Mrs. Reed told her how Tyler dreamed of expressing himself through lyrics and melodies, and that'd he'd even begun composing simple songs on his guitar during his music lessons.

Meggie, on the other hand, also twelve years old, came from a needy single-parent family. Meggie's mom had been laid off of work for over four months. She'd recently gotten a new job, but the year had been a very tight one for their family. Meggie's passion was tennis, and she'd been glued to the TV during Wimbledon. Emma secretly bought her a good tennis racket and canister of balls that would be distributed to her via the community gift chest, but for the public event on Christmas morning, she had a tennis player statuette for Meggie, too.

Thinking about these children and the many more in town, only served to reignite Emma's resolve to host the event the way she'd planned. She wasn't someone who gave up easily, and she knew there *had* to be an angle she could use, a way she could succeed in convincing Austin to help.

Her laptop buzzed in the next room with the distinctive sound of a video call.

Her parents!

She raced to the computer and was pleased to see them grinning and waving at her from a square in Italy.

*"Buon giorno, bella!"* her dad exclaimed. He was holding up his phone. In the background, Emma could see the distinctive canals, bridges, and buildings of Venice.

Her mom popped into view next to Dad and waved. Emma laughed. Her mom was decked out in a blue-and-white-striped tourist shirt designed to make her look like a gondolier. "You guys look great," she said. "How is sunny Italy?"

"Absolutely delicious," Mom answered. "We've eaten pasta and gelato multiple times so far."

"And had lots of wine," Dad added.

"Oh, yeah. And tiramisu," said Mom.

"Anything interesting besides the food?" Emma asked, still chuckling. They looked like they were having so much fun together.

"It's a little warmer here than in northern Europe—almost fifty degrees today—so we've gotten to wander around outside a bit more. Take a look at San Marco's Square." Dad turned his phone so she could get a decent panorama of their surroundings. Pigeons flew around them, and fellow travelers chattered to each other in a range of languages. The buildings and people cast shadows on the square, and the laugh of a distant child sounded like a bell ringing. In the orange glow of the setting sun, the waters of the Grand Canal sparkled with gold, and the world on the other side of Emma's screen seemed to wrap her parents in warmth.

"Gorgeous," Emma declared.

Her mom nodded. "It's been lovely, and Rafael has an evening of entertainment planned to coincide with dinner. Some sort of traditional Italian dance."

"The tarantella," Dad interjected.

"Right," Mom said. "And tomorrow we're going to a Murano glass-blowing exhibit."

"We'll bring you back a vase," Dad promised. "Or maybe just some nice glass jewelry."

"It all sounds wonderful, but you don't have to bring me back any presents," Emma said, meaning it. "Just knowing that the two are enjoying yourselves is gift enough for me."

"Well, anyway, enough about us. How are you?" her mom asked. "Anything new?"

Emma dearly wished she could share all of the crazy goings-on lately—from her revolving display cabinet being destroyed in a fire to Austin Knightley returning to town—but, again, she feared if she disclosed too much, they'd come rushing home, instead of staying on their romantic trip where they belonged.

"Things are...all right," she said. "There have been a couple of glitches. Nothing I can't handle, though."

"We know you're very good at getting things done, baby girl," her dad said, "but don't be afraid to ask for a helping hand when you need it."

"Yeah, well, I've been trying to do that, but some individuals are not as receptive as I'd like," she admitted.

Her mom sent her a loving look. "Not everyone knows you like we do, sweetheart. They might not be able to guess at what you need, so you might have to ask for their support directly, rather than trying to subtly steer them in the right direction or expecting them to guess your intentions or read your mind...like you sometimes do."

If her mother hadn't said these words quite so gently and tactfully, Emma might have burst into tears. Did even her parents think, like Austin did, that she was trying to get her way by being sneaky?

Maybe, in a way, it was true. After all, men like Austin looked at her like she was some kind of pampered Barbie if she ever asked for assistance. So, she'd learned to resort to hinting, rather than openly requesting. Using her charm and leading them carefully to the right course of action. It was a delicate balance, and she'd always prided herself on doing this fairly well.

"Um, okay," she murmured.

"Don't be sad, honey," Mom said. "This isn't a huge criticism. We know what a good heart you have. We raised you to be kind to others, to get involved, and to help, and you do that beautifully. I just mean that, if it's about something really important to you, don't be subtle. State boldly what you need and what you're willing to do to help make it come together." Mom tilted her head to one side. "Does that help at all?"

Emma blinked back a couple of unshed tears and nodded. "It does, and I think you just gave me an excellent idea."

Mom and Dad blew her kisses and wished her a good rest of the day. And then, after Emma hung up from the video chat, she returned to her inventory of statuettes and thought through everything she wanted to say to Austin.

Today would be her planning day. Tomorrow, however, she would be ready with a new and bolder strategy...and she would get him on her side. "No" wasn't an option! And if she had to lay out on a platter for him every bit of reasoning she had for why this project mattered, she was determined to do just that.

# Six

Austin was starting to think that *every* day of December was like Friday the thirteenth...even though today was a Tuesday.

This morning, David had made himself useful by taking their dad to his cardiac rehab/physical therapy session at the gym. Bethany and Reggie were both at work at the hospital. Connor was out plowing the snow off driveways. And Mom, thankfully, was at a coffee get-together with her book club friends, where they spent a couple of hours talking about their husbands, their kids, and their favorite romance heroes. Not necessarily in that order.

It was only ten a.m., but he'd been on the phone with his current managers for the past two hours, trying to figure out this employee application situation.

He'd interviewed another candidate he really liked and who knew the construction industry inside and out. Only problem? He wasn't willing to relocate to the Twin Cities. He wanted to stay near Albert Lea and manage the newer branch there.

The current manager in Albert Lea was willing to

relocate...but only to the La Crescent branch. She didn't like big-city driving and wanted to be along the Mississippi River.

So that left the current La Crescent branch manager, who'd settled into the area about a year ago and hadn't expressed an interest in moving to Minneapolis/St. Paul. But he just might like it...if Austin could work up the nerve to ask. It was like a large-scale game of musical chairs. If he pulled this off, he'd have an incredibly strong team in place in every locale, but getting there was a delicate operation.

Just as he was about to dial up the guy in La Crescent, the doorbell rang. What now?

When he looked through the window and saw Emma Westwood standing on the front step, a box from Adele's Bakery in her hands, and a strangely persistent look on her face, he almost cursed aloud. Seriously? She came back here today, too?

He held the phone up to his ear as he swung open the door. "I'm working, Emma."

She grinned at him—a heart-melting, eye-shining smile that had him clenching his jaw in order to resist it.

"I don't want to bother you," she said sweetly. "I just brought this for your family." She held out the box of bakery goodies. "And I was hoping to talk with you for a few minutes while you're here alone."

He took the box and instinctively took a step back as she slid through the front door. "How did you know I was—"

"Alone?" she completed. "Oh, I was in downtown Crystal Corners just now and saw your mom at the coffee shop and your dad and brother David at the gym. Your sister always works on weekdays. And I figured with the snow we got last night—"

"That Connor would be busy plowing," he finished for her.

"Exactly. And I needed to see you privately today because, Austin, I have to level with you." She paused and took several deep breaths. Emma was someone who almost always looked poised, but there was something in her expression that alerted him to the fact that she'd taken extra care with her appearance this morning. She looked as perky and as daintily dressed as usual, but she seemed a little less sure of herself.

He set the box of bakery bribes on the hall table, but didn't immediately ask for her too-thin cloak or that nearly useless scarf.

"Level with me about what, exactly?" he asked, starting to get impatient.

"I really need your help," she began, but he interrupted her.

"We went over this yesterday, Emma. You need to look elsewhere. I'm not—" His phone rang. Good. Now he didn't have to pretend to be busy. "Excuse me, I need to take this."

He answered the call, but Emma didn't budge from her spot in the hallway. She just stared at him and listened attentively as he spoke to the Albert Lea manager about the proposed job shifts. "No, I haven't called Carl yet. I'm not really sure how to suggest the position change. Yeah, yeah. I know, Melissa. But he's only been there a year and—" He rubbed his forehead as she offered her own ideas of approach. He listened politely, but his attention kept getting diverted by Emma, who hadn't uttered so much as a whisper, but somehow her presence shouted at him from across the hall.

When he clicked off, he locked gazes with her. She was still staring attentively at him, her head cocked to one side and her lips curved into a tiny smile.

"What?" he said, feeling the edges of exasperation closing in on him. "Why are you looking at me like that?"

"Austin Knightley, you have a problem." She paused.

"But I think I can help."

He raised his brows at her. "You don't even know the situation. How could you—"

Then, in her grating, know-it-all way, she cut him off midsentence and succinctly summarized exactly what his problem was. How she'd managed to understand all of that from just his side of a five-minute phone conversation was a mystery, but he'd give credit where it was due. She didn't miss a thing.

"Sorry for eavesdropping," she added, "but obviously, I was standing right here." She pointed her slender index finger at him and took a few steps closer. "The thing you'll need to do next is to create a list of incentives for your employee Carl that suit his age, his needs, and his temperament. If you really want him to consider the transfer to the Twin Cities, your negotiations will go smoother if you approach it from his viewpoint, not yours. You're not going to focus on asking him to leave a city he's comfortable in and a managerial position he's acclimated to. Rather, you'll want to present to him an array of benefits—specific to his interests and lifestyle—that moving to a metropolis will afford."

Emma pulled a small notepad and pen out of her purse. "C'mon. This is important to you. Let's brainstorm."

And before Austin even thought to refuse, Emma had already listed several key demographic components to consider in his pitch to Carl. As a single, early thirties male who loved rock concerts and major sporting events, there were half a dozen entertainment perks alone that would be appealing. Not to mention a larger dating pool and a huge choice of living options.

Austin answered each of her questions, increasingly awed by how astutely she understood employees and their needs. She would have made a heck of a human resources consultant, he thought to himself before he realized that, in fact, she was a highly experienced one already, thanks to her background with her family's foundation. Emma Westwood knew how to handle people.

She ripped out of the notebook the several sheets of paper she'd been writing on in her near-perfect script and handed them all to him like a gift.

"I think you've got a strong strategy here," she said. "If Carl is the man you've described him to be, I think he'll be very excited about this opportunity."

Austin pocketed the pages and studied her for a long moment. "I think you're right," he finally admitted. "Thank you."

She smiled again. That insanely beautiful smile that lit up her whole face like a Christmas tree. He struggled not to let it affect him, but his efforts were in vain. He was attracted to her, and he always had been. He couldn't help it.

"You're welcome," she replied. "Do you want to make your calls and talk to them all right now? If so, I could come back later. Otherwise, if you have a few moments to chat with me before getting back to your business, I could stay just five minutes longer." The hopefulness in her voice almost undid him.

He cleared his throat. "We can talk now, Emma."

She exhaled. "Thank you. I—I've found that it's not easy for me to openly ask someone for help, but I wouldn't be here now if I didn't truly need yours." She paused and looked to be gathering her thoughts, maybe running through a mental lineup of things to say. "This Christmas morning event is really dear to my heart, and to make it work, I need a rotating display cabinet that can hold—"

"I'll help you," he heard himself say, heaven help him. "But—"

"Oh, thank you! Thank you, Austin." She squealed a little and sort of jumped up and down like a bunny. "I've got the picture right here." She pulled it out of her purse and thrust it at him. "And I can tell you the exact specifications for the dimensions and the—"

"Oh, no, no, Emma. Wait." He thrust the picture right back at her. "I said I'll *help* you. I did not say I'll do it *for* you. There's a difference."

She squinted at him. "I'm not sure I understand."

He almost laughed. Legit, she looked pretty confused. He took a step closer and spoke more slowly. "I'll help you make this thing. With wood and nails and stuff," he couldn't help but add, mimicking her words from yesterday. "But if you really and truly want it, we'll be working on it *together*. Which means you'll have to actually do something more than hand me a photograph and expect magic to occur."

Her blue eyes were big and round as she took in these provisional terms, but nevertheless, she nodded. "Okay. W-What, um, do I do?"

At this he did laugh. As usual, she was dressed too impractically to do anything but, perhaps, put on a fashion show or attend high tea at some posh restaurant.

"Step one," he said, ticking the first finger on his left hand, "is to go home and do whatever you need to do to clear your schedule for tomorrow. I have a lot of work-related things to get done today, starting with that phone call to Carl—and, once again, thank you very much for your assistance with that. But if all goes well, tomorrow will be a much easier day for me, too."

"Okay," she said agreeably.

"Good. Step two," he said, ticking his second finger, "is when you come back here tomorrow around nine a.m., dress casually. Very casually. In clothes you can get dirty, you hear?"

"Like play clothes," she murmured, her forehead scrunched up as she considered this.

"Right. Like play clothes, only we're going to *work*. And that's step three." He ticked his third finger. "Be prepared to work on this all day." He nodded toward the photograph she was holding. "From the look of the carousel cabinet you have in mind, and given the other obligations we both have, it might take us a whole week to make it. So, let's get in a good day tomorrow and make some headway. Deal?"

She nodded quickly and did that little bunny bounce thing again. "Deal! I'll be here tomorrow morning at nine o'clock sharp, ready to help."

"In casual clothes," he reminded her. "And shoes."

She glanced at her feet in those teetering black boots. "Um, sure. Play clothes *and* shoes." Then she grinned at him—a smile that could only be measured in watts. "Thanks, Austin! I'm so excited. I'll see you tomorrow." And she bounded out the door, down the walkway, and to her car, like a little girl going home after a playdate.

She'd been such an odd juxtaposition today of a wise woman and a joyful child, he found himself drawn to her and wanting to spend more time with her. He had no idea, really, what he'd just gotten himself into.

What was this Christmas project anyway? All he knew was that he was increasingly curious about the mystery lady behind it, however unwise that curiosity might be.

# Seven

### *One Week to Christmas*

Austin started checking the time every five minutes from eight thirty a.m. onward.

"Why are you so antsy, man?" his brother David asked as he got ready to take their dad to PT again. "Expecting an important phone call or something?"

"Or something," he replied, glancing at the hall clock and willing his beloved family members to leave the house, and quickly. Emma would be arriving in less than twenty minutes.

Once David and Dad were out the door, though, there was still Mom, who was lingering in the kitchen as if she knew someone was coming over. Specifically, someone female.

"Sweetheart, before I go to the grocery store, can I make some muffins or a fruit salad or anything tasty for you?"

"Oh, no, Mom, thanks. I don't need anything."

"But what if someone stops by? You'll want to be able

to offer him—or her—some refreshments. At least let me brew a fresh pot of coffee."

It was now ten minutes to nine. He swallowed. "Coffee sounds like a great idea, but why don't you let me make it? It's busy at the market this time of year. You'll want to get there early to avoid the lines."

His mother raised her brows slowly. No doubt about it, she had to have guessed that something was up. Under normal circumstances, he might have copped to it already, but working on a project with Emma Westwood wasn't exactly a "normal" circumstance. It would be bad enough later when his mom, dad, and kid brother all returned and Emma was there in the house. But if any of them were hanging around to greet her upon arrival, it'd be awkward. And he didn't need this to be any more awkward than it already was.

Surprisingly, Mom didn't voice any suspicions aloud. She just kissed him on the cheek, slipped on her winter coat, and grabbed her keys and shopping list.

"I'll be back in a few hours," she told him. "Maybe a little longer if I stop at Adele's Bakery. Those sugar cookies and cocoa-caramel bars that Emma brought us were delicious. I might have to get more." She paused and smiled...*almost* guilelessly, but he wasn't fooled. "Be sure to thank her if you see her before I do."

"Of course," Austin managed. Four minutes to nine.

Miraculously, his mother had actually pulled out of the driveway and was down the road before Emma drove up and parked in the front, curbside.

Nine o'clock sharp.

She knocked on the door, and he forced himself to wait five full seconds before opening it.

"Good morning," she said brightly, holding up a large white paper bag containing something indistinguishable with her right hand while she waved at him with her left.

"Good morning, Emma." He invited her inside.

"Thanks for parking on the street, but you didn't have to."

She laughed. "I didn't want to block the driveway." She nodded in the direction of the garage. "I'm sure your dad and brother are already at the gym. And I just saw your mom's car pull out. I imagine the three of them will come back at some point." She handed him the bag. "A snack for all of us for later. Or lunch, perhaps. I hope you like curried chicken salad on butter croissants."

He peered into the bag and was struck by her thoughtfulness—both with the parking and with the sandwiches. "Wow. Thank you. Did you make these?"

She shook her head. "No, but it's a favorite of mine, and one of Jennings's specialties."

He felt an unwelcome bolt of jealousy. "Who's Jennings?"

"He's our family's chef and the reason why I'm such a terrible cook." She gave a short, self-deprecating laugh. "I never had to learn how to make anything substantial, not with Jennings in the house. And my few attempts at baking were truly embarrassing. Between Jennings and Adele, I always have wonderful meals and desserts. I leave the tough stuff to them."

He didn't know how to respond to that. He'd never thought of Emma as being unable to do anything she might want—just that there were some things she considered beneath her. Maybe that wasn't the case, though. Maybe what he'd always pegged as Emma's damsel-in-distress act was more a crisis in confidence.

Austin motioned for her to follow him into the kitchen, where he put her offering in the fridge and offered her a mug of hot coffee, which had just finished brewing.

"Let me take your coat," he said, pleased that she was wearing a thicker one today, "and then let's grab our coffees and head downstairs to the workroom. We've got a drafting board and tools. Today's going to be all about planning and collecting materials, okay?"

"Okay." She handed him her coat and then eyed him with a slight air of nervousness. "Am I, um, dressed correctly?" she asked.

He gave her a quick once-over and absorbed as many details as his eyes could take in. Her perfectly manicured fingernails, which would probably get chipped to bits when they brought back the wood this afternoon and started working on it. Her golden ringlets, not a hair of which was out of place. Her big blue eyes and rosebud lips...

*Oh, c'mon, Austin. Focus on her question. The clothes.*

True to her word, she was dressed in an affluent version of "play clothes and shoes" or, at least, sneakers that weren't remotely as ratty as Austin would have liked, but they were a far sight better than those pointy, ankle-breaking boots. She also had on a slightly baggy blue sweatshirt that complemented the color in her eyes and a pair of jeans that were marginally faded, although they weren't baggy at all. In fact, they fit her extremely well.

He exhaled. "Yeah. You look great," he murmured, not liking at all just how much he meant it.

"Thanks." She smiled. "All right, Austin. Coffee and then work. Let's do this!"

"Yeah, let's do this," he repeated.

So, steaming coffee mugs in hand, they headed downstairs to the workshop where Austin's dad had taught him how to measure and cut his first two-by-four. Bringing Emma into this world was like letting her inside a private part of himself. Like revealing a secret.

He watched her gaze thoughtfully at the equipment, the tables, the tools. Or, as she would probably say, the "wood and nails and stuff." Waited for her reaction.

She nodded as she glanced around. "This is really cool." She pointed to a plaque he'd made in woodworking class in high school—the one with his family's last name on it. "I remember when you showed me that on the bus." She paused and nibbled for a moment on her lip. "I'm glad you still have it. It must have been exciting to learn how to use all of these tools when you were growing up."

"It was," he admitted. "My dad and his brothers were all into carpentry and woodworking. It was just a hobby for them, but they made beautiful pieces. End tables. Desks. Some bookshelves. My uncle Jeff even made a rocking chair once. It's still my aunt Kay's favorite piece of furniture."

He offered Emma a chair at the drafting table. "And then I got the building bug. My focus was more on larger construction, but making anything with wood, really, is of interest to me." He pulled out a fresh sheet of paper and a drawing pencil. "Let's take a closer look at your display case picture, and you can tell me about the dimensions you have in mind. I'll sketch a model with measurements and draw up a list of materials we'll need to purchase today. My plan is to hunt down all the wood required at the lumberyard and get it with a graining you love. The sooner we have that, the sooner we can get started on actually building it."

Emma had been listening attentively to him as he blathered, sipping her coffee and nodding along. Now, however, she pulled out the photo of this rotating cabinet of hers and stroked the image with her fingertip, as if caressing the real item.

"What's important to me is to get the design to look as close to this one as possible." She pointed at the picture. "Do you see all of these cased-in compartments here, behind the glass?"

"Yeah." They were hard to miss, and they'd be a pain to replicate on such short notice.

"I need to make sure there's room for a couple hundred statuettes on the enclosed shelving," she informed him. "That part's critical."

Statuettes? Seriously? "You mean, like, little trophies?"

"Sort of. They're mostly figurines, and they *all* have to

fit somewhere in the rotating case."

Austin studied the photograph a little more closely. "Does it *have* to rotate? Because I think I could—"

"Yes," she interrupted. "I'm sure you're really creative, Austin, and that you can come up with amazing and innovative designs, but this is exactly what I've had in mind all year, and it's exactly what I want us to build."

He nodded. "All right," he said to her. Sort of rigid and uncompromising, he added to himself, but, hey, this was her dream project or whatever. He began sketching.

Turned out, the general design wasn't the *only* aspect of the display case that Emma felt strongly about. Emma proved to be *very* particular. When she said she wanted it to be *exactly* like what she'd ordered, she wasn't kidding. The wood staining had to look a certain way. The glass doors had to be curved just so. The width of the shelves needed to be a prescribed distance apart.

Her promptness and thoughtfulness this morning were a plus. And after taking her advice yesterday—regarding what turned out to be an extremely successful and productive conversation with Carl—Austin had begrudgingly found several traits in Emma Westwood that he'd begun to admire, besides just her physical beauty. But this inflexibility of hers wasn't one of them. Neither was her stubbornness.

"I'm not sure I'll be able to get pre-cut glass, curved and weighted to fit your specifications, in Crystal Corners," he told her dryly. "That's going to require a trip to a larger town. But we can worry about the doors and hinges later in the week. We're going to have our hands full just building the display case itself. The shaping, sanding, and staining of it."

"That's great," she replied. "Just show me what to do next." She rubbed her hands together. Then, like a kid on a road trip, she said, "How much longer before we can go to the lumberyard?"

*This*, he thought with a heavy sigh, *is going to be a really long day*.

And initially, at least, he couldn't have been more correct.

For more years than Austin could remember, he'd wanted to see the perfectly proper Miss Emma Westwood look a little disheveled for a change. As they were rummaging through stacks of wood at the lumberyard (Curly Maple proved to be her favorite), inspecting the graining on each plank for good matches (she was as picky about that as she'd been about everything else thus far), and piling all the winners into the back of his pickup truck, Austin got his wish. Emma looked good and messy, and they hadn't even plugged in the circular saw yet.

He laughed and plucked a woodchip from her hair that had somehow gotten lodged in a ringlet. "Hey, hold still a sec. I want to make sure there isn't more in there."

Austin didn't know how, exactly, the bit of wood had found its way from the rough lumberyard shelving to Emma's naturally curly strands, but he was a little envious when he touched it. He'd never felt hair that silky.

She wrinkled her nose. "Is it all out? I don't want to get a splinter in my scalp."

"Let me check you over one more time," he told her, but Austin had been thorough. He knew all the woodchips were gone. Still, for her sake—and, okay, maybe also for his—he ran his hands from the crown of her head all the way down to the ends of her ringlets, letting the long tresses flow through his fingers like a golden river.

"You should be fine now," he declared. But when he pulled his hands away, she was looking up at his face, studying him with an odd expression.

"Um, thanks, Austin. M-Maybe I should tie my hair back in a braid or ponytail before we start measuring and sawing, or I might end up with an unexpected haircut."

He laughed at her joke but stepped quickly back from

her and into his truck. What was he doing? It was one thing to agree to help her with some community project. It was altogether another to be within touching distance. First a caress. Then a hug. Then a kiss—

No.

He couldn't take mental leaps like that. An actual relationship wasn't going to happen. Not with *her*.

Although, she had dated Mack. Even if it'd been for just a very short time, it still proved that Emma wasn't completely opposed to going out with a townie that she'd known since their school days.

"May I turn on your car radio?" she asked politely, breaking into his thoughts and distracting him dangerously from driving.

"Yeah, sure."

She tuned in to Z-104, the station that had been playing constant Christmas music for weeks already. Some new hipster version of "All I Want For Christmas is You" was on. He was tempted to roll his eyes, but his sister would have approved of Emma's song choice.

"Bethany's big into Christmas carols," he said, just trying to make conversation. "She plagues me by playing them in the car and threatening to sing along. What about you? Do you like to sing carols, too?"

She chuckled. "Sometimes, sure. Mostly, I just dance to them, though. But I won't be doing that in your truck as we drive through the middle of Crystal Corners, I promise."

The image made him laugh in spite of himself. "Well, I wouldn't stop you, Emma."

She shook her head, those ringlets fluttering around her shoulders in a dance of their own.

"Maybe we'll need to take a dance break in the downstairs workshop this afternoon," he suggested, enjoying getting to tease her. "Stop, drop, and waltz through 'Silent Night.' Do a little tap number with 'Jingle Bells,' perhaps."

"I took five years of tap," she informed him, just as they were pulling into his parents' driveway. "And seven of ballet. My parents were deluded into thinking it would make me graceful," she told him with a laugh, again being self-deprecating. Second time that day. And also stunningly inaccurate. He'd rarely met anyone who moved as gracefully as Emma, even when she was wearing those absurdly impractical boots.

"You're graceful," he managed to say, parking his pickup and hopping out.

"You still think so? Even after I rammed right into you on the sidewalk last week?"

He'd almost forgotten about that. Had it only been a few days ago when that happened? It seemed like an eternity. "You were probably just preoccupied, not klutzy. However"—he pointed to the bed of his truck—"I need you to be especially mindful of where you're walking as we bring in these planks. They're not heavy, as long as we don't try take in too many at once, but carrying them inside and downstairs will be awkward."

"All right." She slipped on her mittens, not just to ward off the cold but also to protect from splinters. He'd warned her about that when they first left the house, and he liked that she'd been paying attention.

She was so funny about this entire process, though. So clueless. He had to explain the littlest of things to her, step by step. Not that she wasn't responsible, intelligent, or willing to make an effort. But she was clearly inexperienced with these sorts of practical, manual tasks.

Case in point, she'd offered to drive her little silver sports car to the lumberyard, obviously not realizing just how much room long planks of wood would take up and that her car's compact trunk was nowhere near spacious enough. She didn't have any idea how to navigate her way around the yard either—she trailed after him like a lost toddler—but she absolutely insisted on paying for every single item they'd purchased. He appreciated that, but he had to admit, he'd rarely seen someone who'd looked quite so out of place for quite so long.

"You just help me steady these, Emma," he told her, making sure he was handling the bulk of the weight. "Let me do the tricky part."

Somehow, they managed to make their way with the first load of planks into the house, but they didn't get far. Mom, Dad, and David swooped in on them moments after they stepped through the front door.

"Oh, Emma!" his mom cried. "How lovely to see you again. And what on earth is my son making you do?" She shook her head at Austin.

He didn't even have a chance to open his mouth to defend himself before Emma piped up and said, "Austin's helping *me*—"

But then David jumped in. "Let me take this side from you, Emma." Then, to Austin, "Is this going downstairs to the workshop?"

"Yep," he replied as their dad popped his head into the hall, too.

"Is there more wood in the car? I can get—"

"No, Dad," Austin and David said together.

"We'll take care of it," Austin insisted.

"But I'm supposed to help," Emma said, forced by David to let go of her side of the load.

Mom put her hands on Emma's shoulders and steered her away from the door. "I'm not sure what you two are up to, but it's lunchtime. You can help by explaining this project to me while I finish getting our meal together. Plus, I saw a bag of some delicious croissant sandwiches in the fridge. Did those come from your house?"

"They did. But they're for all of us..." Austin heard Emma reply, her voice trailing off as she followed Mom into the kitchen.

He and David were halfway down the stairs to the

basement when his kid brother made a funny face and whispered, "*This* is a story I gotta hear."

Austin just groaned and made David help him with the remaining loads. By the time they were done bringing in all of the materials, Mom had steamed a big bowl of broccoli and cauliflower, cut up an array of colorful fruits, and placed Emma's curried chicken salad sandwiches on a platter in the middle of the table, which Dad was setting. For all five of them.

"Austin," Emma said, when he walked into the kitchen, "your parents requested that we have lunch up here with them. But if you'd prefer to continue our work downstairs, we could—"

"Nonsense," Dad interjected, grinning at Emma. "It's not healthy to work without taking breaks. I hope I taught Austin better than that." Then he shot Austin a look that said in no uncertain terms that he and Emma weren't going to escape to the basement anytime soon.

Austin cleared his throat. "Of course we should take a break for lunch. But Emma does have a deadline for her display case, so we're still going to try to get as much done as we can this afternoon. Right, Emma?"

"Right!" she said brightly, and then she gushed to his parents and brother for three or four minutes nonstop about how helpful he'd been and how much he'd taught her already ("I just *love* the beautiful graining of Curly Maple") and how amazing the finished product would be. "Truly," she told them all, before taking the first bit of her croissant, "I can't thank Austin enough for coming to my rescue on this project."

Dad looked proud. Mom looked curious. And David looked downright smirky. But all three of them nodded at Emma and then sent him glances he couldn't entirely interpret.

Lunch lasted a millennium.

At least it felt that way to Austin. By the time he and

Emma finally made it back to the workshop downstairs, it was midafternoon.

"Okay," he said, steeling himself for several hours of explanations to Emma and endless questions from her in return. He could almost hear them already: "What is beveling?" "How do you 'plane' a plank?" "What do we have to do to make sure the grain matches and is going in the same direction?"

But they'd barely gotten further than the measuring and cutting of the wood before Emma's cell phone rang.

"I'm so sorry, Austin, I have to take this." She tugged off the safety goggles he'd made her wear and answered her phone. He heard her say the name Ginger Mae. Then, "Oh, no!" Then, "Of course, I'll take care of it for her." Emma sunk into a chair. "May I speak with her please?" A longish pause. "Just worry about getting well, Ginger Mae. I'll go over to the community center right now and make sure it all goes as planned." Another pause. "Yes, I've got it. Not to worry."

"Problems at the community center?" he guessed. Ginger Mae Jones was like an institution herself there.

Emma sighed. "Ginger Mae caught a chest cold, but it's been getting worse instead of better. She went to see the doctor today and was admitted to the hospital for tonight. Given her age, her doc is concerned it might turn into pneumonia. But today's the last day for the holiday food drive, and Ginger Mae needs someone at the center to manage the collection and deliver the inventory to the volunteers who are doing the cooking. So, unfortunately, I need to leave right now." She looked around the workshop regretfully. "Would you be free to continue with me tomorrow? Nine a.m. again?"

He found himself nodding. "Of course. We'll just put everything here on pause until you can return."

She smiled at him. "Thank you." Then she gathered her things and raced up the stairs, stopping only for half a minute to thank his parents for lunch.

Austin felt strangely lonely in her absence. He glanced at the wooden planks and then picked up the saw, realizing how easy it would be for him to push ahead and do the next several steps in the building process without her.

But no.

The deal they'd made was that they'd work on this *together*, and he had to keep up his end of that bargain if he expected her to do the same.

Still, it had been an odd day with her here. He'd never imagined anyone could look cute in an old pair of safety goggles, but somehow Emma managed that. He was starting to think that being fashionable had nothing to do with clothes and accessories and everything to do with the air and bearing of the person wearing them.

"Well, you're certainly deep in thought," came a voice from the stairs.

Bethany.

"You shouldn't sneak up on people who are holding very sharp objects," he told his sister, raising the circular saw so she could see the flash of the blade. Then he unplugged it and put it away.

"And you, big brother, shouldn't be keeping secrets from your closest family members," she chided. "Mom texted me to come over, but I couldn't leave work early. Apparently, though, I'd just missed seeing Emma Westwood here. That's...interesting."

Austin exhaled. "Nah, nothing too interesting about it, sis. She just needed help with this display case of hers. A massive wooden carousel for statuettes or something. I don't know why. But she did me a favor yesterday, so I'm reciprocating. And that's all there is to it."

Bethany laughed. "Yeah, sure. If you say so."

"I do say so." And then, because he was starting to feel irritated and defensive and, oddly, at a loss for understanding his own weird emotions, he added, "Besides,

I can't be done with this project soon enough. She doesn't know anything about building, but she's insanely particular about each and every detail. And kind of bossy and stubborn. The whole thing is a headache, and I'm already regretting having agreed to work with her on it." This last part wasn't entirely true, but Bethany was annoying him, and he wanted her to stop smiling at him so knowingly.

His sister did stop smiling. Instead, she squinted at him. "So, you don't even know what she *does* with her statuettes, right?"

He shook his head. "Does it matter?"

"Yes, actually." Bethany walked over near him and grabbed a broom to sweep up the sawdust on the floor. "Emma spends all year personally purchasing and collecting figurines to give out as gifts to all the children in the town on Christmas morning. She's an only child, Austin, with a really big heart. I think this is a way for her to connect with the kids in Crystal Corners. Kind of like surrogate siblings. And to give each of them something beautiful and unique."

He swallowed away a lump in his throat and gulped some air before he spoke. "She'd mentioned the case was for the community, but she didn't say in what capacity. She didn't explain that these statuettes were gifts."

"Of course she didn't. People who are truly charitable don't brag about their generosity." She patted him lightly on his shoulder. "It's okay, big brother. Everyone misses signs once in a while. But you need to stop seeing Emma through some old adolescent lens. She's a grownup now." Bethany finished her final sweep and handed him the broom. "And so are you."

# Eight

Emma woke up the next morning with a tired body but an excited spirit.

Sure, she'd been up late helping out at the community center and making sure the food drive donations got where they needed to go. But it was all for a good cause. And before visiting hours were over, she took a break to make a quick stop at the hospital to check in on Ginger Mae.

The older lady had been full of additional instructions, feisty as ever, and giving the nurses a hard time, which, in Emma's opinion, was an excellent sign.

"She's on the road to recovery," the evening nurse told her with a smile. "But we need to take precautions to ensure that happens. Keeping her here for observation tonight is the best way. But even when she returns home, she shouldn't be going to the community center for long hours or interacting with a lot of people. Her immune system is weak, and she could easily get a secondary infection if she isn't careful."

Emma took this as the warning it was, and she immediately assured Ginger Mae that she'd oversee getting others to cover all of her commitments. "And if I can't find another volunteer, I'll personally take over the task myself," she told her friend. "So just concentrate on getting well."

"I'll try, girlie," Ginger Mae said. "But if they keep pokin' me and stuffin' me with Jell-O, I can't be held responsible for my actions."

Emma laughed at that last night and again this morning, remembering the half-feigned, half-genuine fury on Ginger Mae's face. Emma's schedule was going to be busier than she'd anticipated this week, but she welcomed the activity. It helped her keep her mind off the fact that—except for community events—she'd be alone on Christmas.

And then, of course, there was Austin. Whom she'd be seeing again in less than an hour.

She showered, quickly gobbled the fresh blueberry pancakes Jennings had made for her, and put on some absolutely atrocious clothes that would hopefully be deemed appropriate enough by Austin for woodworking. Then she headed out the door, stopping only at Adele's Bakery for a box of her Peppermint Mocha Cupcakes before driving to the Knightleys' house.

Nine a.m. sharp!

Austin's mom answered the door and gave her a warm hug. "What delicious delights have you brought us today?" Pam Knightley asked when Emma placed the bakery box in her hands.

"Some of Adele's sinful cupcake creations," Emma admitted. "Although, Austin and I will be lucky to have time to eat one with our coffee later. Our construction time got cut short yesterday, so today it'll be *all* work."

His mom nodded thoughtfully. "Yes, he told me as much." She pointed at the door to the basement. "He's downstairs in the workshop already, getting set up. But even you young people can't live on cupcakes and coffee alone. I'm off to run some errands, but I'll be making a simple spaghetti with meat sauce for lunch. How about you let me bring you and Austin a bowl of that around noon?"

"Thank you. That sounds delicious." Emma grinned, thinking of her parents, who were now in Florence and eating pasta daily. She mentioned this to Mrs. Knightley and added, "My mom and dad have been torturing me with their Italian food pictures, which are as stunning as the gorgeous sites and scenery."

"Oh, that's right," the other lady said. "I'd heard they were going away on a European vacation. But they'll be back for Christmas, won't they?"

Emma hadn't been quick to divulge this fact to people in town, but she wasn't about to lie, if asked directly. "No, not Christmas. But they'll be home for New Year's, so we'll get to celebrate together then."

Austin's mom studied her face so kindly that Emma felt the woman was looking right through her, seeing everything she'd left unsaid.

"Well, I'm glad to hear that," Mrs. Knightley replied. "And I know you're a busy bee with lots of commitments in town. But we're having a big family dinner on Saturday night, and we'd love for you to join us if you're free."

"Oh, that's so sweet of you! But I don't know if—"

"Good morning, Emma." Austin appeared at the top of the stairs and glanced between her and his mother. He looked awake, attractive, and...suspicious, for want of a better word.

"Hi, Austin." She'd been hedging about the dinner invite, not because she wouldn't enjoy it, but because she wasn't sure Austin would. He'd been far less hostile toward her recently, but he still seemed frequently exasperated. And yesterday at lunch, he'd looked uncomfortable having her there with his family. She didn't want to force her company on him for longer than necessary.

"Oh, honey," his mom said, "I was just telling Emma about our Saturday night dinner and how lovely it would be to have her join us. Don't you agree?"

Emma tried to project an air of nonchalance, so Austin wouldn't feel obligated to agree, but nevertheless, he said immediately, "Yes, I do. If she doesn't have other plans, of course."

Both of them turned their attention on her.

"Just some community center details to take care of later in the day," she admitted. "But I should be done by six p.m. or so."

"Perfect timing!" Mrs. Knightley declared. "We were planning to gather at six thirty." She patted the bakery box. "Now, let me put these in the kitchen and get on with my errands in town. I know you two have work to do." With that, she bustled away.

And then there were two.

Emma and Austin locked gazes. He was the first to speak.

"Don't let her railroad you into anything you don't want to do," he whispered.

"No, I'd love to come. That was really thoughtful. I just figured you might be sick of me after so much time together this week."

He shook his head. "Nah. You're kinda growing on me." He inclined his head toward the basement. "C'mon. We've got a ton to do."

He wasn't joking. In the workshop, they spent the next several hours "planing" and "sanding" the wood, so it would be straight and smooth. Although he had a machine to facilitate the sanding, he also showed her how to do some of the finishing touches by hand, which was surprisingly meditative.

But her favorite part of the process came in between the planing and the sanding: The grooving.

"So, you *do* get down and dance while you work," she joked. "Is there seventies music involved in this somehow, or will Christmas carols suffice?"

He laughed. "Not that kind of 'grooving,' Emma. This has to do with cutting a slot into the wood to help with the 'joinery'—or the fastening of one piece of lumber to another. We want that so the joints are stronger."

"Okay. I guess I won't force you into a disco dance-off just yet then."

"You wouldn't get far if you tried," he said, pushing his dark hair away from his face and shaking his head. But she liked the fact that he was grinning at her. "I'm not much of a dancer, disco or otherwise. We need to do this kind of grooving, though, before we can move on to the next step, the 'beveling.' That involves cutting at an angle along certain edges or ends of the wood, both for functional reasons—like we must have a forty-five-degree angle on the ends of some pieces to connect them—and also for decorative reasons."

"So it'll be beautiful, too, like the display case in my photograph," she said.

"Exactly." He tapped the end of one of the wood planks. "The goal is strength as well as beauty. To achieve that, we'll use a specific kind of connection—the 'splined miter joint.' And to make it, we'll need to both groove *and* bevel. Let me show you how that's done."

Emma was so caught up in learning these new skills and admiring Austin's mastery of them, that she barely heard his mom when she came downstairs with two steaming bowls of spaghetti, hot coffee, and a pair of cupcakes.

They thanked her and promised they'd finally eat something, but it was a half hour at least before they stopped for a break. The pasta was tepid and the coffee was cold by then, but Emma didn't care. This entire process was fascinating.

They spent the afternoon fitting the frames together for three individual shelving units. "Eventually, we'll attach the three main segments together," Austin explained, showing her how the case would look like a triangle from the top. "We'll drill holes in the bottom and add wheels, so it can rotate. And we'll also screw in the hinges on each of the three sides, so we can attach the glass doors."

"Wow," she breathed, still in awe of how this piece was coming together from just a picture and a stack of wooden planks. It was like three bookshelves, without the shelving inside of them yet, and seeing them being built made her appreciate just how complex it was to craft them well.

"You like it so far?" he asked.

"I love it so far, Austin. Honestly, I had no idea the skill it took to make something like this. You're amazing."

He chuckled and looked away, but not before she saw the blush creep across his cheeks. "We did it together," he murmured. "And we're not done yet."

He explained that they needed to stain the individual pieces next and leave time for them to thoroughly dry, and that was better done at an outside location for ventilation purposes. "Like a garage," he said. "We need cover overhead to keep the wood safe from the elements until it's fully stained. Also, we don't want to connect the three pieces down here in the basement because it'll be a lot harder to move it afterward than it is to bring each of the sides separately up the stairs now."

"That makes sense," she agreed, and immediately suggested that they relocate the project to her parents' garage for the staining and attaching. "It's a three-car garage, and right now, we've only got two cars in it, so there's a big open area available."

"Great idea," he said, and those words were just barely out of his mouth before his youngest brother came clomping down the stairs.

"Hey, I'm *super* bored," David complained. "Can I do something to help?"

Austin raised his eyebrows and then winked at Emma. "Actually, little bro, weren't you just bragging during our recent snowball fight about how much you'd been lifting weights at your university?"

"Uh, yeah..." David said.

"Let's put those new muscles to good use." Austin told him about the transfer of the pieces to Emma's garage.

David bounded up the stairs to get his coat. Then the three of them loaded Austin's pickup truck with the individual pieces of the display case, wrapped in blankets for protection. David sat in the back of the truck, making sure they stayed secure, while Austin followed behind Emma's car as she drove to her house.

Once they got there, Austin and David set out a large plastic drop mat on the garage floor and carried in the larger pieces while Emma grabbed the unattached shelving.

The three of them were looking at the wood and talking about the best stain for Curly Maple when David's cell phone beeped.

"Aw, sweet!" he exclaimed, reading the text. "Just heard back from my buddy Jonathan," David said. "He's finally back home from UCLA." He grinned at Austin. "So, uh, since I was so helpful today, can I borrow your truck for tonight? Jonathan and I were thinking of going to a movie in Montgomery Falls. And I've missed driving."

Austin rolled his eyes. "You do not need to go to a city an hour and a half away just because you miss driving."

"Oh, come on, bro! I'll be careful with your baby. I'll even drive the speed limit, I promise."

"David, if *anything* happens to you, Mom'll have my head—"

"It won't, it won't." He looked pleadingly at his older brother. *"Pleeeeeassse?"*

Emma couldn't help but laugh aloud at these brotherly antics. She'd never experienced such things herself, of course, but being with the two of them made it easy for her to imagine what it must have been like growing up with a sibling. It was obvious that Austin and David loved each other...and just as obvious that they knew how to push each other's buttons.

Finally, Austin heaved a heavy sigh and turned to her. "If I let my goofball brother take my truck, would you be kind enough to drive me home later?"

"Of course," she said, while David, in reaction, boogied around the garage for a moment before giving her an enthusiastic high five.

"Thanks, Emma! You're *so* awesome." Then he held out his hand to his brother. "Thank you very much, Austin," he said, wiggling his fingers until Austin placed the keys in his palm.

"Drive. Very. Responsibly," Austin said before David, who was now jingling the keys and boogying his way to the truck, managed to disappear.

"I will," David called out from behind the wheel. And then he was gone.

Emma and Austin watched the truck zip down the street before he broke the silence and said, "I'm already regretting letting him out of my sight."

She smiled. "He seems like a good guy, though. You probably don't have to worry about your pickup."

He shrugged. "I don't care about that. I just don't want anything to happen to my brother. He's such a people person, like my other siblings. He never stops going, going, going."

"You're more reflective, though," she said, recognizing that this had always been the case for Austin. It was more than just that he was an introvert rather than an extrovert. It was that he was a deep thinker and a candid observer, too. He was someone who probably needed a lot of time for contemplation. She'd realized today how relaxing and Zen-like some aspects of the woodworking process could be and understood at least one of the reasons why he might have been drawn to it.

"I guess," he said, not elaborating. He checked the time

on his phone and grimaced. "The hardware store is closing in ten minutes, so we probably don't have time to get the stain tonight. Plus, I don't want to completely overwork you." He semi-smiled at her. "We should cap it for today and start fresh in the morning."

The sun had set and the streetlamps had come on. It had, indeed, been a full day.

"I'm fine with that but"—she paused and considered whether this question would be wise—"I'm also starving. Would you like to have dinner with me before I drive you back?" She pointed in the general vicinity of the house. "Jennings told me he'd be making chicken fajitas tonight, and trust me on this, there'll be plenty to share. So, um, if you'd like to grab a bite..."

"That sounds really good, thanks. Let me text my parents and let them know not to hold dinner for me," he said, pulling out his phone and typing in a message. Then, "Okay, lead the way. I've been wanting to meet the man behind those delicious curry chicken salad croissant sandwiches."

She laughed. "He'd be thrilled to hear that you said that," she said, clicking the garage door closed and motioning for him to follow her through the door that connected the garage to the inside of the house. "Unfortunately, Jennings won't be here now. He has family visiting from overseas, so I've been encouraging him to leave early while he can and spend time with them."

Austin trailed after her but was walking slowly and glancing around in every direction. "This is a beautiful house, Emma. And really big."

*Ah, that's right.* Austin probably had only seen her house from the road. He'd never been inside. "Thank you. But I can't take credit for it. It's my parents' house, not mine. One day, when I buy my own, it'll be a lot smaller. It would've been silly, though, for me to purchase something when I moved back to Crystal Corners. We run my family's foundation from here, and I knew I'd be spending most of my time in this house anyway."

"So, while your parents are away on their trip, there's no one here but you?"

"Jennings is here for part of the day and Darla, our housekeeper, is here for a bit longer. But at night, no. It's just me then, although they'll both be back in the morning."

He paused several times more on their stroll to the kitchen to comment on the artwork or the architecture. It had been a long time since Emma had seen her home through the eyes of a new friend. It was an impressive place, she supposed, but it would be more beautiful to her when her mom and dad were back in it and she could hear the sound of their laughter.

True to his word, Jennings had all the fixings for a fajita feast in the fridge: Homemade salsa, homemade guacamole, corn chips, grilled chicken strips, grilled peppers, onions, and mushrooms, sour cream, shredded cheese, rice, refried beans, lettuce, large flour tortillas, and lime wedges for squeezing. She watched Austin's eyes widen in surprise with each new item she pulled out and placed on the kitchen island.

"Okay, so you weren't lying about there being plenty to share," he murmured.

"Your whole family could've stopped by for dinner, and we'd still have leftovers. So, please, Austin, eat. A lot."

He nodded and helped her warm up the flour tortillas and the grilled chicken and veggies. Then they each built massive fajitas and dug in.

Around a mouthful, Austin said, "This is amazing but, please, don't *ever* let my brother-in-law Reggie into your family's kitchen."

"Why's that?"

"He and my sister invited us over to their place for Mexican one night, and I don't know how many hot chili peppers Reg put into the meal, just that none of us could talk because we were too busy just trying to breathe." He laughed. "Seriously, I couldn't feel my tongue for, like, three days."

She laughed along with him, enjoying his company and the lighthearted conversation more than she wanted to admit.

When they were finished, she waved her hands between their now-empty plates and said, "See what I mean, though? There's no need for me to learn to cook."

"Ah, don't shortchange yourself, Emma. Jennings is an incredible chef. That much is obvious. But there's also something really satisfying about learning new skills and creating something yourself."

"Maybe so," she said, thinking about Austin's large hands and the deft way he handled the Curly Maple planks, shaping them into something usable and lovely. "But to tell you the truth, cooking just for myself isn't as appealing as learning to make something for others. Like *you* do in your construction business."

She caught his surprised expression as she said that and, again, a slight blush that he tried to hide. "Granted, you're not making the display case all by yourself—at least not yet," he teased. "But what you're doing with it *is* something unique that *you* created."

Now it was her turn to blush. "I didn't, um, I hadn't mentioned—"

"I know. But when I told Bethany that the case would hold statuettes, she knew immediately what you were using it for. I wish I'd have known sooner."

"Would you have been nicer to me?" she asked with a laugh.

"Probably not," he said, grinning. "But I might have agreed to help sooner."

"The important thing is that you *did* agree to help. And now we're...friends, right?" She held her breath, a little stunned to realize just how much weight his response to this question carried.

"I hope so." He met her eye and smiled.

And for a moment—just a split second, really—something tender and soft and infinitely sweet passed between them. She smiled back.

Then, abruptly, he jumped up. "Let me help you put these things away."

So, they loaded the dishwasher with their plates and wrapped up the leftover food before returning it to the fridge. And, somehow, she ended up giving him a little tour of the public rooms in the house that he hadn't yet seen.

In Emma's opinion, he seemed to notice everything. Not just the structure and decor, but the *feeling* each room inspired.

He said he loved the "coziness" of the breakfast nook, the "cavernous freedom" of the downstairs rec room, and the "magical combination of light and warmth" of the living room. It was like inviting him to traipse around in the sacred space of her soul. But, thankfully, he was gentle with it.

And then he saw her bulletin board.

"What's this?" he asked, pointing to the recipe she'd printed out and tacked up.

"A chocolate and apricot torte," she told him, explaining how her parents had loved the dessert in Vienna and that, once they were back and the holiday chaos had settled down a bit, she would give the recipe to Jennings to make for them.

He leaned in close to the page and read through it. "Why wait for Jennings to do it? We could totally make this."

"What? N-No, Austin. It looks delicious but complicated. I mean, someone like Adele could pull it off, but—"

"And so can we," Austin insisted. He pulled out his phone and took a picture of the recipe. "Listen, Emma, I've got some work calls to make first thing in the morning, but I'll be here with the stain by nine thirty, ten a.m. at the latest. Once we do the staining, though, we're going to need to let the pieces dry for a couple of days—until Sunday at least, maybe Monday—before we can attach the three big pieces together and add the extras, like the hinges, wheels, and glass. If you want to coat the case with a lacquer, it'll need even longer. So, what I'm saying is"—he flashed his phone at her—"we're gonna be done early tomorrow."

"But...Jennings will *be* here. In the house. I mean, he could help us, I guess—"

Austin laughed. "No. I'm a very utilitarian cook, Emma. In my condo in Minneapolis, I could've survived with just my microwave for cooking. I've never baked anything from scratch in my entire life, so this'll be an adventure for us both."

"And if we completely wreck it?"

"So what? It's not like we have to show anyone. You wouldn't believe how many woodworking projects I messed up when I was first learning. At least if we destroy it, it's a dessert. We can snack on our mistake."

"I suppose if you put it that way..." she said, already starting to eagerly await this new project with Austin. "We should have most of the common ingredients already here."

Turned out, after reading through the full ingredient list, there were only a handful of items not currently stocked in Emma's pantry or refrigerator.

Austin made note of the others on his phone. "I'll get these in the morning and bring them over. This is gonna be fun. I'm looking forward to it."

"Me, too," she agreed, which was so true it kind of frightened her.

Then it was time to drive him home, and for the first time in hours, she began feeling nervous around him again.

He slipped into his coat and helped her into hers. They

both hesitated in the foyer, searching for words that didn't seem to come easily to either of them.

"Thanks for, um, dinner," he said.

"Thank you for all the woodworking you did," she replied. "And—and for showing me all of the planing and grooving and beveling and sanding." She sort of motioned to hug him, and he leaned in toward her, too.

Their embrace lasted only about three seconds. The big grandfather clock struck eight, and the two of them sprung apart and laughed, as if they'd been caught being naughty instead of nice.

They rode back to his house in silence. But just before he got out of her car, he covered her hand with his and squeezed lightly. "Good night, Emma. See you in the morning."

"Good night." And as he walked into his parents' house, she was filled with as much anticipation and excitement for tomorrow as she'd felt for today.

It was like a Christmas gift she hadn't expected—selected and wrapped just for her.

# *Nine*

Austin made quick work of his business calls that morning. He was in the process of ironing out the transfer details with Carl, Melissa, and the team, so he could officially hire Zach, the new guy, to start in January. This was helping to solidify Austin's own plans, too. Once everybody was in place, he could focus on rebuilding his life here, in Crystal Corners.

His parents were beyond delighted by the idea, and the thought of buying some land in town and building his own house over the next year was appealing. Even more so after having talked so much with Emma yesterday.

He loved that the two of them shared such similar values when it came to being near their families and helping out in whatever way they could. It reminded him of the conversation he'd had with Connor at the sports bar about important versus unimportant ways of being "opposites." Walking around her parents' huge house and listening to her tell him about her preference for a smaller, more intimate type of abode, only underscored that what she cared about were the *people* she was with, not the finery.

And there was a lot of finery in the Westwood house. Gorgeous artwork, beautifully designed architecture, tasteful decor, and so much space a person could get lost in it.

But it was clear Emma was lonely there. That she wanted more coziness, more company. Seemed the two of them shared a few unexpected similarities, despite not appearing to be that much alike on first glance.

After getting dressed in clothes that were already ratty and worn—they were *staining* today, after all—as well as packing an outfit change just in case he needed something nicer later, Austin headed out for the day.

His first stop was the hardware store, where they had a selection of stains. He chose the one he thought Emma would like best—essentially, the one that was closest in color to the picture of the wood for her original display case.

Next, he zipped over to the First Street Market where he hunted for the remainder of the chocolate torte ingredients. Emma had the butter, white sugar, confectioners' sugar, eggs, cake flour, water, and heavy cream covered, thanks to Jennings and his scrumptious meal making. However, for both the cake part of the torte and the icing, semisweet chocolate was needed, and for the filling, a jar of apricot preserves and a few tablespoons of dark rum were in the recipe. He grabbed just those three items and turned to stride toward the register—it was already quarter to ten and he didn't want to get there late—but he almost plowed right into Harriet Smithwick.

"Why, Austin, how are you?" she said.

"I'm doing well, ma'am, thanks." He was pleased to see she had a cart this time. Less of a chance for runaway produce.

She studied the items he was holding. "Oh, my! What a beguiling combination of groceries you have there.

Chocolate, apricot jam...and is that rum? What *are* you making, dear?"

He laughed. "It's for a cake. The rum is actually optional, which is why I just got a small bottle of that, but I had to get a large bag of the semisweet chocolate. The recipe calls for a ton of it."

She patted him lightly on the arm. "It sounds delightful. Chocolate is the food of the gods. And your cake sounds like a heavenly creation. Perfect for sharing with someone special, I think. Am I right?"

Austin hesitated a little, but he wasn't going to fib. "I'm not making it alone, so, yes."

"Ah-ha! Then I know your recipe will turn out beautifully no matter what." And even though she didn't press him to divulge the name of the person he was baking with, she winked knowingly. There were few secrets in Crystal Corners. Then, with a cheery grin, the older lady pushed her cart down the aisle and left him free to race to the checkout lane.

He made it to Emma's house at two minutes after ten, which, all things considered, was pretty good time.

The housekeeper—Darla, if he remembered correctly—answered the door. She told him Emma was already in the garage, waiting for him.

"Do those need to be refrigerated?" Darla asked, pointing to his bag of groceries.

"No. But they're probably safer in the kitchen than in the garage."

She smiled. "I can put them on the island for you."

Austin thanked her, handed her the grocery bag, and told her he knew the way to the garage. It was a straight shot down the hall and to the right.

"Very good," Darla said. "Best of luck with the staining."

He waved the two canisters of wood stain at her before grinning and walking down the hall.

He heard Emma out in the garage before he even opened the door. There was Christmas music blaring inside, and the door separating the house from the garage was cracked open.

He peeked in on her. She was in her faux play clothes and shoes, not full-on dancing, but certainly swaying and singing along to "Winter Wonderland." He laughed under his breath, wishing he wouldn't have to interrupt her because she just looked so cute.

When she finally spun around and saw him, she froze, so he stepped into the garage, a canister of stain in each hand, and danced his way to her along with the music.

She burst out laughing. "You're grooving now, Austin."

"Don't tell on me. I doubt I'd ever live it down if my siblings knew."

"Your secret is safe with me." She pointed at the canisters. "What was the verdict?"

He presented the stains to her, like gifts on a platter. "I have it on excellent authority that this shade will work well with Curly Maple. Shall we give it a try and see what you think?"

"Definitely."

"All right. I brought some rags for us to use as well. We'll stain a tester piece of wood first and check the result. If you like the look, we'll do the rest."

Emma may have been a bit more hesitant with the electrical carpentry tools (she'd looked positively terrified of the circular saw on that first day), but she was a natural when it came to staining. Even though she'd never done it before and she managed to get herself legitimately messy—hair hastily pulled back into a makeshift ponytail, streaks of stain across her formerly clean pink sweatshirt, even smudges on her face—she enthusiastically took part in every step of the process.

He didn't understand how or why this was so, but he was convinced Emma looked even prettier in this disheveled state than she would in an elegant dress with perfect hair and makeup. Not that he'd mind seeing her that way, too. He remembered her wearing this incredibly fancy purple ball gown once when they were kids. She had looked beautiful then, but there was something to be said for a woman who could be stunning even when splattered with wood stain.

She clapped her hands as she dropped the last dirty rag into the garbage and surveyed all of the stained pieces on the garage floor. "The color is so beautiful, Austin. I can't wait to see it once it's had time to dry."

He couldn't help but feel a ribbon of pride at her words. Had he actually thought only a week and a half ago that she was too hoity-toity to mess up her manicure? She'd proven him wrong with astonishing speed.

Sure, she was new to all of this, but she was a quick study across the board. And for him, simply learning more about her and why this project meant so much to her went a long way toward his understanding of why she'd been so particular about getting every detail right. It wasn't about perfection for perfection's sake. It was about people. People she cared deeply about.

That couldn't have been more clear than when he asked her where all of these statuettes were that would be filling the finished display case.

"Oh, I'll show you!" she said, brightening even more and clapping her filthy hands again. "Let's just, uh, wash up first, maybe?"

He wiggled his equally filthy fingers at her and said, "Yes, please. I even brought a change of clothes."

"Oh, good. I don't think Jennings would let either of us anywhere near the kitchen if we looked like this." She showed him to their downstairs bathroom, supplied him with scented soap and fluffy towels, and then ran upstairs to wash up herself.

When they reconvened fifteen minutes later, it was like

getting to begin the day anew.

"I keep the statuettes in an old playroom of mine that my parents were mostly using for storage after I left for college."

She led him on a labyrinthine trek through the house that could probably double as a cardio workout. When they got into the room, though, he could immediately see what she meant. It was yet another very large, very well-decorated space—this one with a kid-sized model castle in one corner, several shelves filled with children's books, and a significant amount of area devoted to cardboard boxes.

"There," she said, pointing at the boxes. "They've all been inventoried and gift-tagged with the children's names, so I know they'll all get one. And I made sure to purchase just a few extras in case there are any new youngsters that just moved in and aren't on the official town record yet."

Austin wandered over to a box that was open with two statuettes wrapped lightly with tissue paper inside. He glanced back at her.

"Those are for the Highbury kids," she said. "You can pick them up and look, if you'd like."

So, Austin unwrapped the first one. It was a figurine of a runner, racing down a track.

"That's for Joey Highbury," she explained. "He's ten and one of the fastest boys in his grade. He loves sprinting."

Austin nodded and unwrapped the second statuette. This one of a girl on a swing set.

"That's for Mimi, Joey's little sister. She's six and a daydreamer." Emma smiled. "She told me once that when she's swinging, she can imagine all the scenes from her life that haven't yet happened. That they played out in her mind like a movie. I loved that."

Austin could see the truth of it. Emma genuinely *did* love learning all of these personal tidbits about the children in town. He could so easily see her as the grade school girl she once was, only now he knew more about what was behind those bright blue eyes. That she was probably very much like little Mimi Highbury—a daydreamer of futures yet unknown.

He wondered what featured in her imagination now. What she dreamed about as an adult. She was no longer dressed in play clothes and looked very much like that ultra put-together young woman he'd bumped into around town when he first returned to Crystal Corners. And yet, there was still something decidedly playful and childlike in her air.

He nodded at the castle. "Yours, I presume?"

She chuckled and sort of shrugged. "What can I say? I had a thing for Sir Lancelot when I was little."

"And now?" he asked.

"Now? Oh, I don't know." She looked away, and he couldn't read her expression. "Maybe none of us ever give up completely on the things we loved as children."

He pondered this. It was true enough for him. He still enjoyed many of the activities and experiences he'd liked as a kid. Working with wood. Playing soccer. Reading novels. Being with his family. Getting to know pretty, spirited girls like Emma.

But what about her? Aside from knights and castles, flowing dresses and frequent conversation, what passions had persisted for her over the years?

He wasn't given the opportunity to ask, though, because she motioned for him to follow her.

"I can smell the pizza. Jennings is making us lunch before we start our baking adventure," she said. "C'mon."

Austin finally got to come face to face with the man behind the meals. Jennings was short in stature but big in personality. A distinguished-looking forty-something man, he wore impeccable whites and chopped vegetables with awe-inspiring precision.

"I want to learn how to make salads like him when I

grow up," Austin whispered to Emma as Jennings, with his nimble but powerful fingers, finished slicing the last of the cucumbers for their large Italian salad.

The chef then pulled out a beautiful sausage and cheese pizza with a homemade, hand-tossed crust that he placed in the middle of the island and presented both items to Austin and Emma.

"Lunch is served," Jennings said with a nod at the food. "Shall I mix the salad for you, Miss?" he asked Emma.

"Thank you, yes," she replied, inhaling. "Mmm. So delicious."

"I hope you will both enjoy it," Jennings said pleasantly. "There is gelato in the freezer, although I know you two will be making a dessert of your own." He eyed the bag of groceries Austin had brought with some apprehension. "If I can, uh, be of service to either of you in that endeavor, I will be available. I have items to stock in the downstairs freezer and wine to add to the cellar."

"My parents shipped home a box of twelve bottles of wine from a winery they visited outside of Paris," Emma explained to Austin. "It just arrived this week."

"And more is coming," Jennings said with raised eyebrows. "From Tuscany."

Emma laughed. "They'll get to have an authentic taste of Europe whenever they want."

"Until they run out of bottles," the cook added.

Austin laughed along with Emma and Jennings. Then the latter left them to their meal, and Austin gratefully dug in.

"That man is remarkable," he murmured after taking only one bite of the homemade pizza. He briefly considered the probability that Emma was right and they just should have asked Jennings to make the European-style torte. It would for sure turn out perfectly then.

But, no.

As the two of them finished lunch and began setting out

the ingredients to make the Viennese dessert, Austin was sure of only one thing: It didn't matter how the cake looked or tasted. All that mattered to him was spending time with Emma.

Emma held up her printed copy of the recipe and began calling out the ingredients, one by one.

"Semisweet chocolate, chopped," she said.

He pointed toward the bag he'd purchased this morning. "Check."

"Butter, softened," Emma said.

"Check," he replied.

"Confectioners' sugar, white sugar, and cake flour," she said.

"Check, check, and check," Austin said in return.

She laughed, a sound that reminded him of Christmas bells ringing merrily. "All right. Then we just need the eggs, separated, and we'll be ready to start the cake part of the project."

He opened the carton of eggs while Emma found two large bowls—one for the yolks and one for the whites.

He placed the required number of eggs in front of her. "Why don't you do this part while I preheat the oven and butter the pan."

"Sure." She paused. "Should we just make one? We've got enough ingredients for at least two cakes."

He considered this. "How about we make one now, and if it's great, we'll know exactly what to do for a second one later today. And if it's not..."

"Then we'll know how to improve the next one," she finished for him.

He chuckled. "Yeah. This first one might be just a 'good learning experience,' as my mom would always say."

"But the important thing is that we're having fun," she stated, grinning at him. And from where he stood, it looked like she was enjoying the process. He could say, without a doubt, that it was the best time he'd ever had cooking in his life.

Between the two of them, they muddled through the instructions for the cake, and while it was baking, they attacked the directions for the filling and for the icing.

"Rum is optional for the filling," she said, pointing at the sheet of paper. "Yes or no?"

He shrugged. "It's your call. But we're legal adults, so it can't hurt, right? And besides, what's our strategy if we hate it?"

"We won't put it in the second one," she said in a mocking tone because he'd recited that line about seven times already. Then she dumped in a couple of tablespoons of rum.

It was all he could do not to reach out and hug her. But, man, he wanted to. He really, really wanted to.

They added in the apricot preserves and the rest of the ingredients for the filling, simmered it in the saucepan until it had thickened, and had it ready to spread in between the cake layers once the cake had cooled completely and had been sliced horizontally.

"So far, so good," Austin observed, feeling rather proud of their handiwork. "Now just the icing."

Emma wrinkled her nose at the recipe. "It looks like it should be so simple to make it. Just chocolate and heavy cream. But I have a feeling that getting the consistency correct isn't going to be easy."

He had to concede that she was probably right. There was a double boiler involved, after all. But he remembered something else his mother used to say and parroted it at Emma. "You can't go too far wrong with a recipe if you're using good ingredients. The icing might be runny, or it might be clumpy, or whatever, but it still ought to taste pretty good."

So they set to work on the final segment, and yeah, while the icing wasn't quite as "spreadable" as the instructions seemed to indicate, they managed to get it onto their chocolate torte in a fairly presentable manner.

They hadn't quite bolstered the courage to slice into it yet (although Emma did take a commemorative picture of it on her phone to send to her parents), when Jennings returned to the kitchen. He eyed their cake and cheered in delight.

"Well done!" he cried. "It looks beautiful. Let me get you some nice china dessert plates for you to enjoy it on."

"Only if you'll stay and have a piece with us," Emma told Jennings. "And if Darla would like to join us, too, all the merrier."

"You might not want to invite anyone else to try it until after we've tasted it," Austin teased. Then, to Jennings, "You may be risking your refined taste buds here."

The cook shook his head and smiled warmly at both of them. "I love seeing Miss Westwood expand her horizons," he said, beaming at her like a proud father.

He left to get the plates and call in the housekeeper, while Austin handed the cake knife to Emma and let her do the honors.

Once the cake was sliced and plated for the four of them, Jennings nodded at Emma and motioned for her to take the first bite.

She exhaled as she lifted the fork to her lips. "Here goes." Austin watched her expression as she tasted the cake and considered the result. "I like it," she told them. "But I'm not sure if that's because it's actually *good*, or if it's because we worked so hard to make it."

Austin, Jennings, and Darla laughed, and all of them dug into it.

Darla declared it "delicious."

Jennings, still glowing with delight, congratulated him and Emma on their "international dessert achievement."

And Austin himself had to admit the end product was pretty tasty. But other than "Mmmm!" he couldn't bring himself to say much because Emma had a splotch of chocolate that was stuck to the corner of her lips, and that was distracting him.

Finally, Jennings and Darla put their empty plates in the sink. Darla returned to vacuuming, while Jennings pulled out a slow cooker and placed in it a thick beef and vegetable stew he'd prepared for them.

"Just let it cook on high for the next three and a half hours, and you can dish it up for dinner any time after that. You can turn it down to low if you think it'll be much beyond four hours before you eat." He pointed to a loaf of French bread on the counter and let them know about various side dishes and snacks that were awaiting them in the fridge. "But you probably won't have an appetite anytime soon," he said before heading out for the day. "Not with half of that fabulous cake left on the counter."

Emma and Austin thanked him, and soon after, Darla popped in to say her goodbyes for the day as well.

"I'll be back in the morning, Miss," she told Emma. "And it was a pleasure meeting you," she said to him with a nod.

Austin got the distinct impression that he'd unwittingly passed some sort of test. That in the absence of Emma's parents, it was important to her family's longtime staff that they check out any new visitors of hers and determine their approval or disapproval.

Emma practically said as much aloud when, after both Jennings and Darla had driven away, she remarked, "They both really liked you."

"It was mutual," he said, meaning it. He appreciated their kindness to him and also their protectiveness of her. He liked that they all had a caring relationship with each other, built from years of consideration and respect.

In their absence, however, the house was eerily quiet.

Before he could think of something to say, Emma asked him, "So...should we make another torte?"

"We still have half of this first one," he replied.

"True, but I was thinking of how nice it might be to bring one over to your parents' house for your family dinner tomorrow night." Emma smiled sweetly at him. "I think your mom and dad might enjoy it, and I imagine your siblings will be really impressed, too."

He grinned. "That they would." He pointed to the fridge. "Let's pull out all of the ingredients again and see if we can improve the consistency of the icing this time."

"Good plan." Emma paused and stared at the remaining cake on the kitchen island. "I'll bet a slice of this will brighten up Ginger Mae's night. She just got released from the hospital. So, after we're done, I think I'll run over and bring her a piece."

Austin was once again bowled over by Emma's generous spirit and thoughtfulness. It inspired him to act accordingly. "I can drive you there, if you'd like," he offered. "And I know someone else who might like a slice, too." He told her about running into Harriet Smithwick at the market this morning and her inquiries about the ingredients he'd been buying.

"I know she'd love a surprise like that," Emma said, readily agreeing to stopping there as well.

So the two of them rallied their efforts to bake their second chocolate-apricot torte of the day—with a few modifications—and, this time, while they were waiting for the cake to cool enough so they could cut it and spread the apricot filling inside, Austin tried to work up the nerve to ask her on a proper date.

"Um, you know the Crystal Corners Christmas Festival is going on this weekend," he began.

"Oh, yeah."

"And, uh, well, they've got those little booths with warm apple cider and frosted sugar cookies and fruitcake."

She crinkled her brow. "You *like* fruitcake?"

"Eh, actually, no...but I just thought it might be fun to walk around there later tonight. There's a bonfire by the old mill. And a snowman-building competition, too. And they have hot chocolate and ice skating at the outdoor rink in Lingonberry Park—"

"I know all about these events, Austin. I've lived here full time for the past four years, and I haven't spent a single Christmas away from home in my entire life, not even during college." She shook her head at him and golden ringlets swung around her shoulders like ribbons. "I always go to the festival, but I don't recall ever seeing *you* there— at least not since we were kids. You don't have to force yourself to go to it just so I'll have company. I mean, I know your mom probably invited me over tomorrow because my parents are away, but I don't want you to—"

"Emma Westwood, I'm trying to ask you on a date here," he blurted, and he watched her eyes widen in surprise. "Clearly, I'm doing it badly, but much as I enjoy working on projects with you, I'd kinda like to spend some time with you when we're not hands deep in wood stain or chocolate glaze."

She laughed. She was in the process of mixing the icing and her hands were currently splattered with chocolate. "So, this isn't some kind of pity date?"

He shook his head. "It most assuredly is not."

"Well, in that case, we've suddenly got a busy evening ahead."

True words. By the time they finished baking, filling, and frosting the second torte, cleaning up the mess they'd made (which was sizable), checking on the state of the display case pieces drying in the garage, eating the stew Jennings had prepared for them, and driving to both Ginger Mae's house and Harriet's house to drop off slices of cake, the downtown holiday festivities were already well underway, with hours of activities still ahead.

Emma hadn't been exaggerating. Austin hadn't taken part in the town festival—even when he was at home for Christmas—since he was a teen. For years, he'd considered himself a little above it. But being in downtown Crystal Corners with Emma by his side made for an experience that was markedly different from his sullen high school days. Seeing the world through her eyes made for a joyful and almost magical evening.

They grabbed some warm apple ciders and sugar cookies by the bonfire, strolled past the ice rink and admired the skaters, and ended up joining forces to build an enormous snowman with a handful of kids that Emma knew.

She and the children joined hands—and they made him do it, too—and then they circled their snow creation, singing "Frosty the Snowman" at the top of their lungs, until they all collapsed from laughter.

They did not win the snowman-building competition, but Austin couldn't remember the last time he'd laughed so hard.

After that, he and Emma warmed up with cocoa, and Austin was even considering giving that fruitcake a try—if only to prolong their evening out together—when he heard someone call out his name and Emma's.

"Mack!" Emma exclaimed, skipping over to Austin's old friend and giving him a warm hug.

Austin didn't like the sudden pinch of jealousy that this gesture inspired. He also didn't like the look of pure curiosity on his high school buddy's face.

"Where's Lila?" Emma asked.

Mack pointed to the ice rink. "I promised to get her some hot cocoa and cookies if she promised to let me off the hook as far as skating." He laughed. "Her skills on ice are far better than mine."

This was Mack being unforgivably modest. Austin remembered hearing about all the years his friend had played with a traveling hockey league. He was as stellar on ice as he was on their championship soccer team.

But Emma didn't roll her eyes or tease him for

downplaying his talent. Instead she said, "Oh, that's so sweet. I highly recommend the chocolate and vanilla twists."

"And how about you, Austin?" Mack said, his grin just a little too gleeful for his own good. "What do you recommend?"

"I—uh, agree with Emma. Those twist cookies were great."

"You agree with Emma," Mack murmured. "That's...awesome. And how did you two end up here? Did you run into each other, or come together?" He asked this with a deceptively innocent tone, but Austin wasn't fooled.

"We were working on a project earlier," Austin informed him, not bothering to explain which project or why. But Emma, of course, wasn't nearly as circumspect. She told Mack about the wooden display case and the chocolate-apricot torte, too. And she gushed about how helpful Austin had been.

Mack looked so amused by this that the guy could barely keep a straight face. "Wow, Austin. I had no idea you were so, um, handy in the kitchen as well as in the workshop."

Austin narrowed his eyes. This may have been good-natured ribbing on Mack's part, but never before had he wanted to slug his friend so much. Mack Morales needed to Stop. Talking. Now.

But Mack did not stop talking. Or smirking. Or mocking him in some form or another.

Mack turned to Emma. "Lila and I are looking forward to your Christmas morning surprise for the kiddies. If you need any help getting the display case over there or setting up the statuettes, just let me know."

Emma had started to nod agreeably, but Austin heard himself saying, "I'll be there to help her." And he shot Mack a warning look.

His old buddy bit his bottom lip and took a step back.

"Well, okay. If anything changes, though, you can give me a call...um, Emma."

"Thanks so much, Mack," she said, patting him gently on the arm. "See you and Lila soon."

"Yeah, you two take care," Mack said, and Austin could distinctly hear his friend chuckling as he strode away.

*I'm behaving like an insecure adolescent,* Austin thought to himself. *What is wrong with me?*

From the odd look on Emma's face, his absurd behavior hadn't gone unnoticed by her either.

He exhaled. "I'm sorry. I just made that conversation unnecessarily uncomfortable, didn't I?"

Emma answered his question with another question. "You realize I talk to a *lot* of people in our town. Every day, right?"

"Yeah."

"And my life wasn't actually on pause during the many years that you were away, Austin."

"I know that, too."

"Good. Because I'm *still* going to be speaking to guy friends of mine, even if you and I go on another date sometime. You understand that, don't you?"

Austin exhaled again, struggling to get a handle on this bizarre new emotion that was plaguing him. In all of his past relationships, including his long-term one with Taylor, he'd never felt quite this envious and territorial before. But he did more than simply feel it now. He'd acted on it, and Emma was right to call him on this.

"I do know that, and you should feel free to talk to whomever you want—male or female—no matter who you might be dating. You're an independent woman," he added, remembering Mack's words about Emma the week before. He'd known then that this was true, but now, this trait mattered more to him. It had him worried that Mack might have been right: That Emma was too independent to want more than a few casual dates with a guy from her hometown, while Austin was quickly realizing that she might be one of the biggest highlights for him about being back home again.

But there was no way he could voice something like that. Certainly not this soon. It was crazy enough that he was even thinking it.

"I am independent in a lot of ways," she agreed. "But that doesn't mean I lack loyalty. If I were to ever make a commitment to someone, I wouldn't take it lightly."

With just a few well-placed words, she'd very effectively put him in his place. She was more than capable of being loyal, but an insecure boy masquerading as a man wasn't going to inspire it.

Point taken.

Then she nudged him. "Hey, look! The town tree is lit. It's like a postcard."

She was absolutely right. It was stunning. He didn't know how many strings of lights the volunteers had used in decorating the tree, but it sparkled in the distance and added little bursts of color to the night.

"Want to walk to it?" he asked.

"Yes," she said. "And the gazebo right next to it is where I'll be giving away the gifts to the children." Then, much to his shock, especially after their recent conversation, she reached for his gloved hand with her mittened one. She squeezed and then tugged gently. "C'mon," she whispered, meeting his gaze and holding it.

And in that moment, he knew that—somehow, someway—she'd seen his flaws and, nevertheless, forgiven him.

His heart melted into a puddle and he couldn't speak. But he could move, and that he did.

Austin let her lead him to the tree and the gazebo.

Several residents were milling around, and nearly all of them called out greetings to them. Emma answered every person with a smile and a kind word. Austin waved and made an effort to be as warm and welcoming as his companion, but he knew (for him, at least) that something significant had changed inside of him.

And when, on their stroll back toward the festival, they passed Santa, who was ho-ho-ho-ing and listening to little kids as they took turns sharing their Christmas wishes with him, Austin caught the twinkling eye of the older gentleman. Though not a word was exchanged between them, Austin could have sworn that the man in the red suit had guessed his own personal Christmas wish: To have more days and nights like this—with Emma by his side.

# *Ten*

It was hard for Emma to keep her mind on the paperwork she was dealing with at the community center on behalf of her family's foundation. With dinner at the Knightley house in less than an hour, her thoughts kept drifting off to the items she planned on bringing there, what she was going to wear, and why she was feeling simultaneously so excited and so nervous.

But no, she couldn't think about Austin right now. Or his family, for that matter.

She couldn't take time to reflect on their day of wood staining, cake baking, or festival going yesterday—let alone her growing feelings of warmth and contentment when she was in his company. The last time she'd gone on a date that she wished wouldn't end was...never. But it had happened last night with Austin.

Emma made herself refocus on the documents in front of her face as she signed or initialed upwards of fifty sheets of paper. Her mom and dad were going to be thrilled by the completion of this initiative and so, so proud.

Westwood International, in conjunction with Crystal

Corners High School District #85, was creating a series of scholarships for local students to help support them in their educational efforts after high school. This project had been the dream of her parents ever since Emma was a high school senior herself. The upcoming graduating class would be the first to benefit from the education grants her parents had developed and put into trusts. Emma was simply finalizing the scholarship distribution, so they could make it official.

Some of the funds were tagged for university tuition, others for trade schools and community colleges, and still others for local apprenticeships and training programs, but all were earmarked for hardworking students who could use the financial boost. And with the rising costs of higher education, who couldn't?

She slipped the stack of documents into a large manila envelope and handed it to her friend Kent, who'd agreed to run through the financials one last time before submitting the offer to the school board.

"They're going to love this, Emma," Kent said, referring to the board members who'd be reviewing the scholarship applications that would begin to flood in once the grants were official.

"I hope so," she said, smiling at him and marveling at how serious and businesslike he looked when he wasn't dressed in workout clothes.

He tucked the envelope under his arm, picked up his coat, and strode toward the door. "Oh, hey, I forgot to ask," he said. "Did you and Austin finish making the display case?"

"How did you know we were—"

"His dad and his brother David," Kent supplied with a grin.

"Of course." She laughed, not surprised that the Knightley men had been oversharing at the gym again. "Well, we're almost done. Just waiting for the stain to dry fully before adding the finishing touches."

"Good. Sounds like you'll be ready for Christmas morning then," he said. "If you need anything before, during, or after the event, just give Jason and me a ring, you hear?"

"Thanks, Kent."

After he was gone, it didn't take her long to pack things away and clear out herself. There'd be a ton of activities here at the community center tomorrow that she'd have to oversee on Ginger Mae's behalf, and even more foundation paperwork to complete at home for her parents but, for now, her brain was already halfway down the road, preparing for an evening with the Knightleys.

When she got to their house at six thirty on the dot—with the second dessert torte in one hand and a freshly purchased poinsettia plant in the other—Emma couldn't deny that excitement had overtaken nervousness for predominance in her gut. But just barely.

The front door swung open, and Bethany welcomed her inside.

"I beat out my big brother in getting to greet you," Austin's sister said with an expression that was equal parts delighted and devious. She lowered her voice. "I can't tell you how awesome it's been thwarting him at every turn since he's been back home. Makes me feel like a teenager again."

Emma laughed. "You're only twenty-four. It wasn't that long ago."

"Still. Sometimes it feels like a lifetime. You know what I mean?"

Emma *did* know. Far too often lately she'd been feeling the edges of adulthood responsibilities without the corresponding perks. Yes, her family's foundation and her community volunteerism were rewarding, but she'd had the persistent sensation that she'd been treading water in her life too much in recent years with nothing major really changing.

Except when she was with Austin.

"I've missed having an older brother around to annoy," Bethany confessed. "It's fun to needle him, but he's a good guy." She stopped to hold the poinsettia plant and the torte while Emma removed her coat. "Don't you agree?"

"Well, yes. Definitely." Emma glanced around. Where *was* he, anyway? "Austin has been incredibly kind and helpful."

"Austin—kind and helpful? *Really?*" said a male voice from the room next to them.

A moment later, Emma came face to face with Connor Knightley, the sibling between Bethany and David in age and a guy she'd probably talked to only a handful of times in her life before tonight.

"Let me take that for you, Emma," Connor said, reaching for her coat and hanging it up. "Our *kind* and *helpful* older brother," he added in a mocking tone, "is currently in the garage, unearthing a box of ancient ornaments for our parents."

"Ancient ornaments?" Emma repeated, imagining turn of the twentieth century keepsakes or family heirlooms.

"Ridiculously silly ornaments we made as kids," Bethany explained. "Mom and Dad like to string the lights when we first set up the tree, but they tend to save the actual ornament decorating for closer to Christmas. Usually at a time when we all can be together."

"That's so they can embarrass us by reminding every single one of their children that we were sucky artists," Connor interjected.

"Speak for yourself," his sister said. "I wasn't good, but you were a *lot* worse."

"Oh, c'mon, Bethany. You made that skunk-cat 'creature'—for want of a better word." Connor rolled his eyes dramatically. "That ornament terrified me as a kid."

"It's the Knightleys' favorite Christmas tradition," Dr.

Reggie Jefferson, Bethany's husband, said, rounding the corner into the hallway and waving at her. Then, to Bethany, "You know I love ya, sweetheart, but I've gotta agree with Connor on this one. That skunk-cat of yours is frightening."

Connor burst into laughter, high-fived his brother-in-law, and blew a kiss at his sister, who glared at them both with mock fury. Emma absolutely adored her parents, but never before had she wished so hard that she could be part of a large, funny family like this one.

"Emma," Austin said from behind her, coming through the door with a big plastic box in his hands and a dusting of light snow on his head. "You're here."

"I am," she replied, unable to get over how just the sight of him immediately lifted her mood even higher.

"Well, now the party can get started!" Austin's mom called out from the kitchen.

And, suddenly, everyone seemed to be in the hallway with them at the same time.

Pam Knightley joined them, a dishtowel in her hand, and exclaimed at the gifts of the poinsettia and the dessert.

David came up from the basement bearing a couple of bottles of sparkling grape juice.

And Austin's dad, Ned, trailed his eldest son into the house and stomped the snow off his boots. "Flurries just started up again," he said. "Let's stay inside and light a fire while we decorate."

"Love that idea," Reggie said with a wide grin. "We never had fires during Christmas when I was growing up."

"That's because you lived in New Orleans, honey, and it was, like, the tropics there compared to Minnesota." Bethany snatched her mom's dishtowel and batted her husband with it. He pretended to run away.

"We'll do the decorating after dinner," Austin's mom commanded. "But *now* we're going to eat. So wash your hands, guys." To Emma, she said, "I cooked us a little turkey and some stuffing. Bethany brought over a platter of raw and roasted vegetables. And Reggie made us a veggie and rice dish."

"*Cajun* rice," David mouthed to Emma behind Reggie's back, raising his eyebrows and clasping at his throat with both hands.

"Be careful with that one," Austin warned, whispering in her ear. "It'll be hotter than my dad's fire."

"I'll remember," Emma whispered back with a smile.

David and Austin weren't kidding. Reggie's Cajun rice was spicy enough to bring tears to her eyes...but she *loved* it.

In fact, the entire meal was delicious, but it wasn't only the food that made it so. The conversation at the table had her in tears, too, but that was due to laughter. It was clear this was a family who loved each other dearly and delighted in demonstrating that love by teasing each other and praising each other—often in the same breath.

Austin sat across the table from Emma and kept catching her eye, as if to check on her reactions. She didn't know if she was able to fully convey nonverbally just how much she was enjoying herself, but she hoped he felt at ease having her with his family. Certainly, she couldn't have been more appreciative of having been included tonight, although it was bound to make the rest of the nights in the following week seem dreadfully dull by comparison.

When it was time for dessert, Emma explained how she'd heard about this European torte from her parents, that Austin had initiated their first attempt at making one, and this was their hopefully improved second attempt.

Bethany's jaw dropped. "You and my brother made *that*? Wow."

Reggie bowed, first toward Emma and then toward Austin. "Seriously, I'm impressed."

Connor said, "It looks amazing, Emma. If it tastes a

little off, though, it'll be because Austin was involved."

"Hey!" Austin said, crossing his arms and glaring at his brother with indignation while his family laughed.

David, who was sitting right next to his eldest brother, nudged Austin and said in a snarky voice, "You two are just creating *all kinds* of things together this week. Anything else we should know about?"

Austin didn't reply, but he nudged him back hard enough that David wobbled in his chair and almost fell out.

Connor and Reggie snorted. Bethany clapped her hands. Austin's parents laughed aloud. And Emma felt herself blushing as she and Austin locked gazes across the table.

"Behave yourselves," their mom said threateningly, waving the cake knife at Austin and David. To Emma, she sighed heavily and added, "They're always like this." And then she sliced into the torte and dished it up for each of them.

It was a huge hit.

Emma couldn't have been prouder of her own efforts in making it, but she was especially pleased for Austin, who was also lavished with praise and appreciation by his family. She could tell that meant the world to him.

After dinner, his dad built a fire as promised, and his mom lifted the lid on the plastic box and began pulling out ornaments.

"C'mon, everyone. Yes, Emma, you too," Austin's mother said. "We need to decorate the tree."

"Whoever sees Bethany's skunk-cat first will have bad luck until New Year's Eve," Connor joked.

"Connor, you brat!" his sister hollered. "Fine. I made a striped cat ornament that looks more like a skunk. I was seven. *You*, on the other hand, made that dreadful so-called 'elf' that looks like an exorcist monkey." She reached into the plastic box and pulled out a very strange-looking clay ornament that was glazed with brown and green paint. She waved it in the air triumphantly. "And you made this monstrosity in high school!"

Connor doubled over with laughter. "Oh, man, let me see that thing. I swear, every year it looks worse."

Bethany handed him the 'elf,' and then reached into the box to uncover a few other childhood treasures. She grinned and walked over to Emma and Austin, who were standing by the Christmas tree.

To Emma, she handed a glass angel, and said, "Austin gave this to our mom when he was in junior high. She still loves it." Bethany pointed at the tree. "Why don't you find a good spot for it."

Emma nodded and placed it near one of the strings of lights, which made it sparkle beautifully with color.

"Perfect," Bethany declared. Then she stealthily passed a small ornament to Austin, all but smuggling it into his cupped hands. "Reggie gave this one to our parents last year," she explained to Emma, but Emma couldn't see the ornament itself.

Austin narrowed his eyes at his sister, who shrugged and said, "Someone has to put it on the tree."

"Bethany—" he began in a warning tone.

"Oh, don't be a spoilsport, bro," she chided, cutting him off and pointing at the Christmas tree like a bossy little sister.

Emma didn't understand what was going on until Austin lifted the ornament to attach it to a branch, and his sister shouted, "Freeze! Mistletoe!"

Sure enough, the ornament was crafted from a sprig of real mistletoe and preserved in some kind of clear lacquer. It had a metal clasp at one end that allowed it to be clipped easily to the tree. But Bethany hadn't given Austin enough time to do that, and he was caught holding the mistletoe ornament in the air, dangerously close to the top of Emma's head.

"You know the rules," Bethany informed her brother,

while the rest of their family looked on, amused.

"You don't have to kiss me if you don't want to, Emma," Austin murmured, shooting dagger glares at his sister.

But Emma wanted to kiss him. She *really* wanted to. And yesterday after the festival, he'd only hugged her good night. It was a very nice hug, but she'd been imagining something more ever since.

She glanced at Bethany, who winked at her, and then Emma turned her full attention on Austin. "But those are the rules," she said, grinning at him and stepping nearer so he'd know she meant for him to follow through.

"Okay," he whispered back, and still dangling the mistletoe ornament above her head with one hand, Austin pulled her closer to him with the other hand and brought his lips down to hers.

It was a light kiss. A gentle one. But the very intimacy of it drew Emma in and made her float, as if on a magic carpet.

In the background, she could hear the whistling and cheering of Austin's relatives, but they seemed distant, almost too far away to reach them. In Emma's mind, body, and soul there was only Austin and her...their hearts beating together for an infinite moment.

When he pulled away, the noise and presence of his family came rushing back, and Emma drew in a shaky breath.

There was an expression in his eyes that she couldn't fully read, but it held a question she wasn't prepared to answer just yet.

Austin blinked and took a step back. He rolled his eyes at his relatives, and parroting the words his mom had uttered at the table, said, "Behave yourselves."

They all laughed, and soon, the family had moved on to other things.

But Emma didn't.

Oh, sure, she played along with their lighthearted antics and participated in their humorous discussions, but she was still mentally by the tree, under the mistletoe, kissing Austin. Her private, internal world trembled from the twin strands of joy and fear that were entwined inside of her, tying her into knots of indecision.

What was happening here between her and Austin? This couldn't ever be a serious relationship, could it? She'd all but given up on finding a soul mate in *any* location, let alone in her hometown. The odds of Austin Knightley—the boy practically next door—being "the one" for her were miniscule, weren't they?

She didn't have any definite answers, just more questions. And they were pummeling her—one after the other—and giving her an unexpected headache.

So, at the earliest polite opportunity, she profusely thanked Austin and his family for the warm and memorable evening and escaped back to her parents' house, where it was silent and dark, lonely and lacking in holiday decorations, but at least it wasn't nearly as confusing as being with Austin that night had been.

# *Eleven*

Austin's family wasn't known for their subtlety or their restraint.

Literally twenty-two seconds after Emma drove away (he clocked it), his nearest and dearest relatives started blasting him with questions, like snowballs in a snowball fight.

Bethany lobbed the first shot. "Emma looked lovely tonight, don't you think, big bro?"

He didn't even have a chance to answer before Connor broke in. "Yeah, but she didn't *stay* that long. Why d'ya think she bolted so fast? Could it have been the kiss?"

His sister snickered.

Again, Austin only got as far as opening his mouth before his youngest brother felt compelled to speak.

"Maybe she was tired of Austin wasting so much time," David suggested. Then, to him, he said, "Aren't you guys done with that display case yet? I mean, you've been doing almost nothing else all week."

"Just because you helped them bring the pieces over to Emma's house does not give you the right to interrogate your brother," their dad interjected. Then he, too, turned to Austin. "But David's got a point. You typically work faster." His father grinned.

Austin usually loved his family's sense of humor. Not tonight.

"We've been working as hard as we can, given both of our schedules," Austin finally managed to reply, struggling to control his irritation. He could live without being ganged up on. "We just did the staining yesterday morning. So, we only have to attach the hardware and the glass now." Which reminded him, he hadn't yet placed the order for the case's glass doors, and the closest town he'd be able to purchase them was in Montgomery Falls. He made a mental note to call them in the morning.

But, okay, he'd admit this to himself if not to his relatives—he wasn't exactly *rushing* to get done with the project. He liked spending time with Emma. And he'd really like to get to spend more of it with her.

Connor waggled his eyebrows suggestively. "You haven't been working *that* hard. Mack Morales told me he saw you and Emma together at the Christmas festival last night."

"And let's not forget, they've been *baking* together," Reggie contributed.

Austin sent his (usually beloved) brother-in-law a less than appreciative look. "She was going to wait until after the holidays to ask her family's chef to make it for her, but I knew she wanted to taste it sooner. After I read the recipe, it just seemed silly not to do it ourselves."

"You *read* the recipe?" his sister asked, her tone incredulous. "In advance?"

"You've never wanted to bake cakes with *me* before," his mother mused with a sly smile. "I'm feeling left out."

"That's enough, you guys," Austin blurted. "I like Emma, okay? But it's nothing serious—"

"You've liked her for a long time," his dad observed.

"Since high school at least," Mom said.

"Wait—what?" Austin couldn't believe what he was hearing. His parents had guessed he'd had a crush on her way back then?

Bethany jumped in. "Oh, you thought we didn't know?" She bubbled with laughter. "That's so cute."

"I hardly knew her then—" he began, in a weak attempt at defending himself.

But Connor snorted. "Oh, c'mon, Austin. She's totally your type."

"The *real* question," David said, "is does she like you?"

Not exactly encouraging words, especially given Emma's speed of departure, post-kiss.

"I'm going to bed now," he announced to a room full of laughing relatives. "Good night, everyone."

They hugged him, tried to get him to stay, whispered things like, "You know we love you, right?" And he *did* know. They meant well. But he also knew he needed time away from his outgoing family members to reflect on the evening and on his recent reconnection with Emma. Their date yesterday. Their kiss tonight. Their growing closeness, and if it meant half as much to her as it did to him.

He was already down the hall, headed toward his childhood bedroom and feeling very much like a confused kid, when he heard Reggie's voice behind him.

"Hey, hold up, Austin."

He turned and leaned against the wall, feeling drained from the sheer weight of his thoughts. "If you're just gonna tease me, Reg, I'd appreciate it if you'd postpone the jokey fun until tomorrow. I'm beat."

But his brother-in-law shook his head, looking serious, and leaned against the wall next to him. "I didn't grow up around here, so I don't know Emma Westwood or her parents the way your family does. Until tonight, I'd just seen her around town and talked with her a few times." He paused. "She sweet, Austin. And she's got heart. I know her rep around Crystal Corners is that she's a rich girl who's into everyone's business. But the woman I saw here this evening wasn't trying to network or manipulate anyone." He shrugged. "I think she's just trying to figure out her life and what she wants—like the rest of us."

Austin took this in and nodded. "Emma's got a lot going for her. She's got money, education, connections, as well as brains and attractiveness. She doesn't *need* anyone to complete her, although I get the sense that she wouldn't mind a romantic relationship. Maybe. With somebody."

"Somebody other than you?"

Austin struggled to put this feeling into words. "A friend of mine said Emma is independent, and in my book, that's a positive quality. I wouldn't want to be with someone clingy. But her past relationships have been so brief. Maybe an attentive boyfriend is a commonplace thing for her. Maybe, to her, I'm just another guy in a long string of interested guys."

"Maybe," Reggie agreed. "Or maybe you're 'the one' for her. I can't tell you that." He pointed down the hall toward the living room. "Your parents and siblings can't tell you that either. Only you and Emma can figure out the truth of her feelings." He patted Austin on the shoulder and took a step back in the direction of the family. "But this much I'll say. *Your* feelings seem pretty clear."

The next morning, Austin woke up early and attempted to wrap his brain around the day ahead.

He immediately tried to call the glass company in Montgomery Falls, figuring he could drive out there and pick up the very specific type of glass doors Emma had requested for the case, so he'd be ready to attach them whenever she was free.

But that plan was instantly shot down the minute he heard their phone recording. They were closed on Sundays.

Fine. He'd call first thing tomorrow. It was an independent company and he knew one of the owners. They should be able to have the glass ready by Monday afternoon—or by Tuesday morning at the latest. But Tuesday was Christmas Eve, and that was cutting it close on time.

Austin wandered into the empty kitchen to fix himself some coffee and a bagel...even though what he was really in the mood for was a huge slice of chocolate-apricot torte. Not that there was any of that left. The eight of them had polished off the entire cake last night.

He grinned at the memory.

He took his coffee and his bagel into the dining room and sat where he'd been sitting last night, imagining Emma across the table from him.

It was an odd sensation to be here alone after all of the activity in their house last night.

Reggie and Bethany had returned to their condo not long after Austin went to bed. He saw them drive away. Sometime later, Connor had gone back to his own place, too. Mom and Dad had left a note by the coffee maker saying that they were attending the early service at church this morning. And David, while technically still here, was fast asleep.

He wondered what Emma was doing (and saying...and thinking...) at eight twenty-four on this bright but chilly December morning. And it occurred to him that there was no reason why he couldn't find out.

He finished his breakfast, rinsed his dishes in the sink, and got dressed for the day. Then he went in search of her. And Austin, because he'd been hanging on her every word last night, knew exactly where to start looking.

He heard her in the Crystal Corners Community Center meeting room before he saw her.

"Now, listen up, everyone." She clapped her hands and the cacophony being made by the swarm of junior high kids surrounding her subsided ever so slightly. "Group A is going with Ms. Adele to the kitchens. There are cookies to be made. *Lots* of cookies. Wash your hands very well before you start." A dozen or so kids broke away and pranced toward Adele, who led them out of the room and, presumably, to a place where they would soon be making a happy mess with flour, butter, eggs, and sugar.

"Group B," Emma continued, her voice firm and commanding, "needs to follow our parent volunteers." She pointed toward a trio of adults on the other side of the open area. "Mrs. Barden, Miss Sanchez, and Mr. Redmond will lead you to the gift center. I know you'll all do a beautiful job wrapping the presents. But the edges of the foil can be sharp. Beware of paper cuts."

A few of the kids shouted, "We will," as they, too, left the room.

"And all of you in Group C," Emma continued, "are staying here with me. We've got mittens, scarves, and hats to add to the community center tree and decorations to put up for tonight's holiday dinner. I know you're going to follow my directions exactly as I give them, right?"

A chorus of "Right, Miss Emma!" followed.

Austin smothered a laugh. She was adorably bossy. When had this trait started to charm rather than irritate him?

He leaned against the doorframe, half camouflaging himself from Emma's view. She knew she was in charge and that the fate of all of these projects and activities rested on her slim shoulders. So the lady knew how to take responsibility. Like a general.

In answer to his own question, he started to admire her—rather than be annoyed by her—the minute he realized her behavior came from a place of caring, not control. And, somehow, his family had recognized that about her long before he had.

She suddenly spotted him across the room and raised her hand in a wave. He returned it and listened as she issued a stream of orders to the kids, who, Austin sensed, appreciated her directness and clarity. Certainly, none of them were openly complaining. Then, when it seemed her crew was well underway with their mitten/hat/scarf project, Emma skipped over to him.

"Fancy seeing you here," she said with a smile that was welcoming if, perhaps, a little guarded. "Is everything okay?"

"It is. I was just...just thinking about you," he said, which was the pure, honest truth.

"It was fun with your family last night," she said.

"Was it?" He swallowed. "I mean, I know we all loved having *you* there, but did you really enjoy it, too?"

She answered without a hint of hesitation. "Yes. They're wonderful, Austin. You're lucky to have a big family who loves you like that."

"But they can be a bit much sometimes. Like my sister engineering that kiss." He paused and tried to read the expression in her eyes, which were bright but still holding something back.

"You didn't like it?" she asked him, worrying her bottom lip with her teeth.

He laughed. "Are you kidding, Emma? I *loved* kissing you. I want to kiss you again right now, only you're in a room with a whole bunch of eleven- and twelve-year-olds." He feigned a glare at the junior high kids, who were decorating their tree in between stealing glances at him and Emma.

She smiled and relaxed. Marginally. But she didn't speak.

"I'm just sorry if you felt Bethany put you on the spot," he explained. "You left, um, sooner than I would've liked last night."

At this, she winced. "T-That wasn't because of Bethany. And...and I'd wanted you to kiss me, Austin. I just, um, I guess I'm just trying to figure something out." She paused. "About myself."

He exhaled. He was an introvert. He fully understood that process. "Do you need space from me to do that? I can go. I don't want to bother you while—"

"You're not," she interrupted. "You're not bothering me." She reached out and tugged on the sleeve of his coat. "Why don't you come in the room? You can help us."

"Sure. I'd like that," he said, realizing as the words left his mouth that there was nothing else he'd rather do. Nowhere else he'd rather be.

To Austin's delight, it turned out to be an incredibly fun day of community work. Local volunteers kept popping in and out of the center, looking to Emma to give them instructions and to pass along news of Ginger Mae, who was well on the road to recovery.

"Hey, girlie, I want more of that cake," the older woman said to Emma via cell phone. "That was good stuff."

Emma relayed this message to him, and Austin had to admit, he was pleased. "Glad she approved," he said. "We should make her another one soon."

"Maybe right after Christmas?" Emma suggested.

"Done," he said. "I'm clearing my calendar for December twenty-sixth."

She laughed, and, man, he *loved* the sound of that. Which was a good thing because he got to hear it often throughout the day.

One of his favorite moments was when, after the party room decorations for the holiday dinner were completed, one of the kids turned on the overhead sound system, which piped in music from the office radio.

Emma tuned it to Z-104, effectively filling the community center with a steady stream of Christmas songs.

From all corners of the building, he could hear kids and adults alike singing along.

Jenny, one of the girls in Emma's group, got pretty excited when "O Christmas Tree" came on. She and a few of her friends linked hands and asked the other kids—as well as Austin and Emma—to join them around the mitten tree.

With all of them together, they were able to encircle it completely. And then Jenny led them all in singing along as they slowly moved around the tree.

Austin was next to Emma, holding her hand on his left and the hand of some lanky young boy on his right. Everyone was singing, moving, and laughing. Austin's heart was in his throat watching Emma's face and hearing her sweet laughter. No doubt about it, he was falling for her. Hard.

He knew she enjoyed his company. But what he was feeling toward her was more than just casual affection.

Yes, she *liked* him. He recognized that and was grateful for that blessing. But what he wanted to know was this: Could she *love* him?

# Twelve

It had been an action-packed Sunday for Emma.

As was often true for her, the vast majority of the weekend had been spent in charitable pursuits. But while this was incredibly rewarding in and of itself, she'd been surprised by how much more enjoyable the activities at the community center had been for her personally, simply because Austin was there with her.

She was meditating on this very subject, having just parted from Austin for the evening, while making her final stop of the day at the library. The building was closed until morning, but she had a big box of romance and mystery novels to drop off in their metal donation bin and figured there was no time like the present.

As she was slipping each book into the bin, a car came up behind her with a friendly toot. "Emma!" a voice from the car window called.

The car pulled to the curb to park and the driver slid out. The very pregnant driver.

"Vera!" Emma left the books and went over to hug her friend. "How are you? How's Steve?" And she nodded at

Vera's belly. "And the little one?"

Vera laughed. "Oh, you've gotta feel him." She placed Emma's hand on her bulging belly, underneath her coat, and Emma was rewarded with a definite kick from the other side.

She gasped in awe.

"We're convinced he has a promising career as a World Cup soccer player," Vera said with a laugh. "Or maybe he'll love martial arts like Steve and me. He's got quite a kick."

"He? Then you guys know for sure?"

Her friend nodded. "The ultrasound confirmed it. Now I just need to make it to Valentine's Day so this kid can be born." Vera paused. "Not that I'm gonna be anxious to do this again anytime *soon*...but maybe the next one will be a girl. I've already got her name picked out." She winked at Emma.

Emma grinned. She couldn't have been more thrilled that Vera and Steve were so happy together. And, yes, this was on account of Emma having set them up initially, but they'd taken their relationship to the next level beautifully even without her.

"You shouldn't be out here in the cold," Emma told her. "Go home, get warm, and please give my best to Steve."

"I will. I've got some books to return." Vera pointed to the book return slot by the side of the library. "But I saw you here and just had to stop." She paused and studied Emma's face. "Maybe this is a hormone thing, but I've been more aware of auras and sensations and other New Age-y stuff lately. And you, my sweet friend, look a little different somehow. In a good way," she hastened to add. "There's an added light." She waved her palm in a circular motion by Emma's eyes.

Emma laughed. "Really?"

"Yeah. I don't know. You're just giving off a slightly different vibe. I hope that means lots of new and lovely things are ahead for you." Vera squeezed Emma's arms. "Pregnancy is really weird, though, and I'm gonna go now because it's been only, like, twenty minutes, and I have to pee again."

They laughed together, then Emma watched Vera waddle to her car, drive to the book return on the other side of the lot, and then head down the road.

She finished putting the book donations in the bin and went back home, too, thinking about her friend's newly developed intuition and—because she couldn't seem to stop herself—reflecting some more about Austin.

He would be here again tomorrow to assemble the stained wood shelving and attach the main parts together. Then they would just need to add the wheels, hinges, and glass doors...and the display case would be done. Much as she'd been looking forward to the completion of this project in time for Christmas, she couldn't deny the acute sense of disappointment that she and Austin wouldn't have something to keep working on together.

No, that wasn't true.

They'd already planned to make a chocolate torte for Ginger Mae the day after Christmas, and Emma intended to hold him to that. Maybe, if she got really creative, she could think of other projects that might interest him.

It was *good* to be productive, she reminded herself. Even if this little romance thing between Austin and her didn't last beyond the holidays (when had she ever dated anyone for more than a few weeks anyway?), it was still nice, right?

There was something distinctly unsettling, though, about putting Austin in the same category of guys as her ex-beaux. She felt nothing but pleasure when she saw Mack with Lila. Or Ben with Sonja. Or when she ran into other ex-boyfriends, like Sam, Dean, Jack...

She shook her head in the middle of her parents' empty house. No, no. She wouldn't feel calmly at peace if Austin started dating someone else, and that realization made her catch her breath. Why *was* this relationship different than any of her prior ones? Why was *he* special?

She checked the time. She had a scheduled video chat with her parents, set to begin in ten minutes. She needed to get her head together before then.

When they called, they told her all about Rome—"The Colosseum, the Circus Maximus, the Roman Forum, oh my!" her dad exclaimed—while she, in turn, filled them in on the details of the educational scholarships and how most everything had now been finalized.

"What fantastic work you've done for our foundation, sweetheart," her mom gushed. "We are so very proud of you. Thank you for being there and for representing our whole family in our absence."

Emma's heart swelled at these words.

"We've really come to count on you," Dad added. "But when we return next week, you'll probably need a vacation."

"Yes!" Mom enthused. "Think of all the fun things you'd like to do. Maybe take a trip somewhere yourself? In any case, we're giving you some time off."

How crazy was it that the first thing Emma thought was that she didn't want to leave Crystal Corners if Austin wasn't with her?

"But not until after we're back from Greece," her dad said. "The Acropolis and the Temple of Athena still await."

"And the *baklava* and the *souvlaki* and the *moussaka*—" Mom began.

"It might be hard for me to get your mother out of Athens, especially with all that good food," Dad joked. "But knowing we'll be spending New Year's Eve with our baby girl should get her on the plane."

Emma grinned at them through the screen of her laptop. "I can't wait to see you both in person." And, as had been the case every time she'd talked with her parents while they were away, she missed them and, simultaneously, felt a longing for the type of relationship the two of them shared as a couple. She knew she had a very good life and that she could be reasonably content on her own. But she was increasingly aware that getting involved in community projects and making herself useful wasn't fulfilling the part of her that wanted the kind of love story her parents had found. A few tears sprung to her eyes, and she quickly brushed them away.

Not before her mom noticed them, though.

"Oh, honey, what's wrong?" Mom gazed at her in concern.

And Dad said, "What can we do for *you*, love?"

Emma tried to dispel their worry, but they knew her too well. Finally, she confessed that she had started seeing someone and was dealing with some new and confusing emotions.

"Austin Knightley," her dad said, even though she hadn't told them his name.

"How did you know about—" she started to ask.

Mom cut her off. "Oh, Jennings and Darla give us reports. We heard all about your chocolate and apricot torte, too."

"Very impressive accomplishment, by the way," Dad said.

In spite of herself, Emma had to chuckle. She hadn't even sent them the picture she'd taken of it yet, but there was no getting around the Crystal Corners gossip grapevine. Not even with her parents five thousand miles away.

"Here's the important thing to remember, sweetie," her mom said. "No matter how confusing a relationship might be at first, just ask yourself this: Does having him in your life bring you more happiness or less?"

"Basically," Dad added, "are you better off with him or without him?"

Emma appreciated her parents' guidance and considered their suggestions long after they'd hung up. The thoughts she had as a result were surprisingly clarifying.

For her first twenty-six years, Emma had led a privileged life, and she'd discovered that the more enriched her own experiences were, the more she had to give back to others. This was important to her.

The joy she felt in Austin's company was undeniable. But more than that, it was a particularly special gift for her because she didn't just have fun with him, she also learned new things and grew as a person when they were together.

Other boyfriends had been very *nice* to her, and she'd liked that, of course. But her mind and spirit hadn't expanded by being with them, so she quickly became restless around them.

Not so with Austin.

Being with him had positively impacted her world. And as much as she loved her newly expanding worldview when she was with him, she appreciated *his* openness to learning and changing, too. It wasn't a one-way street, and in Emma's opinion, that made them both stronger and better people.

Maybe this relationship stuff, while still full of unknowns, wasn't as confusing as she'd thought. Or maybe, she'd just grown up enough to appreciate the beauty of the mystery.

At ten o'clock the next morning, Austin showed up at her front door with a toolbox, looking altogether too handsome and handy for a frigid Monday in December.

Nevertheless, Emma motioned him inside. Soon, the two of them set to work assembling the finished wooden shelf planks and securing them with numerous shelving brackets.

"I should have called in the glass order earlier," he told her apologetically, "but I hadn't realized until I tried to reach the company yesterday that they were closed on Sundays. I'm sorry to be cutting things close for you. I'd hoped to pick up the glass doors from Montgomery Falls today, but they won't be ready until tomorrow afternoon."

Emma surveyed the display case parts currently in the middle of her parents' garage. At this point, it looked like three complete, freestanding bookshelves, but she knew there were important steps still ahead.

"That's okay, Austin. We should still finish on time, right?"

"We will, yes. I never leave a job unfinished. Not ever. It's an unwritten but guaranteed commitment that I make whenever I agree to do a project. It'll get done for sure."

"What exactly do we have left to do?" she asked. "I know we need to attach the units and add something so the whole thing will rotate. And we need hinges for the glass doors. Is that it?"

"Pretty much," he said. "I was originally going to just fasten the three shelving units together and add wheels to the bottom, but you're going to be out in cold weather, and the gazebo floorboards are uneven. So, I think the rotating cabinetry would be more secure if the three units were attached to a circular stand that could spin. Rather than turning on its wheels, the stand would remain steady and just the wooden cases would turn on a rotating pillar, as if it were a carousel. It wouldn't change the external appearance of the display case that much, but I think it would add more stabilization whenever the piece is being rotated."

Emma agreed that sounded good, even if it deviated a bit from her original display concept. She'd learned to trust Austin's expertise in these matters.

"So, what does that leave us to do today? We aren't going to put on wheels, so we don't have to drill the holes for those. We don't want to put on the hinges until we have the actual glass doors, right? And, unless you have one of those circular stands in your pickup truck—"

He laughed and shook his head. "I'll need to get that in Montgomery Falls tomorrow, too."

"Then, is that it for today?"

"As far as the display case? Yes. We need those two important items, but the good news is that, once we have them in front of us, the time it'll take us to add the carousel base and the glass doors is minimal. An hour or two, tops." Austin studied the cases and walked around them, looking at them from every angle. "This will be pretty unwieldy to handle once all three shelving units are connected. Plus, with the weight of the glass that you wanted me to order, it'll be significantly heavier. My brothers and I can help you transport it, along with all of your statuettes, to the gazebo on Christmas morning."

"Thanks, Austin. That would be wonderful." Emma smiled at him, but her heart was in her throat. Sure, they still had a handful of tasks left to do on this project, but tomorrow was Christmas Eve and the following morning it would all be done. She ran her fingertips across the beveled edge of one of the shelves, suddenly feeling extra sentimental about this display case and all the work that went into it.

Naturally, the children would be thrilled with their figurine gifts on Wednesday, but aside from that, the cheeriest part of this entire project was how it had brought Austin and her together. She wasn't ready for it to end.

"I don't want to impinge on any other plans you might have for the day," he said, "but just because we don't have more woodworking to do right now doesn't mean I'm gonna go home and take a nap or anything."

She laughed. "After all of the community center activities this weekend, I have the next few days off. I hadn't scheduled anything else—other than this—today."

"So, you're saying you're free?"

She nodded. "I am."

He walked over to her and stood a hair's breadth away, facing her. "We've already done woodworking and baking together. I suppose you think dancing is the next most natural step in the progression, right?" And with that, he pulled her into his arms and waltzed her around the garage for a few minutes, humming "Silent Night" with maniacal intensity until she dissolved into a pool of laughter.

"I know that cooking wizard who hangs out in your kitchen would probably make us delicious lattes if we asked, but I don't want to bother Jennings," Austin said. "I would, however, love to treat you to a hot beverage of your choice. Any interest in going out for coffee with me, like...now?"

"Crystal Corners Coffeehouse it is," she said, hoping he could hear the pleasure in her voice at his request. "Let me just change into my going-out clothes."

When she removed her old sweatshirt and put on a fuzzy red sweater, he winked at her and pronounced it to be "lovely."

When she slid out of her sneakers and into her high-heeled leather boots, he raised an eyebrow but only added, "They're growing on me."

When she put on her cloak and scarf, however, he flicked at the edges of the designer material and sighed. "It's not that you don't look absolutely beautiful in what you're wearing, Emma, I'm just worried about you catching a chill. Both of these things are *so* thin."

In looking out the window and considering his comments, she knew Austin was right. Temperatures had been dropping steadily, and neither her fine woven cloak nor her paisley silk scarf were intended for warmth. She held up her index finger and rummaged through the hall closet until she found her down jacket and a wool scarf that was both fashionable and functional.

"Better?" she asked him, slipping into the jacket and holding up the scarf.

He took it from her hands, felt the woolen material, and then nodded, lassoing her with it and drawing her close to him. "Much. Thank you." He planted a soft kiss on her forehead, wrapped the scarf snuggly around her neck, and then led her outside to his truck.

At the coffee shop, Mrs. McBride bustled over to their table to welcome them and exchange hugs with Emma. Austin had already ordered their drinks, but the owner insisted on bringing over a complementary platter of espresso brownies, vanilla lady fingers, and crunchy almond biscotti.

"For dipping in your lattes," she insisted. Mrs. McBride put her hands on her hips and grinned at them. Then to Austin she whispered, "Your lady friend is my favorite customer. Be good to her."

Austin nodded solemnly. "I intend to."

"All right then." The older woman blew them a kiss and strode away.

"You have some devoted fans in this town, Miss Emma Westwood," he told her with a grin. "Well deserved, too."

As had happened a few times when in his company, Emma felt herself blush. "People in Crystal Corners are very nice to me—"

"*You*," he interrupted, "are very nice to people." Then he put down his biscotti and took her hand in his. "Yesterday at the community center you said you were trying to figure some things out about yourself. I don't know if you've found the answers you were seeking yet, but I did want to tell you a few things that I've noticed about you."

He paused to inhale, exhale, and repeat. "I love how much you care about the people in this town. How involved you are with them. How generous you are in supporting their needs. People know you, stop to talk with you, ask you questions, and share things with you because they know they can rely on you. When we were kids, I didn't understand that your ability to communicate with people, manage their problems, and put them at ease were special talents of yours. I didn't recognize them as the tremendous gifts they are. I'd like to think I'm a *little* wiser now." He smiled at her. "I see the many things you do for others, and I just want you to know that you're appreciated."

Her body was flooded with emotion at his words. He *did* see her. With him, she felt *known*. For a long moment, she couldn't even respond. But, finally, she found her voice and knew exactly what she wanted to say.

"Austin, my parents used to tell me when I was little that I'd just know if I'd met my knight in shining armor. I didn't believe them...until this past week."

She squeezed his fingers with hers. "Yesterday, when I was trying to figure out what I was feeling, I talked with them. They didn't tell me what I should think or what I should do, but they did remind me of something important—my values. And that's what I've loved about getting to know you again. I hadn't realized when we were kids that we shared so many core beliefs. I admire your devotion to your family and your desire to learn new things. I feel as though we've known each other forever and shared a childhood, and yet, when I'm with you now, you show me a brand-new world. It's like I'm walking in a place I already love, but I'm discovering beauty on the path that I'd never seen before." She paused and saw a gleam of raw emotion in his eyes. "I love that, Austin."

"How is it possible that you can read my mind?" he whispered. "Because what you're describing—that's how I feel when I'm with you."

Somehow, they managed to finish their lattes and nibble on their tasty treats while still holding hands and hardly breaking eye contact. It was the best coffee break Emma had ever had in her life.

After leaving Mrs. McBride's lovely little shop, they went for a long, meandering walk in the snow, holding hands and laughing for no real reason. Emma only knew that this feeling was the definition of pure joy.

They exchanged Christmas greetings with a handful of townspeople and saw several couples taking sleigh rides down the snowy path.

"Any interest in a romantic ride?" Austin asked her. "It's, um, lovely weather for a sleigh ride together...with you."

She appreciated the offer, but she shook her head. "This is all I need today. All I want."

So they just walked and wandered, talked and shared thoughts and dreams. And when a smattering of flurries fell on their heads and dusted the path before them, Emma giggled and started to sing, "Let It Snow."

To her delight, Austin joined in.

Then, when there was no one around to gawk or comment, Austin kissed her in the middle of their winter wonderland.

And it was so warm and so sweet that she didn't even feel the cold.

# *Thirteen*

### *Christmas Eve*

Emma wasn't generally a fan of channel WHMN's regional daytime programming—she tended not to watch much TV during the work week anyway—but she was especially unhappy with this morning's broadcast.

Darla had turned on the television while dusting the living room, and as a result, Emma caught the entirety of the weather report.

"It's Christmas Eve Day!" the far too cheery lady meteorologist, Shelley-somebody, enthused. "And guess what?"

She waited for her TV colleagues to cry, "What?"

"It's going to be a white Christmas!" Shelley declared.

Emma rolled her eyes, feeling like a petulant teen who needed to correct erring adults. "It's already a white Christmas," she informed the lady on the TV screen in a tart tone. It had snowed on and off for all of December. There was at least half a foot of white powder covering the ground. No way would it all melt by tomorrow.

Darla chuckled and continued dusting.

The meteorologist, however, kept jabbering with delight and pointing to a map of North America. "Take a look up here, folks." She indicated something in the general vicinity of Saskatchewan. "This powerful Canadian weather system has been making its way across the northern provinces, gaining speed and strength. It's already pushed east to Winnipeg, dumping over fourteen inches of snow across southern Manitoba, and now it's crossing the border, changing directions, and heading our way."

Darla stopped dusting and stared at the screen.

Emma's jaw dropped as the weather map changed to show the path of the winter storm. Snow was going to blanket most of Minnesota—that much was certain. The question was when would it hit Crystal Corners and how much would they get?

Emma glanced out the window. The day looked clear right now, but she'd grown up in the Midwest and knew how fast weather conditions could change.

Shelley on TV had worked herself into a delighted frenzy, obviously sensing that she'd captured an audience, and was talking about highway closures, various activity cancellations, travel advisories, and the like. "This is a *major* weather event affecting our whole state," she announced. "Do not get out on the road unless absolutely necessary." And then she launched into a scary segment on car accidents and driving fatalities, urging all viewers to take these warnings seriously.

Emma did not like this meteorologist or the network she worked for, but she had to concede that what the lady was saying was the truth. She took Shelley's grave warnings with the utmost seriousness.

Studying the predicted path of the storm, Emma could tell that the towns closest to the northern border would be hit hardest and were, in fact, already seeing significant snowfall. Further south, where they were in Crystal

Corners, the amount of expected snow was still to be determined.

Making it even harder to call were the unpredictable wind patterns. If the wind shifted before the storm reached them, a city just an hour or two to the east or west of Crystal Corners could see a ton of snow...or none at all. They would just have to wait and find out.

For the first hour or so after the broadcast, Emma didn't think beyond the city limits. Crystal Corners was a small town, but they had lots of private plowing services, like Connor Knightley's company, as well as community-wide public ones. There were only a few main roads here, but they would be clear and passable on Christmas Day, even if their area got several more inches of snow tonight.

But then she remembered.

Austin was driving to Montgomery Falls today to pick up the glass doors and the carousel stand. That city was an hour and a half due north.

She grabbed her cell phone and checked the time. Eleven twenty-six. Austin said he was going to pick up the items this afternoon. But maybe, just maybe, he hadn't left yet.

She texted him. Waited (not quite patiently) for ten minutes. No response.

So, she called him. Got his voicemail.

"Argh!" she cried, after leaving only a brief message, asking him to please call her.

She exhaled, thought about who might know his whereabouts for sure, and called his parents' house.

His mom answered on the second ring. "Hello, Emma," she said, her tone holding an edge of worry, which, of course, made Emma worry, too.

"Please tell me that Austin didn't actually leave for Montgomery Falls yet—"

"About forty-five minutes ago," Pam Knightley said with a sigh. "His father and I both tried to stop him."

"Oh, no." Emma sank into the nearest chair and glanced outside. Those large puffy snowflakes had begun to fall. Slowly for now, but that would likely change.

"He insisted that he had a big heavy truck," Austin's mom said. "And that he would be completely fine."

"I want him to turn around and come home," Emma said, meaning every word. Yes, the display case wouldn't rotate or have glass doors like the original one that had been burned up in the fire, but this was a small price to pay for Austin's safety. "I'm going to keep trying to reach him on his cell. But please let me know if you get ahold of him first. Tell him to just come back before the storm gets worse."

"I'll do that," his mom said. "And please tell us if you manage to talk with him before we do. Mothers always worry."

As Emma hung up, she added to herself, *And so do girlfriends*. The thought made her smile and then grimace. After yesterday, she knew she and Austin were genuinely a couple. She couldn't bear it if she'd finally found her soul mate only to lose him.

No. That wasn't going to happen. She would be persistent, and she'd call and call and call his cell phone until he answered her and listened to reason.

Turned out, she only needed to call one more time.

"Emma," he said. "How are you?"

"How am *I*? I'm fine. I'm *at home* in my nice safe house. The question is where are *you*? And, here, let me give you the correct answer, which is 'driving back toward Crystal Corners right now.' Got it?"

He laughed. "Wow, you're, like, *super* bossy. Even more so than usual. But before you get offended, let me just say that I've started to think that's a pretty cute trait."

"Um, thanks. Listen, Austin, about this trip. Call it off. Please."

She heard him inhale on the other end of the line. "You

realize that's not how I roll."

"Why not?" Emma huffed in exasperation.

"Because I have a job to do, and I *always* complete my jobs. Besides, I'm here at a gas station, refueling, grabbing some snacks, and I was just getting ready to reply to a few texts and messages, including yours, when you called. Never, ever text and drive," he said lightly.

"That's a great motto. Now, please, put away your phone, forget about your work ethic for one afternoon, and just drive home. I'm worried about you. Your mom's worried about you. And there's a massive snowstorm—"

"Stop worrying. I'm an excellent driver, and I have a full-sized pickup truck with four-wheel drive, state-of-the-art suspension, a 5.3-liter V8 engine and—"

"Save the motor vehicle commercial for someone else, Austin. None of that makes you invincible."

"But I'm most of the way to Montgomery Falls already. The glass company isn't going to deliver your specialty doors to you like a pepperoni pizza, Emma. If I don't pick them up, I can't attach them tonight."

"It's okay. *Really.* We'll figure something else out." She had no idea what...but there had to be another way. One that didn't involve putting Austin's life in jeopardy and allowing him to drive into the heart of a blizzard.

"Nah," he said. "I'm gonna stick with my original plan. The snow's not coming down that hard. Just normal Minnesota winter stuff. Say hi to my mom for me," he added with a laugh. "Tell her I'll be back by dinner. And I'll see *you* later tonight." He blew her a big kiss through the phone line and promptly hung up on her.

Seriously, if he made it through this harebrained plan of his alive, she was gonna kill him.

Bad weather had a way of sneaking up on a guy.

The storm really hadn't been that unusual starting out. Austin hadn't lied to Emma about that. It was pretty normal winter snowfall—at least initially.

But the further north he drove, the heavier it got. And by the time he arrived in Montgomery Falls, he was aware that the dangerous sheet of ice just beneath the newly fallen snow was a recipe for driving collisions and roadway disasters of all sorts.

In just the last five or ten miles before getting into town, he'd spotted seven cars in ditches and three tow trucks. He took the exit ramp at less than half of the posted speed, and his truck still skid a few times before he made it off the highway.

Austin was stubborn, yes, but not stupid.

However, he had a dilemma to resolve and just a short window of time to do it. Should he stay in Montgomery Falls long enough to wait for the glass to be ready...or hightail it home before conditions worsened?

The National Weather Service had put out their official bulletin after he'd already begun the drive up here. If he left Montgomery Falls within the next twenty or thirty minutes, he might be able to make it back before the storm hit Crystal Corners.

But then he would have come all this way for nothing. To come up here, be so close, and *not* get the rest of the supplies for Emma's display case? He just couldn't concede defeat that quickly.

And no matter what she said, Austin knew she'd had her heart set on completing this project just the way she'd envisioned it. There was a chance that he wouldn't have to wait the two or three hours expected before the glass was ready to be picked up. If he could at least get that part, he could jury-rig something else for rotation—possibly go back to the previous wheels-on-the-bottom idea—but the glass doors were nonnegotiable. Not if he wanted the final piece of furniture to resemble what Emma had been so excited about them making.

It took all his skills as a winter driver, not to mention all of the fine steering and handling features of his truck, but he made it to the center of the city and scored a parking spot in a covered garage. Downtown traffic was a mess, not only because of the snow and the salt trucks on the road, but because many businesses were closing early, even on Christmas Eve Day, on account of the crummy weather.

He brushed handfuls of snow off his coat before he pushed through the front door of Fairfax & Churchill Glass and, within minutes, found his buddy Ray Fairfax.

"Hey!" Ray said. "You're a crazy dude. You came all the way up here in this?"

"I know, I know," Austin replied. "But it didn't get bad until...well, the last ten or fifteen...okay, the final twenty miles pretty much sucked."

His friend shook his head. "I know we received your order, but I wish you'd called before driving so far. The guy who usually handles the specialty glass didn't even come in this morning. Car trouble. Then this insane snowstorm started, and we couldn't get anybody else to jump in to cover for him. And the rest of us have been swamped."

"So, it's not going to be done today at all?"

"It could be, yes. I was going to have Nate finish it, so it'd be ready for you by three thirty or four-ish this afternoon, as promised. But that's still a few hours away. If you're angling to get back home early, it's not likely that we'd be able to have it done much sooner. On a normal day, maybe, but not on Christmas Eve Day in the middle of a blizzard. I'm sorry, Austin."

He understood. If a customer had come into his construction company's headquarters in the Twin Cities, looking for a custom carpentry order, for instance, several hours in advance, would he have tried to help? Without question, yes. But there was no guarantee he'd be able to do it, especially when there were extenuating circumstances like a major holiday or unusually bad weather.

"Oh, no worries, Ray. I wanted to ask, just in case, but I get it." he said. "Maybe I'll wander around Montgomery Falls and do a little Christmas window shopping while I wait," he joked.

Ray grinned. "You could. Or you could head back to Crystal Corners while you still can. There's chatter on the radio about the highways being closed because of all the accidents. The conditions out there are treacherous, buddy. And the exits into and out of town are especially icy from what I hear."

Austin knew this was true from his personal experience. But the city hadn't had a chance to salt the interstates and ramps yet when he first drove into town. He figured he ought to give them an opportunity to do that at least. He could check in with Ray and his crew in a couple of hours. Maybe the wind would shift or the snow would stop. Conditions in the later afternoon might actually be better than the current ones. It'd happened that way plenty of times before.

And, legit, he did have a little Christmas shopping left to do. He might as well make the most of his time here...or his captivity.

He called Emma and explained about having to wait for the glass. He downplayed the dangerous road conditions, but he did admit to her that it wasn't ideal driving.

"Not *ideal?* Austin, you numbskull," she all but shouted on the phone. "Don't you dare try to drive back tonight. Even if, by some miracle, the weather clears up where you are, it's still a mess down here. In Crystal Corners we've gotten four inches of snow already, and there's more ahead. According to the online forecast, Montgomery Falls is expecting *an inch an hour* between now and midnight. Before this storm moves on, the city you're in might get a foot of snow or more."

"Okay, okay, Emma. I agree that doesn't sound encouraging for travel. But maybe—"

"No, Austin. There is no 'but maybe' this time. Remember yesterday? You got aggravated with me for planning to go outside wearing only a thin cloak and a silk scarf. So, what did I do? I *listened* to you. I realized you were right, and I wore heavier items instead. Now, it's your turn to listen to *me,* and it's about something much more perilous than proper outwear." She paused to let those words sink in. "I don't care if you stay with a friend or crash at a hotel or spend all night at a 24-hour diner stuffing your face with all-you-can-eat pancakes, but do *not,* under any circumstances, drive back here until the roads are safe again. I mean it!"

"But I really want to be with you tonigh—"

"I'm falling in love with you, Austin. If you care about me *at all,* stay put."

The combination of worry and sheer exasperation in her voice made him pause, but it was the words themselves— and what they meant—that made him listen.

"Emma, I'm falling in love with you, too. You know that, right? I was doing this *for* you. What about your Christmas morning event with the kids tomorrow? If I don't come back tonight, then—"

"I'll figure something else out, okay? I'm not helpless. In the grand scheme of things, this is a very small problem. I realize that now. But you listening to me and demonstrating you have some brain cells left in your head that haven't been completely frozen by the ice and snow yet...that is a much bigger problem."

In spite of everything, he laughed. And he was considerably cheered by the fact that she laughed along with him. He knew that Emma (and his mom, and his sister, and practically everyone who had his cell number and had called or texted him) were correct about the weather conditions and that he shouldn't risk the drive. He was man enough to concede this fact, even before the decision was taken out of his hands.

Not ten minutes later, he heard from one of the shop owners that the state police had closed down the highway outside of Montgomery Falls and, except for service and emergency vehicles, no one was getting out of town until midday tomorrow. At the earliest.

When the implications of what this meant fully sunk in, though, Austin muttered a silent apology to Emma and buried his face in his palms. Now, he just felt guilty. Because, if he'd only listened to her and to his parents in the first place and returned home when he was at the gas station, he might not have had the glass doors with him, but he would have been there to help her. Help by not only coming up with a revised plan for the display case tonight, but also help in getting it to the gazebo tomorrow morning as he'd promised. As it stood now, he'd not only taken a bad situation and made it worse, he'd let Emma down in the process.

On the upside, he did manage to find a room at a quaint bed and breakfast downtown that, fortunately, had a vacancy because of a last-minute cancellation. ("On account of all this snow, you know," said the clerk. "No one should be driving in that.") It was within easy walking distance of the parking garage, which was just across the street, so he didn't even have to move his truck.

He picked up a handful of toiletries from a corner pharmacy and an extra T-shirt to sleep in, then proceeded to order a carryout dinner of hot dogs and potato chips. A far cry from the Christmas Eve plans he'd originally had with his family and with Emma.

But he didn't have the luxury of feeling sorry for himself.

For one, this situation was his own fault. Not Mother Nature's part in it, but his insistence on ignoring the weather and Emma's wishes. And, two, he needed to spend the evening helping her from afar, even if he couldn't be there in person.

As soon as he'd talked with his parents and assured them he'd checked into a B&B and was safe for the night, he set about calling his most reliable friends in Crystal Corners and the family members he knew he could count on to do some heavy lifting, asking them all for help on her behalf.

His brothers were immediately on board.

David said, "Dude, c'mon. I was already gonna help you bring the display case over to the gazebo tomorrow. I was gonna wake up, like, three hours early anyway. I'll totally do whatever Emma needs. I could even drill the holes at the bottom of the shelves and add in the wheels, if she still wants that."

And Connor said, "I've got a lot of snowplowing contracts tonight, so I'll be out late. But there's a team of us, and I can send some of my guys to cover things if Emma needs help in the morning. Give her my private cell and tell her to call anytime, okay?"

Austin was grateful to his brothers and even—sort of— to his sister.

Unasked, Bethany texted him and informed him that she'd already offered to lend Emma a hand with setting up the statuettes at the gazebo. "I want to be there for moral support, too," his sister added. "Since, apparently, Emma actually cares about you and won't be happy until you return." This was followed by a row of emojis with rolling eyes.

Great. Bethany's idea of "moral support" was a terrifying thing. Then, again, she'd had the wisdom to select an awesome man as her husband and bring him back to Crystal Corners.

He called Reggie, too. Not only to ask him to assist Emma in whatever way he could, but also, for advice—

which he seemed to be needing.

Austin's brother-in-law took his call in a private room at work and listened as Austin explained the depth of his feelings for Emma and his disappointment in having let her down. "I just really want to make things right, but I know it's more complicated than that. This is just one situation. One event. What I'm wrestling with is bigger than what'll happen on Christmas Day."

"I knew at the dinner with your family on Saturday night that you cared a lot about her, Austin. But what are you saying? That you're already thinking beyond the dating stage?"

Austin groaned. "I know it's nuts, given that we've only just officially become a couple, but I can't help but feel we were meant to be together. No relationship I've ever been in has made *sense* like this. I just—am I delusional, Reg? I mean, how long had you and Bethany known each other before you knew she was the one?"

There was a burst of laughter on the other end of the line. "Do you want to hear the *real* answer...or the answer I give everyone?"

"There's a difference?"

"Oh, yeah," Reggie said. "The answer I give everyone is 'four months' because that sounds reasonable, right?"

"Right," Austin answered dutifully.

"Yeah. About four months into our relationship I was sick with the flu. Really bad. I could barely sit up. Your sister made me a pot of chicken soup and brought it over to my apartment. It was *so* bland and in need of spice that it was practically inedible until I added a cup of sliced jalapenos. Thankfully, I always keep bagfuls of them in the fridge, and I managed to chop some and slip them in there after Bethany left. The gesture was super sweet and thoughtful, though. I couldn't help but fall for her. But, um—"

"But what?"

"But that's a lie," Reggie said. "I mean, sure, I loved that she did that. But I was already deeply in love with her by then. I fell for her about thirty seconds into our first conversation, even though it took me a couple of weeks to find enough guts to ask her out. We hadn't been dating a week before I'd already worked out how I wanted to propose." He paused. "Sometimes, the heart knows the truth long before the head."

Austin thought about his brother-in-law's words long after their phone conversation ended. He knew, with bone-deep certainty, exactly what Reggie had been talking about. And unlike Bethany and her wise husband, Austin and Emma actually had a shared history that went back a couple of decades. Society in general might consider it premature for him to think of their relationship as a "lifetime love" already, but he did. That was a fact, and there was no way around the truth of it.

He called in a few other favors from friends back home, all of them agreeing to be of help to Emma tonight or tomorrow, based on whatever assistance she needed.

Finally, he swallowed his pride and texted Mack Morales, too.

Mack texted back in under a minute.

"Listen, Austin, Lila and I will do anything we can for Emma. She's got contact info for both of us, but we'll reach out to her tonight as well. Is there anything we can do for *you*?"

"You can accept my apology for being a jerk at the Christmas festival on Friday," he wrote back. "Sorry."

Mack responded with an "LOL" and several smiley faces. "Water under the bridge, buddy. But...did you seriously try to convince me just, like, two weeks ago that you *didn't* have a thing for her?"

Austin could almost hear his friend snorting with laughter on the other side of the phone screen. "You know what," he typed, "when we finally go out for those beers after the holidays, I'll tell ya all about it."

"I'm gonna hold you to that," Mack replied before signing off.

For the next half hour, Austin paced the room, feeling hemmed in despite the beautifully furnished rustic decor, and he watched the continuously falling snow from the window. It made for a picturesque scene. Too bad he couldn't share the view with Emma.

Speaking of which, she'd sent him several cryptic messages that he was unsuccessful in interpreting. Something about "Thinking outside of the box—literally!" was what she'd written the first time. Then she said only that she wanted to work through the details of her plan before she called him, but that she'd probably need his help via video chat.

All of this sounded reasonable, despite being a less than comprehensive explanation. But he could be patient. Kind of. His girlfriend—a happy term that brought a smile to his face despite the day's many frustrations—was a very bright and determined woman. He knew this. And much as he wanted to solve this problem for her, he needed to trust that she could figure it out for herself.

It was after seven p.m. when Emma finally called, her voice bubbling over with excitement, but as she explained her brainstorm to him, Austin knew she had a winning solution.

It took a while before Emma landed on the perfect plan, but by around six thirty or so on Christmas Eve, she'd nailed down the details.

The toughest part wasn't actually the plan itself. It was breaking away from her old way of thinking. She'd been so stuck on her original concept for the Christmas morning event, right down to the display case being precisely the way she'd envisioned it, that she couldn't see outside of the box.

And in staring at the three freestanding shelving units in her parents' garage, that was exactly and quite literally what she needed to do.

When she called Austin that night at his room in Montgomery Falls, she had her new and improved game plan in place.

"Okay, so it turns out, I need to be just a little more flexible in my thinking," she admitted to him. "Even if your brothers helped me fasten the three sections together and add in the wheels, without the glassed-in doors, some of the statuettes would probably fall out when the display case is rotated. If we skipped the wheels and left the three shelving units freestanding, they wouldn't be as stable. They'd still need to be attached to each other or nailed down somehow to keep them from tipping. And this is where I finally saw the problem clearly. This is supposed to be a fun event for the kids, not a dangerous one. The goal is really all about accessibility—both to their individual statuettes and to each other, so they can have this shared experience. And that's when I remembered the sleighs."

"The ones people were taking rides on yesterday?" Austin asked. "When we went for our snow walk?"

"Yes! Although, now that I think about it, we probably shouldn't have sung 'Let It Snow' quite so enthusiastically then."

He laughed at her joke. "You're saying we summoned this blizzard?"

"I hope not. But next year, I'll make you sing 'I'll Be Home for Christmas' instead, just to be safe."

"Oh, Emma. That's a deal." He sighed on the other end of the line. "You have no idea how sorry I am for—"

"You can make it up to me when you're safely back at home, but now I need you to focus," she said, knowing he was probably thinking how bossy she sounded again.

"Yes, ma'am," he replied, but Emma could hear the affection in his voice. "What can I do for you?"

"The two of us made three beautiful units that could hold and protect the statuettes until they could be distributed to the children. They can still do that, but they'd be safer for the kids and more accessible to them if the units, instead of being upright, were tipped on their backs. And if I put runners on the bottom—like a sleigh—the individual cases could be in the snow next to the gazebo—"

"And all the kids would have room to gather around them," he finished for her.

"Exactly. And they'd be lower to the ground, so much easier for the little ones to reach. We wouldn't need the carousel stand at all or any wheels or glass doors."

"Although you'd want to make sure the shelving is completely secured to the brackets now," he told her. "Before, the individual shelves we built were removable. They just rested on the brackets and gravity held them in place. But if you tip the units—"

"Oh, right," she agreed. "So, I'll make sure those are fastened somehow. Nailed, glued, something permanent. And then if I screw in a pair of runners for each shelving unit, the three statuette sleighs wouldn't even have to be lifted once we got them to the park. Your brothers and I would just unload them from the truck, and they could be pulled toward the gazebo, like sleds."

"That's brilliant, Emma."

"Thanks for saying that. Better late than never, I suppose." She sighed. "I shouldn't have been so stuck to my first idea that I wasn't willing to consider other possibilities. Although I guess my stubbornness had an upside."

"That you learned a little carpentry and realized what a creative thinker you could be?"

She smiled and shook her head, although she knew he

couldn't see her. "No, Austin. Because it gave me a chance to get to know you."

"I'm encouraged that you still think so."

"I do," she said. "And I appreciate all the offers of help I've gotten today. For someone who isn't a big fan of socializing, you certainly called in the cavalry."

"Well, now we just need to make sure you get some help with securing the shelves and finding those sleigh runners—"

"Already done," she interjected. "I told you, Austin, you sent in the cavalry. As soon as I knew how I wanted to change the design, David brought over a bunch of tools and various supplies. Connor hunted down one pair of runners. Mack somehow came up with the second pair. And my pals Jason and Kent are going to bring over the third pair, as soon as they can retrieve them from the prop storage room at the theater. They used a real sleigh in a production of *Holiday Inn* once," she explained. "For us, the storm has almost ended and the band of snow seems to have settled farther north. By you."

"Yeah, it's still coming down pretty hard around these parts. And with the interstate closed to all cars except for emergency and service vehicles, I have to wait it out until whenever the blizzard stops and the crews can clear the roads."

"That doesn't get you out of helping me tonight," she said lightly, hoping to make him feel a bit better. "From the beginning, you said we had to *work* on this project *together*, and I intend to hold you to your own rules."

She was rewarded with a hardy laugh from Austin. "You're on. Want to switch over to video chat?"

"Yes. And with your instructions and the help of all these tools you brother brought over, you're going to talk me through the process of attaching the sleigh runners to the wooden units." She picked up a screwdriver from the tool box, switched to video, and once she saw Austin's handsome face on her phone screen, she waved the screwdriver at him. "Where do I start?"

The finished product looked even better to Emma's eye than the idea she'd envisioned just a few hours before, and it was a significant improvement for her needs over the whole display case thing, however pretty.

Sometimes function trumped fashion. And, hey, she'd learned that Curly Maple was a gorgeous wood, whether vertical or horizontal.

She and Austin stayed up late, just talking, for hours after she'd finished turning the last of the screws. Late enough that the grandfather clock in the house struck midnight, and Emma was able to wish Austin a very Merry Christmas morning.

Even after they finally bid each other good night, though, Emma lay awake, contemplating another idea.

She picked up the knight in shining armor statuette that Santa had given her when she was six, and she rubbed the smooth metal thoughtfully, dreamily...for inspiration.

If she could learn to think outside of the box in one area of her life, she mused, what was stopping her from doing the same in another area?

Nothing was stopping her, she decided. Nothing at all.

# Fourteen

### Christmas Day

Christmas morning started unusually early for Emma.

Despite being up half the night, mentally running through a series of scenarios for the day, she all but leaped out of bed when her alarm rang at quarter to six.

*It's Christmas Day!*

Jennings also had an early start, having arrived a half hour before to make Emma her favorite kind of French toast—extra thick sourdough slices with warm syrup and sliced strawberries.

"I think you just gave me all the energy I need for today," she told Jennings. "Thank you for a delicious Christmas breakfast."

"My pleasure, Miss," he said with a slight bow. "Merry Christmas to you."

She hugged him tightly, and then got online to check, double-check, and triple-check the forecast, both for Crystal Corners and Montgomery Falls.

Current conditions here were fine, and the new blanket

of clean snow only served to make the day brighter and more beautiful. The community Christmas event with the children was set to begin at ten a.m., so she had almost four hours before the festivities to prepare.

As for Montgomery Falls, the blizzard had finally stopped up there, but the roads were expected to remain closed until midday, when the plows would have enough time to fully clear the ramps and main arteries. Which meant Austin was really and truly stuck at that B&B in downtown Montgomery Falls.

But, as she'd concluded in her brainstorm late last night, that was excellent news.

Emma picked up her phone and began texting. Connor first. Then David. Then Bethany and Reggie, and Austin's parents, too, just to keep them in the loop. Then Jason and Kent. Then Mack and Lila, followed by Vera and Steve. Then Adele. And, finally, Ginger Mae.

With all players on the snow-covered field in place and ready to spring into action, Emma grinned and got dressed. This was going to be *fun*.

Austin awoke on Christmas morning to a series of strange and vaguely incomprehensible messages.

They started coming in around seven a.m. and didn't let up for a solid hour and a half.

First, it was his mom and dad texting to wish him a Merry Christmas. That was normal enough, but then his dad, who hated cell phones with a gleaming passion, texted him about fifty-seven consecutive questions that had to do with construction modification ideas his parents were hoping to make to their house in the coming year.

Austin was totally on board with this plan and even had some preliminary sketches drawn up. But why, exactly, his dad wanted to message him about this at way-too-early o'clock on Christmas morning was a complete mystery.

"Seriously, Dad," Austin texted. "It'll be a lot easier for me to just show you the design ideas when I get home later today. I might even be able to leave soon."

"No, no!" came his father's surprisingly fast reply. "It's still not safe out there."

Austin had barely gotten done answering this stream of texts from Dad, when Reggie and Bethany started in on him.

Again, the phone call seemed to begin all right, but then it took a bizarre turn. Under the guise of wishing him a Merry Christmas, they started reflecting on how much they'd both loved the chocolate torte he and Emma had made over the weekend. Within five minutes, which was usually longer than Austin typically chatted with them on the phone, Reg was all but interrogating him about the ingredients in the dessert and requesting specifics about the baking and icing directions.

"I'm thinking of making a spicier version of it," his brother-in-law mused. "To give kind of a Mexican hot chocolate kick to the torte with, you know, a little cinnamon, a little nutmeg, a little cayenne pepper."

"Um, okay. That sounds...intriguing," Austin managed, glad his brother-in-law couldn't see him wincing at that combination. "When, exactly, were you planning to make this?"

"Right now would be good," Reggie declared. "No time like the present."

So, Austin was on the phone for another half hour at least, while Reggie painstakingly searched his pantry for ingredients both resembling and not resembling those in the original recipe and, alternately, asking another eight million clarifying questions about the baking process.

Austin might not be able to drive out of Montgomery Falls, but he didn't want to stay cooped up in the B&B all morning either. The kind owners brought him a tray with a full English breakfast, but he'd been interrupted with phone calls and texts so many times, he'd barely had a chance to nibble on it.

As if he hadn't heard from enough family members, Connor texted him a Christmas greeting not long after Reggie finally hung up, and David sent him a text first, followed by another phone call.

"Hey, bro. You know I'm gonna be graduating from college in May. I was thinking of, maybe, buying a truck this summer. I really like the way yours handles and—"

"I'm not giving you my truck, David."

"Oh, yeah, no. I wasn't asking for it," his baby brother said. "But I did kinda want to talk pickups with you for, like, ten minutes, is that okay?"

His family was effectively driving him insane, but a guy was never too busy to talk to a sibling he loved. So he said, "Okay, Davey."

"Awesome. So, I know there are both compact and full-sized models, but I wondered—"

"Wait a sec," Austin said, cutting him off. "What are you doing chatting with me on the phone? Why aren't you over at Emma's, helping her get the wooden sleigh-like things loaded in Connor's truck? Doesn't she have to have them by the gazebo before ten a.m.?"

"Oh, yeah, we totally did that already," his brother said. "Actually, these friends of hers, Vera and Steve, have a full-sized pickup. A really nice red color that I liked, by the way. Steve and I loaded in the sleighs. And, uh, your buddy, Mack—he was waiting at the park to help Steve unload them. So, anyway, I was thinking about engines and how much horsepower I would need to—"

"Wait, what? David, why weren't *you* there helping Steve unload? Or helping Emma carry over all of those boxes of statuettes? You didn't leave them for her to move all by herself, did you? And then there's the setting up of the—"

"Whoa! Yo, bro, just chill. It's all been done. Everything for Emma's event is ready. Reggie and Bethany were helping out with the statuettes. And so was this other friend of hers. Jason. He's a theater guy. His partner Kent was there, too. It's all cool."

"Okay, fine. So, where's Emma now? If you guys left early and got things set up so fast, you didn't leave her out in the cold or anything by herself, just waiting for the kids to come, did you? Because that's still"—Austin checked the time—"an hour and forty minutes from now." There was a knock on the door. Probably one of the maids coming to collect his breakfast tray...with the meal he hadn't yet finished eating. "Hang on a minute, David."

"Yeah, sure."

Austin got up, cell phone in hand, and walked over to open the door.

It took him several long moments to understand what he was seeing. His youngest brother, waving a cell phone at him and grinning like a demented maniac. And next to David stood another guy that Austin faintly recognized as one of his brother's friends.

"What in heaven's name are you doing here?" he hissed at David. "Are you nuts driving on these roads? How did you even get into town?"

"Merry Christmas to you, too, bro," David said, still sporting that fiendish grin. "This is my old bud, Jonathan. We were kind of in the mood for another movie in Montgomery Falls. They always release some good ones on Christmas Day, you know."

Austin stared at him. "You came up for a movie? At— what, eight fifteen in the morning? That makes no sense. Do Mom and Dad even know you're here? Because I seriously can't believe they would've let you—"

David and Jonathan glanced at each other and laughed.

"Yeah, man, you were totally right," Jonathan said to

David. "He's clueless."

David shrugged. "He's like that." Then, to Austin, "You're gonna want to take all your stuff and go to the lobby. Oh! Except for your car keys. Jonathan and I are gonna need to use your truck again."

Austin shook his head. "Oh, no, you're not. And I'm not going *anywhere* until—"

David stepped into the room, effectively pushing Austin out of the way, and he motioned for Jonathan to follow him. Then, as if he were speaking to a preschooler, David leaned close to Austin and said, "Please. Trust. Me." He gave him a hug so filled with brotherly love that it rendered Austin speechless. "Where's your coat?" David looked around until he spotted it. "Okay, any other personal items? T-shirt...toothbrush...wallet...got 'em." He collected Austin's belongings and thrust them all at him.

Jonathan found the keys to Austin's truck on the bedside table and held them up. "We're going to check you out of the B&B, Austin. And when the interstate opens back up in a few hours, and it's really, really safe to drive, we'll bring your truck back to Crystal Corners. You're parked in the garage across the street, right?"

Austin nodded mutely, pulled the parking receipt from his wallet, and handed it to his brother's friend. He got the distinct impression that his life was no longer under his control. At all. Maybe he should just go with the flow and stop fighting it. There were clearly forces at work here that he didn't understand.

He grabbed the only other thing he'd brought into the room—a small bag with some of his Christmas Eve shopping spree purchases—faced his youngest brother and exhaled slowly. "Okay. I'm trusting you. I'm going down to the lobby now."

"Good," David said, smiling. "Further instructions will be waiting for you there." He patted Austin on the back. "And, um, have fun."

"Thanks. I think." Then Austin left the room.

When he entered the lobby, it was empty. Well, almost empty. Only the morning manager, who was on duty at the reception desk, was in the room. He was nearly convinced that David and his friend had just pranked him when the lady manager spoke.

"Mr. Austin Knightley?" she asked.

"Yes."

"I have a note for you." She reached into a slot under the counter and out of his view and pulled out an envelope with his name printed on it. Emma's handwriting.

His heart started beating faster as he took the envelope and opened it.

*"We've come to rescue you,"* the note read. *"Dress warmly, then walk outside and turn left on the sidewalk. Your coach awaits. ~E."*

"Thank you," he told the manager. "And Merry Christmas."

"Merry Christmas to you, too, Mr. Knightley."

He did as he was told. He put on his coat, zipped it up, added gloves from his pocket, and collected his things. Then he walked outside, turned left, and spotted one of Connor's snowplow trucks. Sitting snugly inside of it was his brother in the driver's seat...and Emma on the passenger side.

She waved her mittened hand at him from behind the windshield and then popped open the door when he approached. She held out her hand to him and waited until he grasped it. Then she tugged.

"C'mon inside, Austin. We're taking you home," she said, scooting toward the middle so he'd have room.

When he was seated in the cab of the truck with the two of them—Emma giggling like a schoolgirl and Connor not quite able to hide his amusement—Austin finally spoke. "What on earth did you guys do?"

"Emma was the mastermind behind this plan," his

brother said, starting up his vehicle and signaling to pull into the street. "I'm gonna let her tell it."

Austin leaned in and brushed a kiss against her temple. "I want to hear every single detail."

And so she told him.

He listened in amazement as his brilliant and beautiful girlfriend explained that she'd heard that only "service and emergency vehicles" could enter or exit Montgomery Falls. That the city allowed public and private plowing services to come through, since many residents and businesses had contracts with companies to plow their driveways, streets, and parking lots. Austin's brother, while not technically working for anyone in Montgomery Falls, had one such acceptable vehicle. And, just to be legitimately helpful, Connor had even stopped to clear some of the snow and ice off the exit ramp that he and Emma took into town.

"Your brother's an awesome guy," she told Austin, and he saw Connor bow his head and try to hide his blush.

"I know," Austin agreed, feeling the truth of that.

"Aw, c'mon, you guys," Connor said with a groan. "You need to stop embarrassing me or I can't drive."

He and Emma laughed. Then Austin remembered something. "Hey, what about your event with the children?" He glanced at the time. "We might not make it there by ten a.m."

"That's okay," she said. "I've got it covered. Thanks to David, Mack, and Steve, we got all the sleighs and boxes with the statuettes to the park early. Reggie, Bethany, Kent, and Lila joined forces to set everything up around the gazebo and unpack the statuettes, so that Connor, David, Jonathan, and I were free to leave and come here to get you. Meanwhile, back at the Crystal Corners Community Center, Ginger Mae opened up the big meeting room for us, and Adele brought in refreshments for the children and any volunteers who arrived early and wanted to go somewhere warm before the festivities began. Your parents and Steve's wife, Vera, have been getting the word out to the people in town that there'll be a twenty- or thirty-minute delay getting started, so we'd have a little extra time to get back. If we're gone longer than that, Jason offered to open the event for me and start giving out the gifts to the kids until we can arrive. But"—she tapped on the dashboard clock— "I think we're going to make it."

He stared at her—impressed, amazed, and head over heels in love. "You've been very busy, Miss Westwood."

She smiled slyly at him. "Let's just say, Mr. Knightley, that I know a little bit about networking." Then she took his hand in hers and held it tight. And Austin knew that, even though they weren't back in Crystal Corners yet, he was definitely home for Christmas.

Although Austin had grown up in Crystal Corners and thought he knew everything there was to know about his hometown, it turned out that there were a few things he'd forgotten, overlooked, or simply never suspected.

Or maybe, it was a function of his heart, which was flowing over with so much love, gratitude, and goodwill (toward men, women, children, and animals alike) that even everyday occurrences had a sheen of the magical about them.

Of course, Christmas Day wasn't an everyday occurrence.

And when it was combined with the heady sensation of realizing just how much he'd fallen in love with Emma Westwood, the result was an overpowering feeling that Austin was walking around in an enchanted world. Literally *every* word he'd heard spoken aloud—from the moment his feet touched the snow-covered pavement on Main Street until he climbed into his childhood bed that night—had a spellbinding ring to it.

Had Crystal Corners always been so charming? Were the residents all so captivating and humorous? So very giving and kind?

Each interval in the day produced a dozen or more enthralling vignettes of human-to-human (or human-to-mammal) interaction that made Austin pause and just appreciate the love that surrounded them.

When they first drove into town, Connor dropped them off at the Main Street entrance to the park. Emma, still holding Austin's hand, raced with him over to the gazebo, where their friends and his family had gathered, along with more children than he'd ever seen in once place.

Jason, who Austin was used to seeing mostly at the gym, waved excitedly at them and then said into the microphone, "The lady of the hour is here, kids."

A huge cheer went up from the twelve-year-old-and-under crowd, as well as from their parents.

Emma kissed him on the cheek before finally letting go of his hand and skipping up the gazebo stairs, where Jason was waiting for her.

He gave her a quick side hug before addressing the crowd once again. "Allllll righttt! This is the moment all of you youngsters have been anxiously anticipating." Jason grinned at the crowd of beaming children and nodded slowly, prolonging their suspense.

Austin couldn't help but laugh along with many of the parents, who were trying to rein in the excitement of their children. They knew what was coming and could barely contain their enthusiasm.

"You all know who I'm here to introduce, don't you?" Jason asked.

And all of the kids, except, perhaps, for the very youngest members of the crowd, shrieked some variant of "Yes!" or "It's Miss Westwood!" or "Emma, Emma, Emma!"

Jason laughed. "Well, Emma," he said into the mic. "Looks like your young public awaits."

She got into the act and rubbed her hands together in anticipation, her face radiating as much delight as the children all around them.

"One last thing before I turn this microphone over to our lovely Miss Emma," Jason said. "I'm sure all of you are aware of how involved Emma Westwood has been in our community. She has a big beautiful spirit and a knack for getting the people who cross her path to be just as involved and excited about her special projects as she is." Several chuckles rose in the crowd, especially among the adults. "No truer was that the case than this year. She really went above and beyond to make sure this Christmas morning event would come together, and I know I'm grateful to have been even a little part of it. Here's wishing each and every one of you a very Merry Christmas, and may the New Year ahead bring you much joy." Jason blew Emma a kiss and then he blew another one to the crowd. Several people blew kisses back. "And nowwwwww!" Jason said. "Without further ado...heeeeeere's Emma!"

Everyone in and around the gazebo cheered wildly for her, none louder than Austin himself.

His sister, who'd somehow managed to find him in the mass of residents around the gazebo, nudged him and said, "Glad you made it back, bro."

"You, Reggie, our parents, and both of our brothers will have to answer to me later for those wacko phone calls and texts this morning," he said, nudging her back. "But, thank you. I love ya, sis."

Bethany laughed. "We love you, too. Isn't it obvious?"

Emma took the mic and did a quick curtsey to Jason and to the applauding crowd. "Thanks, Jason, and thank you all. Thank you *so* much." She smiled warmly at everyone in all directions, even pausing for a moment to catch his eye.

"I appreciate the kind words and all the applause, but I truly could not have done any of this without the help of so many friends," Emma said. She took the time to name everyone and make them raise their hands for recognition—from Jason and Kent, to Bethany, Reggie and the other members of Austin's family, and then she pointed out Steve, Vera, Mack, Lila, and mentioned Adele and Ginger Mae (the two of them were still in the warm community center, offering cookies and cocoa to anyone who needed a treat) and, finally, Austin himself. "I want to give a special shout out to Austin Knightley, who taught me a little bit about carpentry and a lot about thinking outside the box and having fun." Her grin broadened and she winked at him." He felt his heart grow three sizes larger in just that one second. "And it's thanks to him that we have these very cool new sleighs that contain the presents for all of you gorgeous children!"

At this, the kids' excitement mushroomed to a level of frenzy that Austin had never witnessed before, not even at a major holiday event. He supposed that over the past few years, ever since Emma had begun doing her statuette giveaway, that the children's anticipation continued to grow. That they knew what a unique and wonderful experience it would be and recognized just how thoughtful and generous she was. Something that had taken Austin longer to see than it should have, but he was completely on board now.

Emma began with the youngest of the children—the two- through four-year-olds—whose gifts she'd sectioned off in one part of the first sleigh. The little kids and parents crowded around as she gave each personally tagged statuette to either the youngsters or, if they weren't quite old enough yet, to the parents on behalf of their child.

The kindergarteners through second graders were next, and Austin began to see—even with a group of five-, six-, and seven-year-olds—what a beautiful vision for inspiring appreciation of each youngster's gifts Emma had in mind when she created this event. The children knew they would all be honored and their personal talents and passions would be recognized. That certainty must have given them the confidence to not only be pleased by their own aptitudes but also to gain at least a pint-sized degree of awareness of the abilities of other kids.

Between a couple of six-year-old girls, Austin overheard this snippet of conversation:

"Ooooh, that's such a pretty flower bouquet, Lindsay," a dark-haired girl said, pointing at the other girl's new statuette.

Lindsay nodded. "I love flowers and gardens and making things grow." Then she looked at the statuette that the other girl was grasping to her chest as if someone might snatch it from her. "You must love swinging on your swing set, Mimi."

Mimi smiled, a missing-tooth grin that was shining with happiness. She held out her statuette for Lindsay to look at more closely. "I do my best thinking there."

And Austin realized he'd seen that very statuette at Emma's house, and she'd told him about it. That this child was Mimi Highbury. The little girl who had the brother who loved to run. The little girl who was a daydreamer...like young Emma herself.

There were other tender conversations. Other moments of touching acceptance and inclusiveness. Other children who'd begun to learn what it meant to be simultaneously proud of their own talents and still appreciative of those of their peers. That these two skills could exist peacefully out in the world, but they needed to be modeled first. And Emma was doing an amazing job of modeling it.

He was forced to look away from her only when his parents materialized on either side of him and sandwiched him in a parental hug.

"We were worried about you," his mom said. "You

shouldn't have headed into that storm yesterday."

"Sorry, Mom," Austin said. "You were right."

"Moms are always right," she replied.

To which his dad murmured, "So are wives." He raised his eyebrows comically at Austin's mother, and she narrowed her eyes just as comically back at him.

Austin laughed. He hoped—dearly so—that he'd have a strong marriage and a loving relationship with his future spouse, much like his parents had with each other. A future spouse, incidentally, that he'd like to think he may have identified. Recently.

Reggie jogged up to the three of them as they were watching Emma praise the individual children in the final group—the eleven- and twelve-year-olds. She was taking longer with them than with the preschool and early elementary set because, Austin guessed, she knew what a tricky age this was. How very much they all needed to feel simultaneously special and also part of the crowd.

"I remember being in junior high," Austin's brother-in-law said. "Man, did I ever hate that age. Couldn't wait to grow up, get into high school or, even better, leave school behind me for good."

Austin glanced at him. "You chose to become a doctor, Reg. You had, like, a decade and a half of school left."

Reggie nodded. "Yeah, but I didn't know who I was back then. Not when I was twelve. It was different once I had a better sense of myself. A goal I could cling to. A larger purpose. Then the work involved was doable. All the late nights studying. The many long hours of residency. The endless tests and competency exams and board certifications. The gazillion hoops that needed to be jumped...that was just part of the process of getting to where I wanted to be. But"—he nodded toward the group of kids Emma was talking with—"they're not there yet. Most of them probably have no idea. That's one of the reasons why what she's doing is so special. She's shining a guiding light into the mystery." He patted Austin on the back. "You found yourself an awesome girlfriend, man."

"Thank you." He leaned shoulder to shoulder with his brother-in-law and added, "And thanks for your good advice about all that relationship stuff on the phone yesterday. It helped. A lot, actually."

"Glad to hear it. I've got my fingers crossed for you." Reggie checked his cell. "Your sister and I are gonna stay here for another half hour or so to help Emma finish the event, but then we've gotta run. We both have a shift at the hospital this afternoon. I was hoping we'd both get the day off, but at least it's a little more fun to work a holiday when your loving spouse is somewhere in the building."

"So, you're saying you two aren't going home to chow down on that Mexican hot chocolate variation of the dessert torte that you claimed you were about to make this morning?" Austin teased.

Reggie flashed him a dazzling grin that showed off a significant number of the good doc's straight white teeth. "I'm still totally making that dessert. Real soon. And don't you worry. When I do, I'll save you a big peppery piece."

His brother-in-law wished both of Austin's parents a Merry Christmas and went in search of Bethany, who was flitting around the snowy park like the cheerful social butterfly she was.

Austin watched as Reggie spotted her. Saw the way Reg's face lit up like Mom's Christmas tree when she looked his way and waved him over. Austin had admired their relationship from the very beginning, of course, but he felt an even greater kinship with his brother-in-law these days. Austin could recognize the depth of true love now when he saw it.

He spoke with his parents for a few minutes more before they, too, needed to head out. It was a pleasant day for late December, but it was still very much a wintry one.

"We're going to stop by the community center to get

warm and to chat with Adele and Ginger Mae for a little longer," Mom told him. "But then we'll be returning home."

"And I'm gonna grab me a few more of Adele's cookies," his dad confided.

"You've already had three. You're not supposed to eat that much sugar and saturated fat, Ned," his mom said with a glare, and she wasn't joking this time. "You know what the doctors told you about heart health and nutrition."

Dad let out a long-suffering sigh. "I know, I know. But, honey, it's *Christmas*."

He sounded so much like a little kid that Austin had to laugh.

"That's right," Mom replied, tugging on his sleeve in the direction of Main Street. "And we've already seen Bethany and Reggie today. Not that I wouldn't enjoy their company again, but I'd prefer that it isn't at the hospital."

"Maybe just one more cookie?" Dad asked.

Mom groaned in exasperation. "Maybe *one*." Then, to Austin, "We'll see you tonight?"

"I'll be home for dinner this time," he said. "I promise."

"Good," she said, and they left the park.

Austin glanced around and spotted his buddy Mack and another guy (Steve, was it?) loading up the two empty statuette sleighs into the second man's truck. Emma was still finishing up her discussion and gift sharing with the kids by the third sleigh, but he walked over to the men and figured he'd offer his help with loading the last one when she was done.

Mack clasped Austin's outstretched hand and said, "Hey, buddy. Glad to see you here."

"Glad to be here," he replied. Then he offered his hand to Steve, which the other guy shook as Mack officially introduced them.

"Thank you for being such a tremendous help to Emma," Austin said to them. "I'm in debt to you both."

Mack looked at Steve and said, "Yeah, that's code for the first order of loaded nachos and first round of beers are on him."

Steve laughed loudly. "Well, count me in then. But, honestly, it was a pleasure to do something for Emma. She's done so much for me and for my wife Vera." He nodded toward the very pregnant woman who was carefully making her way over to them from the community center, a six-pack cardboard beverage carrier in her hand, which Austin soon learned contained a combination of hot cocoas and coffees.

"Have a warm beverage, guys," Vera said, offering them their choice of drink.

"Thanks so much," Austin said, reaching gratefully for one of the coffees. He smiled. It was hard for him to think of drinking coffee without thinking of Emma. The two of them would have to go back to Mrs. McBride's coffeehouse again soon. He didn't care what kind of hot drink they ordered. He just wanted to hold hands with her across the table and look deep into her beautiful blue eyes as she shared with him her daydreams for the future.

He glanced up and saw Vera studying him, an interested expression on her face.

When Emma got done with her conversation with the children and all the statuettes were happily distributed, Austin, Steve, and Mack started to head over to the last sleigh to collect it. But Vera pulled him aside.

"So, Austin," she said, "I think I've finally figured something out." Vera inclined her head toward Emma, who was in the process of giving her usual detailed directions to several of the volunteers near the gazebo, while Steve and Mack waited by the sleigh. "You're the reason for her different aura, aren't you?"

"Um, what?" he asked.

Vera took a step or two closer and poked at him with her index finger. "She likes you. And when she's with you, she's happier."

"I hope so," Austin said. "It's mutual."

"Good." Vera nodded at him. "It's just—she's a dear friend of mine. So, don't hurt her."

"I won't," he promised. "At least not intentionally."

"Good," she said again. "Because I might be huge and pregnant, awkward and embarrassingly imbalanced right now, but I took fourteen years of jujitsu. So, if you break Emma's heart, you'll be very sorry."

There were no words Austin could say to counteract this loving threat. He just stared helplessly at her until she grinned, poked him with her finger one last time, and waddled away.

After Austin helped Steve and Mack load the third and final sleigh onto Steve's truck, Austin sidled over to Emma, who was issuing more commands (in a very sweet and good-natured way, of course) to one more set of volunteers. He waited with the utmost patience until the coast was clear for a moment.

"You were a rock star today, Emma Westwood." He kissed the top of her head. "Give me instructions, and I'll help you with whatever tasks are left. I ask only one thing."

"What's that?"

"A little time alone with you later. Just the two of us."

"Deal," she said. "Besides, I have something for you."

"Oh, yeah? What's that?"

She laughed. "You think I'm going to tell you? No, no. You've got to wait and see. There's no fun in giving away a surprise early."

He looked forward to that, not that he needed any surprises other than her. Emma was plenty surprising.

As he helped her collect the last of the cartons, boxes, and crates that had contained all the statuettes for the kids, he thought about his most recent conversation with Reggie. About how twelve-year-olds were still trying to figure out who they were. About the Emma he remembered from grade school, junior high, and high school. The girl he *thought* he knew.

He suddenly remembered an incident that had happened on the school bus when he was a quiet, world-weary sophomore and she was a bright and shiny freshman.

It was one of the earliest days of the school year, and there was this new kid sitting alone. He'd just moved to Minnesota from somewhere in California and wasn't somebody Austin had talked with yet. Of course, Austin rarely said anything to anyone on the bus if he could help it, plus this boy wasn't the chattiest person either, except in gym class. He'd already proven he was a natural athlete.

But Austin knew that Emma couldn't have cared less about the kid's skills on a playing field. She just boarded the bus and saw the guy all alone and took it upon herself to keep him company.

Austin overheard her asking Mack Morales if the seat next to him was taken. But what he remembered most was how Mack had smiled at her that day. Not the smile of boy with a crush on a girl. But the smile of a new kid who just needed to know someone was there to welcome him. That someone in his new community wanted to be his friend.

That was the kind of person Emma was. Austin had seen her demonstrating kindness to people again and again—including to him—even as a child, but he hadn't always interpreted her actions in the way they were intended. And maybe that was because she *was* kind of bossy sometimes and chatty rather often and very particular about certain things, too. She was, on the surface at least, the opposite of how Austin saw himself.

But deep down, she was more than the type of person Austin was. She was the type of person Austin *wished* he could be.

The realization of that hit him full force, and he just stopped for a minute to admire her and catch his breath.

Myra and William Elton happened to be walking by

just then, and he overheard them grumbling about the "mess" the children made in the park. They were forever complaining about other people making messes and were a pair of rare exceptions to the legions of kindhearted residents in town.

Most of the time, Austin ignored them. That would have been the case this time, too, except they made the foolish decision to criticize Emma.

"That Westwood girl is always making a 'production' out of something," Myra Elton griped. "We can't have a single holiday in this town without her creating some sort of community 'event' out of it. What a nuisance."

"And just look at the park," her husband whined. "It was so pristine and calm this morning. Now? All the fresh snow has been trampled by those hordes of screeching children." He sniffed. "Maybe we can petition the town council to refuse to allow that woman to host another—"

"Beautiful and giving event?" Austin finished for him. "Which, as you know—or perhaps you don't—is the reason for the season. That Westwood girl knows it well. Better than all of us, I'd say."

The obnoxious pair narrowed their eyes at him but neither dared to contradict his statement.

"Have a *very* Merry Christmas," Austin said, enunciating every word clearly and staring down the Eltons until they'd scurried away.

Good riddance.

"What was that about?" Emma asked, walking up to him, a curious expression on her lovely face.

"Nothing worth repeating," he said and, instead, reached out and hugged her. Hard. "You must be starving after your roundtrip drive to Montgomery Falls and then your long—but totally fabulous—event. Why don't you let me buy you lunch? After all, I wouldn't be here, able to enjoy Christmas Day in Crystal Corners, if it weren't for you."

"Well, when you put it that way..." she said. "I'm up for almost anything, food-wise. But what's open?"

It was true that the majority of restaurants were closed. Even the First Street Market wouldn't open their doors again until tomorrow morning. But he'd hang out with Emma anywhere, even if he had to buy a jar of peanut butter and a loaf of bread at the gas station convenience store and make them sandwiches. Fortunately, he didn't think it would come to that.

"Have you ever been to Overtime?" he asked her. "It's the sports bar just off Chestnut Street. Fairly certain they're open today."

"I haven't eaten there in ages," she admitted to him, "but I remember liking their burgers."

"They also have some pretty decent fries and onion rings, if that appeals to you. Not quite the gourmet side dishes that Jennings would make—"

"But it's just what I'm in the mood for," she professed.

"Let's go then." He reached for her hand. "No time like the present."

# Fifteen

The day had been a whirlwind of activity for Emma.

After all the planning, organizing, strategizing, and networking needed to pull off the Christmas event for the kids—not to mention the extra excitement of figuring out how to get Austin back to Crystal Corners in time—she'd almost forgotten what it felt like to relax. To get to sit in a squishy red vinyl booth, order up a feast of perfectly decadent burgers and fried everythings, and just talk with her boyfriend face to face.

"Can I tempt you with a French fry? Or an onion ring? Or both?" Austin asked, holding up a basket of each because they couldn't decide which one they wanted more when they'd placed their order.

"Definitely both," she said, plucking a couple fries and rings out of their respective baskets and chomping down on one of them. Until that first fry touched her tongue, she hadn't realized just how hungry she was.

Austin, too, looked famished. He joined her in sampling both items, and when their main courses arrived, they eagerly dug in.

But also they talked. And talked.

On the one hand, it felt to Emma like they were a couple of teenagers on a cozy date. As if they'd just gone to one of their high school's basketball games and were now ready to slurp their sodas, polish off their juicy hamburgers, and make predictions about who'd be the next prom king or queen.

But even though a professional NBA basketball game was on Overtime's big screen TV, and on occasion, they'd watch a play or two, check the score, or comment on the athletic performance of one of the teams, Emma was acutely aware that she and Austin were not conversing like adolescents. That there was, in fact, something very adult and increasingly weighty about the direction their discussions were taking, however lighthearted they may have appeared on the surface.

This didn't bother her.

Actually, it was such a welcome change from the years of insignificant, overly casual, and mundane dating experiences that it merely served to give her pause and provide a dramatic contrast to her past relationships that she couldn't ignore.

It didn't surprise her that, with Austin, once he began to feel comfortable opening himself up to her, a flood of deep thoughts, dreams, life goals, and wishes came flowing out.

He told her about how much he wanted to help his parents adapt their house to suit them better as they aged. That he and his dad were already in the planning stages for some updated features in their main living space.

He shared with her that he'd been looking into buying a particular piece of property situated in a lot across town and, for a while, the two of them discussed design concepts. He'd frequently ask her opinion as they spoke, following up with good questions, and taking every one of her suggestions seriously.

He also confided both his excitement and his fears

about running his company from a distance, but he knew his place was here at home in Crystal Corners. She understood instinctively that none of these topics were the kinds of things he divulged to just anyone. That somehow, in the past few weeks, she'd become part of Austin's inner circle.

And, lest she start to think that he couldn't be deep and humorous at the same time, he expressed an avid interest in the lives of his siblings.

"I'm not going to openly suggest to Bethany and Reggie that they hurry up and get started on having a family soon," he stated, his grin turning mischievous. "My sister would strangle me. However, not to be immodest or anything, but I'm determined to be their kids' favorite uncle."

She laughed. "I can see that as a strong possibility. Although, to be fair, your brothers are pretty good guys, too. What do you imagine doing with your young nieces or nephews? Are carpentry lessons in their future?"

"Yeah, probably. If any of them show an interest. But—" He paused and gazed at her from across the table. "I think there are a lot of really great skills for kids to learn. What you've been doing for the children in town—helping to reflect back to them their genuine interests and making them feel good about the things they love—that's incredibly important. I'd want a future niece, nephew...or, um, any other child related to me to be *seen* the way you see people."

And then he began asking new questions about her. About dreams and ambitions she had. About any remaining places she hadn't yet seen that she might want to visit. And about how she saw her own life in the coming years.

"I want to know everything about you that you want to share with me, Emma. All the things you know for certain..."

One thing she knew for certain was that, when Austin

was with her, she didn't feel lonely. Not even a little.

After they finished their lingering lunch, they went on a drive together around Lake Crystal. The small lake on the western edge of their hometown was frozen over, but nothing marred the beauty of the setting. Austin pointed out the lots that most interested him and, again, asked for her opinion.

When she told him her thoughts—she did, in fact, prefer one lot over the other two, although all of them were well situated—Austin just nodded thoughtfully and thanked her for being willing to talk out the possibilities with him.

"Just in case I go ahead and buy it," he said, reaching for her hand, "I want to, you know, make sure that it's a location you'd approve of. A place where you might want to, uh, spend time with me."

She squeezed his hand and nodded. "I'd want to spend time with you no matter where you were living, Austin."

"Good." He squeezed back. "I was hoping you'd feel that way."

They spent the remainder of the afternoon in each other's company. Mostly, they enjoyed simple activities around town, like checking in on Ginger Mae at the community center to see if she needed anything and to make sure she wasn't overexerting herself.

"Do I look busy to you?" the older woman asked, eating one of Adele's frosted sugar cookies and smiling with every bite. "Didn't do nothing today but get to talk to people and enjoy lots of treats. And in a half hour"—she pointed to the clock—"I'm locking up and going to a big Christmas dinner with my bridge friends."

True enough, there were only a handful of residents still hanging around in the large meeting room, chatting in clusters and drinking cocoa. And to Emma's relief, Ginger Mae seemed to be in significantly better health than she'd been the prior week. Emma commented on this.

"Best medicine in the world, girlie, is spending time

with good people." She grinned at the two of them. "You got Christmas plans for tonight? The both of you can join me at Debbie's house, if you'd like."

Austin thanked her but was quick to explain that he couldn't accept her kind invitation. "My parents were, understandably, mad at me for missing Christmas Eve dinner last night," he said. "So I promised I would absolutely, positively be there for dinner tonight. I was hoping I could convince Emma to tag along and help distract them from their irritation with me." He winked at Emma. "They really like her."

"Well, who wouldn't?" Ginger Mae proclaimed. She hugged Emma, expressing her appreciation for all the work Emma had done recently and for taking on so much of the community center activities in her absence. And then she playfully slugged Austin in the bicep with her wiry little fist. "You'd better take care of her, you hear? She's a treasure, our Miss Em." Then she grabbed yet another Christmas cookie and walked away.

Austin laughed. "I can't tell you how many times this week I've been warned by one of your friends to be good to you, and that's not even counting all the lectures I've gotten from my own family. You inspire tremendous loyalty, Emma."

Her heart was glowing from the warmth and happiness she felt. So many good people. So many good happenings. It was almost too much joy to contain.

Austin agreed that "with the possible exception of the obnoxious Eltons," he'd never experienced such a magnificent display of community goodwill and holiday spirit. "I realize just how much I have to be grateful for," he added, looking at her with an expression in his eyes that radiated a universe of kindness, acceptance, and appreciation.

Their mutual feelings of satisfaction at the world and its inhabitants were only underscored when they arrived at the

Knightley house. Mr. Parsons next door was just returning from walking his dogs, and his two golden labs were demonstrating their own brand of holiday celebrations—jumping in delight at the doggie treats their owner had gotten them, dashing through the fresh snow like a pair of reindeer, and licking Mr. Parsons with so much enthusiasm that he belly laughed and was forced to sit down on his front step.

"Merry Christmas!" Emma and Austin called out to him.

"Merry Christmas," the postmaster called back, waving cheerfully.

And it was clear to Emma that this was, indeed, the most wonderful time of the year.

After a delicious supper with Austin's parents, Connor, David, and his friend Jonathan—the latter two having safely returned from Montgomery Falls with Austin's truck and several entertaining stories about their movie adventure there—Austin took Emma back to her house and walked her to the door.

His heart was brimming with a variety of happiness so tangible he could almost touch it. He hated to part with her even now, despite the lateness of the night, but he knew they would be getting together in the morning. After all, they'd promised to bring Ginger Mae more chocolate torte, and neither of them were the kind of people who'd go back on their word.

"Oh! You have to come in," she insisted. "Just for a few minutes. I have something to give you, Austin."

He wasn't inclined to refuse her anything, but he didn't want her to feel as though she needed to go out and buy him presents. Just being with her was enough of a gift for him, and he told her so.

"Besides, I think you've given out more than your share of Christmas gifts today. Between you and Santa, the kids in town made out like bandits."

She flashed a grin at him. "The present I'm giving you isn't something I bought—it's something of *mine*. But it's an item I'd particularly like for you to have," she told him.

So, he trailed after her and waited, more or less patiently, in the living room while she retrieved this mysterious item.

He glanced around the spacious room and thought about the remainder of the holidays. They'd already discussed several things on their individual to-do lists for the week ahead, which, for him, included tying up some loose ends with regard to the manager transfers at the various branches of his company. And for Emma, there were several Westwood International projects she had to complete in addition to attending a charity event or two in town. He was honored when she asked him if he'd be willing to accompany her to one of them.

"Of course. The theater fundraiser sounds fun," he said, which he was startled to realize was the truth. Austin made donations to many good causes, but always privately. That he suddenly considered a very public fundraising event to be something he was sincerely looking forward to, simply because he would be by Emma's side, was a first for him.

Event or no event, all he wanted to do was be with her. The experiences he hoped to share with her kept mushrooming.

Fortunately, they were planning to spend quite a bit of time together, not only with their cake baking or going to that charity social, but also Bethany and Reggie had invited the two of them over to their condo for brunch later in the week. Austin was looking forward to that. And then there was the return of Emma's parents, which was only five days away. Emma had expressed a fervent desire for him to help her decorate the house for New Year's Eve and attend her parents' annual party.

Naturally, he'd agreed to both of those things, too.

But he had to admit there was a growing band of apprehension running through his body at the thought of facing the two most important people in Emma's life—her mom and dad. He couldn't help but worry that things might be different between Emma and himself once her parents were back in the picture.

Even having grown up in the town, Austin had rarely ever spoken to Mr. and Mrs. Westwood. Without a doubt, they were well-respected residents, not to mention bighearted and charitable people who were intelligent and active in their community. But all of those good qualities didn't mean they'd let just anyone get romantically serious with their beloved daughter and only child.

So, as confident as Austin was about many aspects of his life and as content as he'd been about the direction his relationship with Emma had been taking, that particular get-together was one that inspired a degree of trepidation that he was trying to tamp down.

"Okay, I'm back," Emma said behind him, her voice both breathless and filled with excitement.

He turned to face her and, again, couldn't help but be overwhelmed by the admiration, gratitude, and love he felt for this beautiful and gracious woman. He knew he'd do whatever he needed to do to continue to make her smile like that, especially at him.

She had a small but perfectly wrapped gift bag in her hands. The design on the front of the bag featured a charming little town blanketed with snow. "I figured this was an appropriate scene," she joked, "given our recent blizzard."

"Ha. Yeah, I won't soon forget yesterday's snowstorm." He took the gift when she held it out to him. "Thank you."

"Open it," she whispered. "I've been waiting all day to give it to you."

So, he dug into the crinkly white tissue paper until he felt something hard and heavy beneath his fingertips. He grasped the object and lifted it carefully out of the bag. It was the metal figurine of a man on horseback with his sword raised. A knight.

"Wow. What an amazing piece, Emma. It's incredibly well done." He stroked the sides of the horse, admiring all the places where the metal was smooth and all the spots where it was detailed. The craftsmanship of the man and his sword was equally intricate and expertly handled. But for Austin, it was the thought behind the exquisite gift that touched him the most. "This was yours?"

She nodded. "It was my very first statuette. I got it for Christmas when I was six. But I'd like for you to have it, Austin," she said, her tone utterly earnest. "I'd asked Santa for a knight that year, and he gave me this. But now I have a real one...*you*. And one knight—or Knightley—is all I need."

He fought the swell of emotion rising inside of him, threatening to engulf him with its power and poignancy. He could only express how moved he was by her tenderness and sincerity with actions, not words.

Austin swept her into a hug as warm and embracing as he could deliver with only the two arms and two hands available to him and, again, he whispered his thanks in her ear. Then he let her in on a secret that he felt she ought to be aware of tonight.

"I have a present for you, too," he said, "but it's not ready yet. There's something important that needs to be added to it before I can give it to you. But if you'll just give me a week, it'll be yours."

# *Sixteen*

## *New Year's Eve*

Austin had been acting just a little odd since Christmas.

Not rudely, of course, or badly or in any way negatively, Emma quickly determined. Just slightly off what she'd come to regard as his "usual" self.

He was typically a bit more aloof than she was around strangers or even acquaintances he didn't know well. But this strange new vibe she was getting from him happened not only when they were in a crowd but sometimes even when they were all alone.

When she asked him if everything was okay, he immediately replied, "Yes. Oh, yes." And he hugged her. He murmured something about how things were going great, but that it was an unusually busy holiday season.

Which rang true.

Emma recognized that—in addition to Austin's work responsibilities and his family commitments—she herself had added a slate of new activities to his recent schedule.

The day after Christmas, the two of them baked up a

slew of chocolate-apricot tortes in the kitchen. They reserved one for Emma's parents to try after their return from Europe. They personally delivered one to Ginger Mae, who was delighted and didn't even bother cutting the cake before digging into it with her fork. And they made a couple of extras to have on hand to slice up and share with other friends.

Adele was in such raptures after she'd tried a piece that she immediately asked for the recipe. She was determined to learn to make it herself, so she could add it to the bakery menu.

"I'll give you guys a cut of the profits," she declared, which made Emma and Austin laugh.

"Why don't you donate my share to the community food drive?" Austin suggested, and Emma, so pleased with his idea, seconded his response.

"All right," Adele said, "but I promise I'll bake you two a special treat every month in thanks."

Not that her wonderful neighbor and friend didn't already bring Emma plenty of sweet treats, but she knew Austin had to appreciate the thoughtful gesture.

On the day after that, he attended the Friday Night Fundraiser for Friends of the Crystal Corners Theater with her. She'd asked him if he wanted to join her, but truthfully, she had half expected him to decline after all of the holiday events and social activities he'd already participated in on her behalf.

But he surprised her. He readily agreed to go to this, too.

Jason, who was heavily involved in this charity event, was there, of course, along with Kent and about one hundred and fifty other residents of the town, including Austin's parents.

"Never in my life did I think the day would come when our reclusive first born would show up at something like this voluntarily," Pam Knightley mused. "He even looks like he's mostly enjoying himself." She inclined her head in Austin's direction, and they could see he was laughing aloud at something Jason had said to him. "You've been a good influence on my son, my dear. Keep it up."

Not long after that, Jason sidled up to Emma. "Your handsome boyfriend just made a sizeable donation to the programming fund for next year's theater season." He leaned closer to her and lowered his voice. "What did you say to him? And, uh, could you please say it to every other guy and gal in the room?"

Emma laughed. "Honestly, I didn't say anything. Austin is just very generous, especially so once a person gets to know him."

"Well, then, you've caught yourself a good man, Miss Em." Jason hugged her. "I couldn't be happier for you both." He took a step back and pointed between her and where Austin was standing across the room. He was now deep in conversation with Mack and Lila, who were avid theatergoers and dedicated supporters of the arts. "Find out your honey's favorite plays for me, will you? He's officially a platinum-level patron now, and we like to work into the season at least one platinum fave."

"Will do," she said. Then, "Hey, wait a sec. *I'm* a platinum patron, too. What about *my* favorites?"

"Oh, c'mon. You think I don't already have *Pride and Prejudice: The Musical* on the master list, babe?" He blew her a kiss, then turned and jogged over to where the mayor of Crystal Corners and his wife were munching on hors d'oeuvres—and in the perfect position to be cornered.

She grinned to herself and was soon swept into another conversation with someone she knew from their town hall.

Emma and Austin spent a fair bit of time together during the course of the evening, but even when they weren't standing next to one another, he made an effort to catch her eye and smile. She'd always return it.

Seriously, she was so happy she could barely contain

the emotion.

The day following that was a planned Saturday brunch at Bethany and Reggie's, just the four of them at their condo. After all the help they'd given her before, during, and after her Christmas morning event, Emma now considered them both good friends, so the time spent together that day was bound to be delightful.

And, oh, it was.

Austin's sister and her hubby were not only wonderful hosts—providing a spread of both spicy and mild offerings—but they made her laugh until her sides ached, regaling her with hilarious stories from their early dating years and with tales of Austin and Reggie's first outing alone as (soon-to-be) brothers-in-law.

"We got together in Minneapolis one day last spring," Reggie said. "Bethany and her mom were out wedding dress shopping, and Austin and I had, like, five hours to kill before they'd be done. I had no idea what he and I were going to talk about for that long."

"It was an eternity," Austin agreed.

The two men glanced at each other and burst out laughing.

"Who knew we'd end up having a mutual love of late twentieth century sci-fi?" Austin said. "Between the books, the games, the films—"

"The clothing and accessories," Reggie interjected.

"Not to mention those cool old lunchboxes and movie posters."

"We literally spent the *whole* time at a downtown retro toy store, geeking out over *Star Wars* action figures, *Battlestar Galactica* board games, endless Trekkie memorabilia," Reggie added, getting visibly excited.

"Remember the talking Spock?" Austin asked.

"Do I ever! Their *Star Trek* collection was phenomenal."

Austin grinned. "What can I say in our defense? We

loved every minute of it and vowed to go back one of these days."

"Oh, man, we should," Reggie said. "Did you see that wall with all the *Stargate* stuff?"

"Yeah, it was *huge!*" Austin leaned toward his brother-in-law and the two of them launched into an awed discussion of the store's selection and availability of rare collectibles before moving on to a debate regarding *2001: A Space Odyssey* that left Emma mystified but amused.

Bethany nudged her. "Maybe if you and I ever want to go shopping in the Twin Cities," she whispered, "for, um, dresses or anything special, we could bring these two dorks along and drop them off for a few hours at their sci-fi happy place."

Emma watched Austin and Reggie as they laughed together, joked some more, and recounted in absorbing detail what they'd seen in the shop that day, and she knew that she could count on any road trip with these three people to be an amazing time for them all.

"I would *love* that," she told Bethany.

Austin's little sister winked at her. "Let's plan on it then."

And as if there hadn't already been enough activity in their post-Christmas week, the following day was Sunday—but it was hardly a day of rest.

Emma originally thought her parents might choose to skip having a New Year's Eve celebration on account of the fact that they were arriving home on December thirtieth and would, quite likely, still be suffering from jet lag.

But while they did decide against hosting anything as gala-like as the party they threw last year, they told her right before Christmas, during one of their video chats, that they really would like to have "just a small gathering with, maybe, thirty or forty of our closest friends at the house." The idea was to provide an array of tempting appetizers throughout the night and sparkling glasses of champagne for a midnight toast.

So, Darla busied herself making sure their home was thoroughly cleaned. Jennings set to work on an hors d'oeuvres menu that would make a 3-star Michelin restaurant envious. And Emma enlisted Austin's help in decorating the downstairs in honor of the occasion.

They strung yards and yards of white lights around the house with ropes of gold and silver garland. They filled a table with party favors and a range of noise makers, paper hats, goofy glasses, and other festive accessories, and they even set up an enormous blow-up Baby New Year in the corner of the living room, which looked so funny that Emma chuckled every single time she walked past it.

"There," Emma declared. "I think my parents will be pleased with this display."

She looked over at Austin, and he had an expression on his face that she couldn't entirely read. He looked anxious and uncharacteristically unsettled. "Don't you think they'll like it?" she asked him.

He turned to face her, swallowed a few times, and smiled. "I wish I knew, Emma. The truth is, I hardly know them. I'm not at all sure what they'll like or if—" He stopped abruptly.

"Or if what?"

"If they'll approve of me."

Ah. So *that* was what had him all worried.

Emma tried to reassure him that her parents were supremely supportive. "Plus, they've already heard tons about you from Darla, Jennings, and most of all, me. I've said a *lot* of good things about you, Austin."

He looked marginally less nervous after that, but it was obvious to her that his fears wouldn't subside completely until after he'd had a chance to talk with her mom and dad in person.

The first opportunity for that to happen was supposed to be on the day of their arrival. Unfortunately, because of a delay in the Athens to Montreal leg of their return trip, they missed their connecting flight from Montreal to Minneapolis. The end result was that they weren't going to be home from the airport until well after eleven p.m.

Once Emma learned of their updated arrival time, she sent Austin back to his house, insisting it would be too late for him to stay. That she wanted him to meet with her parents after they were all better rested.

"Don't worry," she assured him. "You'll all be able to chat at the party tomorrow night." A comment that only served to make him seem apprehensive all over again.

Nevertheless, he complied with her wishes. "Sweet dreams, sweetheart," he whispered before they parted for the evening.

A couple of hours later, her mom and dad burst through the front door, bringing with them the beautiful ring of their laughter that she'd so dearly missed, endless joyful reunion hugs, and more luggage than two passengers should be allowed to carry. Ever.

"Did you guys import an entire European city to our house?" she asked her parents, laughing as she watched her mom pull item after item after item out of her various suitcases, carry-on bags, and random extraneous travel totes.

"Oh, love, we have so many gifts for you," Dad said.

And Mom added, "We can't even unpack them all tonight. Tomorrow, before the party, if we're really industrious, we should have most everything out of these suitcases and put where they belong, including your belated Christmas presents."

"The best gift of all is having you both back home safely," Emma said, feeling the truth of that deep inside of her. Although she couldn't help but exclaim at how beautiful the beaded Venetian glass necklace was that her parents had picked up for her in Italy. And when they broke open a large package of dark German chocolate packed with raisins and hazelnuts, well, she would have been crazy not to sample at least a few of those delicious pieces.

"I want to hear all about your amazing European adventure," she told them.

"And we," her dad said, "want to hear all about this young man of yours."

Her mom nodded in agreement. "I'm tired, but not too tired to find out more about this grown-up Austin Knightley."

So, despite the fact that it was so late and they'd all had a long day with another big day ahead, the three of them stayed up until the wee hours talking, laughing, swapping stories, and catching up on the details of each other's lives that they missed over the past month.

Emma realized as she was explaining the various events surrounding Christmas Eve and Christmas Day that, although she *thought* she'd told her parents so much about Austin via video chat, there was a great deal more about their relationship that she hadn't shared, simply because of limited time.

"You're saying he taught you how to *bevel* a wooden shelf?" Dad asked, somehow managing to sound both dubious and impressed simultaneously.

"Explain again why he decided to return home and not stay in the Twin Cities? He still *has* a job, right?"

"Interesting that he joined you at the community center and helped with the mitten tree," Mom said. "Does he volunteer in any other capacity?"

"Where, exactly, is this potential property of his? By Lake Crystal, you say?" Dad pulled out his phone and Googled the area.

"Darla and Jennings spoke highly of him, but how often did he come to the house when they weren't here?"

"He was always sort of quiet as a kid," Mom observed. "Has that changed?"

"Aside from dessert recipes, can he cook at all?"

Emma's mom and dad

Emma was convinced the Spanish Inquisition had finally made its way to Crystal Corners. She rolled her eyes. "Seriously, you guys? He cooks better than I do."

"I think it's wonderful that you two attended the Friends of the Theater fundraiser together," her mom commented after Emma mentioned how they'd spent their Friday night. "Hmm. Who else was there?"

Emma could almost hear the wheels in her mother's clever brain spinning and clicking into place as she thought of who amongst their nearest and dearest friends she could pump for additional information about the event. And, presumably, about Austin's appearance at it.

"I'm sure we'll all have a *lot* more to talk about tomorrow night, once we get to chat with him face to face again," Mom said. "It's been years since we've seen him."

"Yeah," Dad agreed with a surprisingly serious— verging on grim—expression on his face. "Ask him to come early."

For the first time, Emma felt a tremor of trepidation that probably mirrored Austin's feelings from earlier in the night. Maybe her parents, while having always been supportive of *her* in the past, might prove to be more cautious in extending that same support to *him*. Particularly if they somehow came to the conclusion that the two of them didn't belong together.

But, no.

That was highly unlikely, and in any case, Emma had no intention of dwelling on what-ifs of that nature. She'd fallen in love with Austin and adored his family. To a person, the Knightley clan had all been very good to her. Emma trusted her own judgment. And although she couldn't make her parents respond to Austin in the same warm and welcoming way that his family had embraced her, she had a strong feeling that, once her mom and dad had a chance to get to know him better, there would be no reason for them to disapprove.

Thus, Emma awoke on the very last day of the year with a spirit of optimism and a heart full of love and anticipation.

She helped her parents finish their preparations for their New Year's Eve party.

She texted Austin a number of times and made sure he knew just how much she was looking forward to seeing him.

She slipped into her newest and, in her opinion, prettiest gown, which was royal purple, silky, and tea length. It reminded her of the fancy one she'd worn for dress-up day in school so long ago.

And she gratefully accepted the many presents her parents lavished upon her. They'd modeled generosity her whole life, and she appreciated the gift of that lesson even more than the beautiful souvenirs they'd brought back to share with her.

While they'd undoubtedly had a remarkable and memorable European adventure, Emma realized that she, too, had experienced quite an adventure of her own, despite having never left the state of Minnesota during all of December.

That "adventure" was a man she'd grown to love, and he arrived on their doorstep promptly at seven thirty, just as her parents had requested.

Austin's pallor was noticeable when her dad, who'd insisted on opening the front door, led him into the living room where Emma and her mom were waiting.

Still, despite his obvious discomfort in the moment, he shook hands with her father, politely gave her mother an elegant winter rose bouquet, smiled at Emma with such warmth that her heart swelled even more, and kissed her on the cheek.

She noticed her parents exchanging cryptic glances as they watched her and Austin together, but she stood determinedly next to him, grasping his hand in hers, and continuing to hold it, even after the four of them sat down on the facing sofas.

Conversation was stunningly stilted.

Emma knew Austin tended to be more reserved than most of the people of her parents' acquaintance. And while he plainly was trying his best to be open and gracious in their company, she sensed how hard this initial meeting was for him.

What surprised her much more was that her parents, who were usually so gregarious and unwavering in their desire to put others at ease in social situations, weren't making it easy on him. At all. They alternated between asking him copious questions—much like their inquisition of her last night—with periods of staring at him for long moments of embarrassing silence. And when she tried to jump in and smooth over the discussion, her mom and dad stared at her, too, with curious and enigmatic facial expressions.

What, exactly, was going on here?

Emma glanced at the clock. Seven forty-seven. The majority of their invited guests weren't expected to start arriving until eight p.m., and it was doubtful that any of them would be inclined to show up early. Her parents, Austin, and she might have to endure this awkwardness for another half hour or forty-five minutes at least, possibly more. Given what Emma remembered of Austin as a kid, this was probably worse for him than the longest school bus ride ever.

Finally, the doorbell rang.

Oh, thank goodness for the punctual Mr. and Mrs. Bates!

Emma had never been so grateful for the splendidly chatty couple with their endless and frequently inane tales about their brood of Persian cats. Emma encouraged them to go into *great* detail as the pair shared one such story, and she was rewarded with an appreciative laugh from Austin.

That effectively broke the ice. She was pleased to see him relax at last and converse more comfortably with her parents' friends than he had with her mom and dad. And fortunately, more and more guests kept arriving.

At one point, Emma, who'd been pulled into a discussion by a charismatic woman who'd once worked extensively with Westwood International on public relations and advertising endeavors, spotted her dad ushering Austin into his private office. She didn't remember when, precisely, Austin had released her hand and slipped away from her side, but she'd seen him in conversation with a few others in the room.

He'd even engaged in a short one-on-one dialogue with her mother near the hors d'oeuvres table. When Emma finally cornered her mom to ask what they'd been discussing, Mom replied, "Appetizers. Obviously." Then she grinned weirdly at Emma and dashed away before she could be questioned further.

But Austin—trapped and alone with her dad in his office? After the stiff conversation between the two men earlier in the night, this was worrisome.

Emma kept an eye on the closed door, but it remained decidedly shut for twenty or thirty minutes at least. Guests stopped her frequently, praising her for the Christmas morning event she'd hosted for the children and for her work with her family's foundation. Truly, she was thankful for their kind words of appreciation, and she spoke to them for as long as she was able, but her mind was elsewhere.

By the time she'd finally detangled herself from a trio of gentlemen who were responsible for various banking enterprises for the foundation, the door to her father's office had been opened again—but neither Dad nor Austin were anywhere in sight.

She raced around the house, at least as fast as her high-heeled pumps (which matched the color of her new gown perfectly!) would let her. When she rounded the corner near the back, she spotted them. Still together. At the entrance to her parents' large library.

Emma's childhood books were housed in her old playroom with the model castle. But this room was devoted to the family's extensive book collection. Shelves upon shelves of adult fiction and nonfiction, rising from the hardwood parquet floors up to the wooden beams that spanned the ceiling.

Her father and Austin turned in unison as they heard her approach.

"Hi," she said brightly, studying the two of them and slowing her walk considerably in an attempt to keep them from thinking she'd been sprinting. Which she had. She could feel a tiny trickle of sweat on the back of her neck. "What are you guys doing?"

"We're talking, Emma," her dad replied.

"A-About what?" she asked, gazing at them both. There was still a noticeable formality between them, but she was relieved to see that there weren't any overt signs of glaring antagonism.

"Um, well—" Austin began.

"Architecture," her dad supplied.

Austin bobbed his head in ready agreement. "Yep." He pointed at the ceiling. "Great beams."

She squinted at the two of them. "Oh, yes. Well, that's...true."

When she'd given Austin a tour of the house that one day, they hadn't gotten to this wing. But she could see why he might like the composition and structure of the building in this part of their home. And he definitely liked books.

Her dad smiled at her. "I don't think I told you how beautiful you look tonight, love."

"Thanks, Dad."

"You do," Austin said, agreeing with her father in this as well. "That's one of your favorite colors, isn't it? I remember you wore a similar dress once before—years ago—when we were kids."

Emma stared at her boyfriend in astonishment. "You remember that?"

Austin nodded. "You're not easy to forget."

She grinned at him, pleased he was speaking freely again and that he was willing to say something that bold in the presence of her father.

Dad glanced at his watch. "It's getting close to midnight, isn't it?" He smiled at Austin first and then at Emma. "I should probably be heading back to the main rooms. I don't want your mother wondering who's going to kiss her when the clock strikes twelve." Then he laughed, as if to an inside joke. "See you both out there in a bit?"

"Yes," Austin replied. And Emma said the same.

"Did you, um, have a chance to see everything you wanted to see in the library?" she asked Austin after her father had disappeared down the hall.

"I wouldn't mind taking a closer look," he told her. "With you."

So they walked fully inside the room, and he listened to her as she pointed out the shelves with her favorite classic novels. There were entire rows lined with leather-bound volumes of Charles Dickens tales, Mark Twain adventures, Lucy Maud Montgomery books, and Jane Austen stories.

And there was something else, too. Something that had her name on it.

It was a Christmas-paper wrapped box that was on the end table nearest the door, and the tag had "To Emma" written in fancy script.

"Is this from you?" she asked Austin.

He shook his head. "No. Actually, I didn't even see it there when your dad and I were talking by the library door. Maybe it's from him?"

"Might be. My parents have been giving me so many belated Christmas gifts since they returned from their trip last night that I've almost lost count."

"Why don't you open it?"

"I will. A bit later, though. It's almost midnight, and I want to spend the last few minutes of this lovely old year with you," she told him.

"Well, in that case—" He paused and reached into his pocket. "This seems to be the time for belated Christmas gifts. I got this for you on Christmas Eve in Montgomery Falls. I was thinking about how deeply I'd fallen for you. How much I love everything about you. But because we've gotten to know each other so much better, I also knew that night just how important your parents are in your life, and that this particular gift of mine wouldn't be complete unless it also had the blessings of them both."

Austin knelt down on one knee in front of her, opening the small velvet box in his hand, and looking up into her teary eyes. "Emma Westwood, I love you. The one thing I want more than anything in the world is to begin the New Year knowing I'll get to spend it—and all the years that follow—with you in my life." He paused, his eyes shining. "Will you do me the honor of marrying me?"

She immediately knelt down next to him, right there on the library's hardwood floor.

"Yes!" she exclaimed, and she kissed him just seconds before the grandfather clock struck midnight.

"Happy New Year, Emma. And thank you for making me the happiest man on the planet."

"Happy New Year, Austin," she whispered, brushing her tears away as he slipped on the sparkly diamond ring and kissed her hand, and then her tear-stained cheek, and then her lips again. "I can't wait for us to begin our new life together."

"Me, too."

When, eventually, they rejoined her parents and all the guests, Austin and Emma officially announced their engagement. There were many cheers, champagne toasts, and lots of good wishes shared.

Her mom and dad, finally able to openly show her now how supportive they were of the match, confessed to being a little more intense in their questioning of Austin than they might have with someone else.

"A *little* more intense?" Emma said. "You grilled him. I had no idea what you guys were up to. You had me worried."

"Your dad and I were convinced you were very serious about him, sweetheart," Mom said. "We wanted to be certain he was equally committed." Then she hugged Emma so tight she thought she might lose all ability to breathe. "But Austin Knightley seems to be quite a stellar gentleman—and I've done a little extra checking, just to make sure." She raised her eyebrows and nodded at the crowd of knowledgeable and well-connected New Year's Eve guests milling around the room. "The two of you are adorable. And, oh, my darling baby girl, you're going to have a beautiful life together—and a very fashionable wedding!"

Emma and her mom shared a laugh and decided they'd get started on the planning and organizing of that event soon. Like on January second.

Sometime later still, when Emma finally returned to the library to retrieve her last Christmas gift, she pulled something unexpected out of the box.

As it turned out, this present wasn't from her parents after all. The tag on the outside said "To Emma," but the note on the inside said, "With love from Santa."

Beneath the pretty gift wrap and tissue paper was a new statuette—this one featuring a beautiful princess in long flowing gown, smiling and carrying her very own intricately crafted silver sword.

# *Epilogue*

### *Six Months Later ~ A Midsummer Knight's Dream*

Connor Knightley slapped at the gigantic mosquito on his arm that was trying to suck him dry like an angry, flying vampire.

Of course, his brother Austin and his new sister-in-law just *had* to have an *outdoor* wedding. In Minnesota. By one of the state's ten thousand lakes. It was being held on one side of the vast property that Austin had purchased a few months back, and the view of Lake Crystal was spectacular. But still...air conditioning would have been nice.

The white canopy billowing overhead was an elegant touch. However, it didn't do a thing to stop the invading insects. The temperature, which otherwise might have been pleasant (it was, after all, mid-June), felt stifling due to the size of the crowd, which swarmed around him. Much like the mosquitoes.

The bride, to be known from this day forward as Mrs. Emma Westwood Knightley, knew just about every living soul in their hometown of Crystal Corners, and Connor was pretty sure that *all of them* were invited to the wedding and currently in attendance. Normally at a joyous occasion of this scope, he'd sneak off for a while, chat it up with a pretty guest or two...or three...or hang out near the bar with a bunch of other guys and talk sports.

But this time he had responsibilities. He was a groomsman—specifically, the best man—and he wasn't about to ditch his big brother on his special day.

Connor smothered a yawn, waved at the well-wishers who were smiling at him and snapping an endless stream of photos with their smart phones, and tried to discreetly wipe the sweat off his brow at the same time.

He loved Austin and Emma. Truly and deeply. He was thrilled that she was finally an official member of the Knightley family. Nevertheless, he couldn't help but wonder for probably the five thousandth time in the past hour: Would this wedding reception *ever* come to an end?

"Connor, get over here," his ever-commanding sister called. "The photographer wants us to take pictures by the floral centerpiece." Bethany pointed at the ginormous display of blossoms, artfully arranged and carefully spilling onto the beautifully set table with its silky black tablecloth and white lace trim, which was reserved exclusively for the wedding party.

For a moment, he pondered the viability of being able to hide behind the considerable cluster of red, white, and pink roses alone. If he scrunched down a little, the photographer might not be able to see him at all.

"Connor!" Bethany bellowed again, this time adding frantic waving motions.

"Yeah, okay, sis. I'm coming, I'm coming." He sighed heavily and made his way toward the table.

Bethany and her husband Reggie had gotten married just last fall so, naturally, she considered herself the reigning expert on all things "wedding." But in this case, her dictatorial impulses came from someplace deeper than that. After years of being the only girl among the Knightley siblings, Bethany finally had been given the sister she'd always dreamed of having in the form of Emma. The two of them, who had been merely casual friends up until Emma and Austin started dating, became close this year. Extremely close. Probably closer than if they'd been biological sisters.

So Bethany, of course, was asked to be a bridesmaid.

And Vera, one of Emma's dearest friends in the community and a new mother to boot, was the matron of honor. Turned out, Vera and Bethany had *also* become good friends, thanks to their mutual adoration of the bride, and the two of them had joined forces to keep everyone else in line—namely, Reggie, who was a fellow groomsman, Austin and Connor's kid brother David, who was a groomsman as well, and Connor himself.

"All right, all of you fun people, if you could gather together behind the table," the photographer guy said. "Let's get a shot of the happy couple standing right behind this gorgeous centerpiece with all of you crowding around them." He clicked a handful of pictures before even half of the attendants were assembled. Connor wouldn't be surprised if he was caught rolling his eyes in a few of those shots, should they make it into the official wedding album.

"Closer still, you guys!" the photographer urged, gesturing for the wedding party to squish together even more. "Emma and Austin, let's see a really good smooch now, okay? Good! That's good."

Connor could hear the camera clicking relentlessly. To his brother and sister-in-law's credit, they gave the photographer exactly the kind of kiss he had asked them for.

The final bridesmaid, who'd been paired with David in the attendant line up during the ceremony, was Emma's former college roommate and good friend from her university days—Tania.

Tania was attractive, well-educated, and single, which made her of great interest to the otherwise unattached men at the wedding reception. But Tania had confided to Emma, Bethany, Vera—and, honestly, to anyone else who happened to be sitting near her during the rehearsal dinner—that she suffered from a broken heart and didn't want to have anything to do with relationships for a while. Something about a fickle ex-boyfriend and how love didn't make any sense.

Connor wasn't one to eavesdrop, but overhearing this lament was unavoidable. He made sure to be especially kind to Tania when they spoke but also to give her plenty of space and not even try to flirt.

For the record, though, he more or less shared Tania's low opinion of relationships. Whereas his big brother Austin had been searching for his soul mate practically his entire life, Connor was convinced that true love was an illusion. At least for guys like him.

He was a practical person. He liked the outdoors and working as a landscaper in the spring, summer, and fall. He even liked plowing snow in winter because it got him out of the house and filled his lungs with fresh air. He wasn't looking for a perfect woman. He wasn't expecting to find somebody who would be his "love of a lifetime." He definitely wasn't hunting for a *wife*. He just wanted to hang out, date a little, and have fun. Was that too much to ask?

"Connor," Bethany said, smacking him on the shoulder.

"What now?"

"I asked you, like, three times already to find out from the florist about the best way to relocate this large centerpiece during the meal, so we don't wreck it."

"Sorry, sis. Didn't hear you before. I'll take care of it right away."

"Good, thanks. Her name is Helena Alexander. Medium height, dark hair, brown eyes. And I know she's walking around here somewhere. All dressed in pink." Bethany shooed him away. "Go. Please. The caterers are waiting." Then she stalked off in David's direction, no doubt intending to terrorize him next.

Connor glanced around. Okay, where was this elusive florist?

He saw Emma's parents, the Westwoods, talking with his mom and dad near the edge of the canopy. The two couples, now joined by the marriage of their children, were laughing and reveling in the joy of the day. Connor spotted the photographer snapping a few candid shots of the four of them. That picture, he had to admit, would be a nice one for the photo album.

He also saw a handful of cute townies—mid-twenties, about his age—and made a mental note to chat them up later. Once the required wedding party waltzes were over, he'd ask one or two of them to dance. Maybe. If he felt up to exerting the energy.

But he didn't see a brown-eyed brunette florist in pink attire of any sort, anywhere.

Connor shrugged to himself. Bethany could snap, crackle, and pop at him all she liked, but he couldn't get the info she needed if he couldn't locate the lady who had it.

He wandered around in search of the florist for a while longer but only managed to run into a couple of his distant cousins, about three thousand of Emma's friends, and his brother—the groom.

"So, dude, how's it feel to be a married man?" he asked Austin.

Austin grinned, a smile that somehow radiated both ecstasy and exhaustion in a single glance. "It's awesome, but I'm probably going to need all of our two-week Italian honeymoon to recover from the festivities," he admitted. "Emma's in her element—so many people, so many conversations—but I need to take occasional breaks and just breathe deeply, a few steps away from the maddening crowd."

Connor laughed. "Yeah, I can imagine a scene this packed would be draining for you. To tell you the truth, it's a bit much even for me."

His brother raised a dark eyebrow. "Everything okay, Connor?"

He nodded. "Yeah, yeah. Just—I don't know—I'm feeling a little restless."

"Ah, that's right. It's been, what? A week? Ten days, maybe, since you dated someone? But this gathering should be prime pickings for you. Just look at all these beautiful ladies." Austin nodded subtly in the direction of cuties that Connor had already scoped out. "You're bound to talk to a few who you'd find interesting. At least for a couple of dates."

"Probably," Connor said, unconvinced. He knew his brother was just giving him a hard time, and Austin had earned that right, especially after all the teasing he'd dished out to his big bro about women over the years.

But if he were to be completely honest with Austin, he'd tell him that he just hadn't been that motivated lately to meet anybody new, or even take part in his usual harmless flirtations. Connor blamed this on too many recent wedding activities. All of this crazy focus on *soul mates* and *lifetime loves* and such. He didn't buy into any of it.

"Or perhaps, instead," Austin suggested, "you'll cross paths with the woman of your dreams. She could be here somewhere, and you might fall in love with her at first sight."

"I won't," Connor countered.

"Why not, bro?"

"Because I don't believe in falling in love at first sight." *Or, really, falling in love at all*, he thought, but he didn't voice this. It was his brother's wedding day, after all. He was trying to stay upbeat.

"You never know, Connor. Love is a powerful drug. A

little drop of it could be life-altering—even for you." Then Austin patted him on the back, took a few meditative breaths, and dove back into the bustling crowd...of which he was king for the day.

Connor let him have the last word, but after Austin left, he smothered another yawn, killed another mosquito, and wandered the perimeter of the canopy. He was just about to concede utter defeat in locating this mysterious florist when he spotted the face of an absolutely gorgeous woman peeking out at him from under one of the tables.

"Uh, miss? Do you need—" he began.

She shook her head and popped back under the black tablecloth and out of sight.

Well, okay. That was bizarre.

He was sorely tempted to just walk away but—wow—she was truly beautiful and—also, wow—that was an extremely odd thing for an adult woman to be doing at a wedding.

His curiosity got the better of him. He knelt down and gingerly lifted the hem of the black tablecloth. The woman's face was right there, practically nose to nose with him.

"May I help you with—"

"Yes," she said. "I lost my necklace, okay? I think it's somewhere around here, though." She motioned toward the grass under the table.

Connor nodded. Well, why not? It was better than running back to Bethany the Wedding Dictator and being yelled at or assigned another errand. He crawled under the table with her, which was seriously awkward, very dark, and kinda funny—all at once.

He laughed.

"Look," she said, her tone stern and not at all amused, "you don't have to help me—"

"I want to," he said quickly, not knowing why but just strangely certain that if he could be of service to her, he would.

As he tapped the grass around him, his pinky touched something that felt distinctly like a thin metal chain. Bingo.

"I think I may have found it." He tugged at the chain until he could gather all of it up in his palm, lifted the tablecloth again so a stream of light could shine in, and held it up for the woman to see. "Is this it?"

"Oh, my goodness, yes! Thank you."

She reached to pull it from his hand and their fingers met. Connor could have sworn there was a bolt of lightning in her touch. It was positively *electric*. He'd never experienced anything like that before. Stunned, he pulled back, lifted the cloth higher, and slid out from beneath the table. He kept holding the cloth for her, too, until she could crawl out.

One of Emma's elderly aunts happened to be strolling by right as they both emerged from under the table. She sent Connor and the very pretty woman next to him a distinctly disapproving look.

He didn't care, though. He could finally see his companion in the sunlight, and the first thing he noticed was that she was even more striking than he'd thought. Maybe Austin was right. Maybe love at first sight wasn't such a ridiculous concept.

The second thing he noticed was the necklace itself, which she was fastening around her neck. It was a silver coin pendant on a silver chain, but it wasn't a currency Connor recognized.

The woman caught him staring. "It's a Greek *tetradrachm*," she explained. "A very old Athenian coin."

"Cool," he murmured, glancing from her face to the necklace and back to her face again. Which when he noticed the third, fourth, and fifth things. She had the most soulful brown eyes he'd ever seen. Very long, very dark hair. And pink earrings that matched her pretty pink dress.

He blinked at her, and she stretched out her hand for

him to shake.

Connor felt that current of electricity zap him again when their palms touched, even before she said, "Thanks again for your help. I'm Helena Alexander."

"Hello, Helena. I'm Connor Knightley, and I've been, um, looking for you." *My whole life*, a quiet voice inside his soul whispered.

# ~End~

# Recipe

## Emma & Austin's Chocolate-Apricot Torte

**Ingredients for the Cake:**
5 ounces chopped semisweet chocolate
1/2 cup white sugar
1/3 cup confectioners' sugar
1 cup cake flour
1/2 cup softened butter
6 eggs, separated into whites and yolks

**Directions for the Cake:**
Preheat oven to 350 degrees F (or 175 degrees C).
Place the parchment paper into the bottom of a 9-inch
circular pan and butter the paper.
Melt 5 ounces of chocolate in the microwave or by using a
double boiler and stir.
Mix the confectioners' sugar with the butter until creamy.

*Add in the melted chocolate, then beat in the egg yolks.*
*In another bowl, mix the white sugar with the egg whites until stiff.*
*Incorporate this into chocolate mixture, then fold in the cake flour and stir.*
*Pour into the buttered pan and smooth the top.*
*Bake until a toothpick inserted into the center comes out clean, approximately 40 - 50 minutes.*
*Cool completely.*
*Remove the cake from pan and discard parchment paper.*
*Slice cake horizontally into two halves.*

**Ingredients for the Filling:**
*1/4 cup water*
*12 ounces apricot jam*
*1/4 cup white sugar*
*2 - 3 tablespoons rum (optional)*

**Directions for the Filling:**
*Bring the water and white sugar to a boil in a saucepan until the sugar has dissolved.*
*When the syrup is clear, remove from heat.*
*Optional: Stir in half of the rum.*
*Brush half of the syrup onto the cut side of the cake bottom.*
*Puree the apricot jam with about a tablespoon of water.*
*Simmer over medium heat in a saucepan and cook about two minutes until thickened.*
*Optional: Stir in the other half of the rum.*
*Spread about half of the jam mixture onto the cut side of the cake bottom.*
*Place the top of the cake onto the bottom.*

Brush the top of the cake with the second half of the syrup.
Spread the second half of the apricot jam over the top.
Refrigerate until it's time to ice the cake.

### Ingredients for the Icing:
10 ounces chopped semisweet chocolate
3 1/2 ounces heavy whipping cream

### Directions for the Icing:
Melt 10 ounces of chocolate until smooth.
Bring the heavy cream to a simmer in a saucepan, then stir
the cream into the chocolate.
Cool and continue stirring until the melted chocolate
reaches a spreadable consistency.
Set the cake on the parchment paper to catch any dripping
chocolate.
Pour the icing on top of the cake and spread it around the
edges.
Transfer to a dessert plate and either eat immediately or
store in the refrigerator.
Serve at room temperature, topped with whipped cream, if
desired.

### Enjoy!

# STORY EXCERPTS

If you enjoyed THE KNIGHT BEFORE CHRISTMAS, check out these excerpts below from Marilyn Brant's "Perfect Pair" series -- two sweet contemporary Austen-inspired romances!

PRIDE, PREJUDICE AND THE PERFECT MATCH (Book One) - Story Summary and Excerpt:

*Would an Elizabeth Bennet by any other name be as appealing to a Darcy?*

*A single mother and an ER doctor meet on an Internet dating site—each for reasons that have little to do with finding their perfect match—in this modern, Austen-inspired story. It's a tribute to the power of both "pride" & "prejudice" in bringing two people romantically together, despite their mutual insistence that they should stay apart.*

*Beth Ann Bennet isn't looking for love. She's an aspiring social worker using an online alias to study sex-role stereotypes. Dr. William Darcy isn't looking for love either. He's just trying to fund his new clinic by winning a major bet. Both think Lady Catherine's Love Match Website will help them get what they want—fast, easy and without endangering their hearts. Both are in for a big surprise.*

*Pride, Prejudice and the Perfect Match...where true love is just a fib and a click away.*

### From Chapter One:

Beth Ann Bennet typed "male" in the box that indicated which gender she was seeking. Her best friend and fellow classmate, Jane Henderson, leaned over her shoulder and studied the university library's computer screen in the afternoon sunlight. The cursor blinked, and Beth's level of nausea rose with each flash.

"So far, so good," her friend declared.

Beth seriously doubted it.

"This has to be illegal, or maybe just immoral." She bit down on her lip again, the one she'd chewed until it'd turned raw and achy. "Somehow I doubt Professor O'Reilly had this method in mind when he told us to gather sociological data."

Jane tilted her auburn head and gave Beth that familiar

when-are-you-gonna-get-with-the-program look. She exhaled melodramatically. "For goodness sake, Beth Ann, this is *research*. It's not like you're going to get emotionally invested or anything. Heaven knows, you'll drop the dimwit like a dead goldfish before he has a chance to ask any questions. Find an appropriate case study, get the info and get out. Kids' stuff."

"For you, maybe," Beth said, wondering for the seven hundredth time why she'd let herself get talked into this. "You've playacted with your identity since you were— what, a toddler? I haven't."

Jane flashed a grin of discernible pride, which was combined in equal measure with deviousness. Beth's spirits sank a notch lower. Why couldn't she be more like her best friend? Jane was light years ahead of her in the deceit department.

"C'mon," Jane said. "Next question."

"Okay. Between the ages of…?"

"Well, you're twenty-six, but you'll be playing it younger of course." Jane squinted at the screen. "Go for men in the twenty-five to thirty-five range."

"Fine." Beth typed in the information. "Located within…?"

"No further than a twenty-mile radius of your Chicago ZIP code."

She keyed that in also, her pulse picking up speed.

"Now, check the 'photos only' box and click on GO. I want to see if the rumors are true."

"You know as well as I do that this is a scam. I mean, seriously. *Lady Catherine's Love Match Website—Where You're Destined To Find Your Perfect Mate?*" Beth forced a laugh. "We may succeed in proving gender-role stereotypes are alive and well in the New Millennium, but there's no way we'll snag a guy who'll prove true love can be found through an e-search."

Jane smirked then aimed an index finger at the screen.

"Scroll down and let's get a peek at your—holy shmoly—
*fifty-four* potential Love Matches. Not that I'm dying to be
a bridesmaid or anything but—"

Beth elbowed her.

"Ouch!"

"Shhh. We're in a library."

Jane rolled her eyes in response.

Beth closed hers before threading her fingers through
her tangled mop of light-brown hair. She felt the split ends
snap.

She groaned and wished she could afford a decent
haircut. But no. March meant paying off the final
installment of her tuition bill and what she made at work
could only stretch so far. Plus, there were necessities like
bread and peanut butter, staple items for a mom with a six-
year-old. If everything went as she planned, maybe by June
she could justify an appointment.

She opened her eyes and glared at the listing of eligible
men, reminding herself that she *had* to choose one. They
swam through her range of vision while the lyrics to
"Looking for Love in All the Wrong Places" flooded her
brain. She tried to block out the tune and focus on the faces
of her research subjects. Who'd make the best candidate?

Jane, quick study that she was, had zeroed in on
someone already. "Oh, Beth. Just look at Number 16. Blue-
eyed. Beefy. And he likes children."

Beefy was right. He had muscles the size of overgrown
cantaloupes. And, oh, he preferred blondes.

"My soul mate for sure." She ignored Jane's protests
and scrolled further down the screen. She had one shot at
this and refused to mess it up. "Number 23 has some
potential, though. He claims to be athletic. And 'spiritual.'
Into fast cars. Watches 'Must-See TV.' And he's seeking
someone in the skinny to slim range. Sounds like an ideally
stereotypical guy."

She kept reading.

Whoa.

"Except he's proud of his Streisand CD collection, his Chia Pet and his Virgo perfectionism. These things could throw off the hypothesis." Beth sighed.

Jane read the name. "Reverend Ezekiel Collins is not typical enough for you?"

"Maybe not."

"Moving on then."

"What do you think of Number 37?" Beth said.

Jane wrinkled her upturned nose.

"Yeah. Me neither," she conceded, "but I'm running out of options."

Then she saw him.

She centered his profile on the screen. Read the bio. Reread it while Jane's giggles bubbled around her. Heaven help her, but Number 49 was The One.

"So, it'll be 'Will Darcy' then, eh?" Jane said. "Likes women of every hair color. Very open-minded of him."

"It's all there," she whispered, marveling at the image of the man before her. "The sports interest. The standard descriptive lines. A professed 'love of the outdoors' and other oh-so-masculine pursuits."

"You're right. He likes camping. Yuck."

"No mention of cooking together, dancing 'til dawn or seeing sappy chick-flicks, like some of these other guys. At least we can't question his honesty. No unusual club affiliations. And he even admits to having strong professional ambitions, although he doesn't elaborate."

"Definitely falls into an acceptable salary range," Jane agreed, pointing to the numbers listed in the right-hand column.

"And just take a peek at what he's looking for. Someone 'attractive, college-educated, height/weight proportionate'—meaning almost anorexic." Beth raised her eyebrows. "Someone 'twenty-one to twenty-five who likes children but has no dependents.' They all want a woman who's young and unencumbered. I swear, this guy sounds like every blind date I've had in the past five years."

Her friend gave her a scrutinizing once-over. "You're slim, pretty, you've got great bone structure and those huge brown eyes, and you could pass for twenty-two without a second thought."

Beth shrugged. So what if she looked young? One's age wasn't something a person could hide forever. "Maybe," she said. "And I'm almost, finally, college-educated. But there's still that little question of dependents…"

"He doesn't need to know about Charlie or your real occupation or even your real name, Beth. Use an alias. Maybe that combination of your parents' names—Charlotte and Lucas—that you pretended was your penname when you were ten."

Jane tapped her chin. "Besides, you might as well try for someone you think is kind of cute. If all goes well, you'll have to spend hours analyzing the guy. Maybe even a few studying him in person—without getting too close of course," she warned. "It's okay to have a little fun with your online profile."

Beth shuddered. The things she had to endure in the name of science. Well, social science.

But perhaps Jane was right. If she had to do this final Sociology 369 "Gender and Society" project, and if she was in the quarter of the class that had to use the Internet as her main research tool, she might as well choose a subject who was at least tall, dark-haired and gorgeous. Nothing stereotypical about her own mate selection, of course, she thought. The irony of it brought the day's first grin to her lips.

She lifted her fingers to the keyboard and clicked on the REPLY button to send Number 49 an email:

*Hello, Will. I'm a twenty-two-year-old child psychology major*, Beth began. She glanced back at her friend.

"Yeah, that's perfect," Jane said. "Use my major. It'll

explain your knowledge of children without giving anything away. I can fill you in on subject details later."

Beth nodded. *I love the outdoors and particularly enjoy playing softball*, she typed, and then grimaced at the blatant lies. The guilt was already eating at her, but she had to think of her son. Nothing could get in the way of her providing for Charlie. She continued, *I'm hoping we might correspond and get to know one another better. My name is Charlotte Lucas and you can email me at...*

In the Regents General Hospital cafeteria a few weeks later, Dr. William Darcy gulped his last swallow of the Mocha-Cappuccino De-latte Delight he'd gotten at the gourmet coffee shop nearby. Then he glared at his cousin. "No, I don't want to bet a hundred bucks on whether or not you can catch a fish stick between your teeth."

Bingley McNamara grinned, crossed his long legs at the ankles and propped them up on the metal chair to Will's left. "Face it, Cuz. You're intimidated by my varied and remarkable skills." He tossed his last greasy fish stick in the air and caught it neatly between his incisors. He chomped down. "I'd have won," he said around a mouthful of deep-fried pseudo-fish. "My talent frightens you."

"The only thing about you that frightens me is your insatiable gambling habit." Will leveled his most disapproving stare at the guy but, as usual, his cousin ignored him.

"Aw, c'mon. Everyone makes a wager now and then."

"Only if 'now and then' means every fifteen minutes." Will scanned his watch. "Go. Get out of here. Although this may be a foreign concept to you, I've actually got a job."

"I've got a job," Bingley said, sounding indignant. "It's just a little less, oh, how should I put it? Obvious."

"Overseeing your trust fund is not a bona fide career. It's a sick obsession. Although how it manages to grow profits, despite your wagering addiction, is a mystery."

"Jealous?"

"No."

Bingley snorted, guzzled his short Colombian espresso then sent Will a semi-serious look. "Listen up. Did you give any more thought to my proposition last month? Any bites online?"

Will turned his back on his favorite and only cousin, who—at present—he wanted to strangle to within a millimeter of the rich party boy's life. He pitched the remains of their lunch in the trash then loosened his tie.

"And what if I have?" Will said finally, knowing he'd regret even considering Bingley's latest ludicrous bet. But, dammit, he needed the help and he needed it now. "Are you prepared to follow through if I can get the lady to materialize?"

"Not just any lady," Bingley reminded him. "A girlfriend who could take an active role in your precious clinic." He sniffed. "That'll give you a shot at wanting to be with her long term. I expect a five-date minimum, and I need to meet her before the second Sunday in May."

"Listen, Bingley—"

"I know you don't believe me, but I'm looking out for your best interests here, Cuz. Before I plunk my money into some do-good operation, I want proof that you've finally gotten a life outside of this, this...morgue." He waved the arm with the Rolex attached to it in a wild loopy arc. "Evidence that you've scored a little balance in your daily life—among other things." He waggled his brows suggestively.

Will marveled at how a guy who resembled him physically could act with all the subtlety of a Saturday-morning cartoon character.

"So keep the movie-ticket stubs from your dates,"

Bingley said. "Learn how to use the camera app on your phone, or even grab your old Polaroid, and snap some pretty pictures of the two of you. Save her emails and make sure she shows up happy and talkative by my birthday. It's on Mother's Day, this year." He tilted his head as if in deep contemplation. "Whoever this chick is, I wanna see her hanging on your arm with lovey-dovey eyes only for you."

Will thought of the one woman he wanted, no, *needed* to win this wager with Bingley. Charlotte Lucas. If only she could be as amazing in person as she seemed online. A youthful but professional twenty-two-year-old future child psychologist. Bright, humorous and a sports enthusiast with a warm heart. Someone who'd fit in perfectly at the clinic, if he'd gauged her right. And someone he could tolerate for five dates outside of it.

She'd described herself as being five-foot-six with light-brown hair and brown eyes, but she held the advantage. She'd seen him—a scanned picture anyway—but he had yet to see her. Maybe, just maybe, after three weeks of cautious emailing, that'd change tomorrow. The clinic's funding depended on it.

Still, this was a devil of a way to make a few million bucks.

"I've got to go," he said. "My rounds start in a few minutes. Talk to you next week."

"Catch you later," his cousin said. "Don't be a stranger."

"They don't come any stranger than you," Will muttered, their standard childhood reply.

"I heard that." Bingley smirked, his fingers scoring his thick brown hair, his lean legs sauntering on his way through the sliding doors.

Will sighed and took to the stairs. The guy never changed. There was always some weird bet, some eccentric agenda in Bingley's quest to "feel needed" or whatever. But this time the ends might justify the means.

Will tucked the flap of his shirt into the dress slacks he'd worn for the administrative meeting today and readjusted his tie with a scowl. He missed his scrubs but formalities had to be observed with the hospital board.

"Hey, Dr. Darcy," a ninety-year-old patient called from her bed on the second-floor east wing. "You my doctor today?"

"Wish I was, sweetheart," he said, winking and making the elderly lady blush. "None of the patients on my roster could hold a candle to your good looks."

"Oh, how you do go on!" She looked away, her head and hands shaking, feigning disbelief, but he could see teeth. She was grinning big.

Parkinson's. Stage Three. He struggled to close his mind to it and move down the hall. The pain of dealing with deteriorating elderly patients would chew him up if he dwelled there. Even though the low-income moms he liked to work with were often in dire straits, it was still less agonizing to watch than the suffering of the elderly.

He slid into an empty room and flipped on the computer. He had huge plans for his clinic. He just needed to get the hospital's final stamp of approval, which he could get if he could secure the rest of the cash.

The board had said so.

This morning.

To get the cash, though, he'd have to get Bingley onboard. To get Bingley onboard, he'd have to get Charlotte Lucas.

Immediately.

He scanned his list of unread email messages, but didn't see anything life-threatening in the subject lines. Clicking on Charlotte's email address, he typed what he hoped would be a hard-to-resist invitation.

Will proofed it for errors, took a deep breath and clicked SEND.

❀❀❀

## PRIDE, PREJUDICE AND THE PERFECT BET
(Book Two) - Story Summary and Excerpt:

*The course of true love doesn't always run smooth—not even for millionaire bachelors...*

*Everyone thought Beth Ann Bennet and Dr. Will Darcy had an unexpected romance in Pride, Prejudice and the Perfect Match (Perfect #1). Now, Beth's best friend, Jane Henderson, and Will's first cousin, Bingley McNamara, begin their own unlikely love story in Pride, Prejudice and the Perfect Bet (Perfect #2), which starts at the Darcy/Bennet wedding when they find themselves in the roles of maid of honor and best man for the newlyweds.*

*Jane is an interning school psychologist and a woman who wears an angelic mask in public, but she's not as sweet tempered as she'd like everyone to believe. Turns out, she may have just crossed paths with the one person who'll unnerve her enough to get her to reveal her true self.*

*As for Bingley, he's a wealthy, flirtatious and compulsively social guru of finance, who likes to wager on stocks and, let's face it, on just about anything that strikes his fancy. But this dedicated ladies' man may have finally met the woman who'll challenge his bachelor ways!*

*Pride, Prejudice and the Perfect Bet...where life's biggest gamble is the game of love.*

### From Chapter One:

Bingley McNamara stood near the altar of St. Andrew's Presbyterian Church, right next to his cousin, Dr. William Darcy—the lucky groom on this lovely September Saturday. The two men watched as the maid of honor glided gracefully down the aisle, every step in time with the distinctive thrum of the pipe-organ music overhead.

Jane Henderson, best friend of the bride, wore a silky, cocktail-length gown with a scoop neckline and some fun ruffly bits around the hem. Given the color of her dress and her auburn hair, she was a vision in dark red. Appropriate, Bingley thought, since, when she spotted him, she shot him a look that was positively murderous.

*This was gonna be a helluva long ceremony.*

He adjusted his equally red bowtie, took a deep breath and nudged Will. "You ready, Cuz?"

Will nodded. "Absolutely. You got the rings?"

Bingley patted the jacket pocket of his tux. "Sure do. Nothing to hold you back now. I mean, if you still wanna go through with it and everything. Which you do, right?"

His cousin stared at him as if he were an escapee from a traveling circus act, planning to cartwheel down the center aisle of the church. "What?"

"All I'm saying is that, you know, there's no *pressure* one way or another," Bingley whispered. "You've got *options* available. If you want them. But I'm pretty sure you don't. I know you love Beth and that she loves you and that you both love Charlie and that everyone in the family loves each other…and this whole wedding idea is just…just a really great thing. To do. Today. Right this very second."

Bingley was well aware he was babbling but, man, his favorite cousin—his *closest friend* in all the world—was getting married in about three minutes. And though the bride was a genuinely wonderful woman and the soul mate his workaholic cousin desperately needed, Bingley knew he'd no longer be the go-to person in Will's life after today.

Aw, who was he kidding? He'd lost his elevated position months ago—the minute Will had laid eyes on Beth Ann Bennet.

Will just shook his head and ignored the jabbering. Bingley sighed. Clearly, his cousin was only focused on his soon-to-be wife and was distracted by her beauty as she prepared to follow Jane down the aisle.

The organ music changed to the stately "Wedding March" by Mendelssohn, and the entire three-hundred-member congregation stood to watch as Beth serenely made her way toward Will, accompanied by her father.

Bingley, of course, was aware of Jane's periodic glances in his direction—which could more accurately be described as *piercing glares*—but even *she* was finally paying more attention to her best friend than to him.

Still, he couldn't help but sneak a few more looks at the fiery maid of honor, remembering the way they'd first met four months ago, around the time Beth and Will became an official couple. So much polite chitchat followed. He'd been on his best behavior (Will's orders) and, yet, couldn't deny his immediate attraction to Beth's dearest friend.

But Jane had seemed so…*nice*, for want of a better

word. Too sweet for him to want to tamper with or tease too much, although Beth hinted there was more to Jane than her pleasant veneer might suggest.

He hadn't believed that at first but, oh, he believed it *now*, as she swiveled to face her friend, shooting another death stare in his direction, then sending a much kinder, warmer look to his cousin and, finally, winking at Beth's six-year-old son, Charlie, who was in the first pew.

Charlie beamed a grin at her that infused his young face with delight, waved at Will and at him, too, and then squirmed to the edge of the pew so he could steal a few glances at his mom before she reached the altar.

"You're gonna be really happy, Cuz," he whispered to Will, who was smiling at Beth as if he'd just won the lottery and it was being hand delivered to him in a pretty package of white tulle.

"Thanks, Bingley," his cousin murmured. "I owe you, you know. None of this would've happened without you."

Bingley swallowed away a sappy emotion he didn't want to succumb to in public and clenched his jaw to keep from saying anything either overly sentimental or just plain dumb. Much as the whole commitment thing gave him hives, Bingley couldn't have been happier for Will. The guy deserved every ounce of wedded bliss.

"Anything for you," he finally managed, meaning it, but unable to stop the wave of irritation that hit him in the gut when he caught Jane rolling her eyes at him from the periphery.

No, she wasn't nearly as nice as she appeared, although he'd thought she was pretty awesome during the engagement party a couple of months back. Jane had downed, perhaps, a few too many glasses of celebratory champagne, and the two of them had ended up in the coat room, making out like teenagers. He quickly learned three other very interesting facts about her:

She wore some *really* racy undergarments beneath her

simple, classically cut clothes.

She could do several wickedly imaginative things with her tongue. Both excellent discoveries, in his opinion.

But her emotions jumped up and down like an insanely volatile stock during a wild trading day.

Bingley exhaled and tried to stop his mind from playing the X-Ray Vision game every time he caught a glimpse of Jane standing demurely by the altar. Although, how could he keep himself from wondering if she had that leopard-spotted bra on underneath her red dress, like the one she'd been wearing in July, hmm? Or, why she had all but sprinted away from him when he saw her again a few days later, and why she'd studiously avoided him at the few other events they'd both had to attend since then... They'd barely made it past second base at the engagement party. Was she embarrassed? Had he unknowingly done something wrong?

*C'mon, man, get a grip!*

He knew from years of experience that he was better off not caring about what women thought of him. Keeping his emotions out of any relationship was the key.

Seeing Will with Beth together had lulled him—temporarily—into believing that whole "happily ever after" thing might happen for him, too. Their connection through that online dating site had encouraged him—briefly—that a "Love Match" wasn't impossible. So he'd entertained the idea of dating more seriously when he met Jane.

Big mistake.

He knew what he was: A lifetime bachelor. And there wasn't a woman in the world who could snag his heart long term. He'd be willing to bet on it.

Still, he had a few assets.

He was young, reasonably good looking, wealthy...and he sure didn't need a pseudo-sweet, temperamental, psychologist chick blowing him off, especially after he'd let his guard down long enough to get close to her one hot summer night. Wouldn't happen again.

Besides, this was a *wedding*. There were plenty of smart, beautiful babes to be found—it'd be like cherry picking Blue Chips in a bull market—and he was the guy to find them. The sooner the better.

He sent the reverend an impatient look as the bride finally reached the altar and Jane took her sweet ole time fixing the train of Beth's wedding gown.

"So," he whispered to Reverend Elton, "what do you say we get this ceremony started so we can move on to the reception, eh?"

The reverend glanced at him with surprise, his cousin with a fresh round of bafflement.

Bingley just shrugged and donned his most charming grin. "I just *can't wait* to start celebrating the joy of love."

As Jane adjusted the lacy train on Beth's wedding dress, her heart was filled with joy for her best friend. *Happy at last!*

Beth had been through such heartbreak and grief, thanks to her deadbeat first husband, Pete Wickham. That stinkin' rat. She'd been left to raise their son alone and had struggled for years—emotionally and financially—until she met Will.

Sure, the unlikely couple had a few rocky moments when they first got together, and Jane admitted she'd had her doubts about Beth's new boyfriend, until she'd gotten to know the guy. But Jane was now fully convinced the two of them belonged together and that their relationship had been a blessing for them both. And for Charlie, too. She was thrilled to be maid of honor.

In fact, Jane could no longer think of a single thing she didn't like about Dr. William Darcy—except for his cousin.

*Bingley McNamara.*

Hmmph. Just look at him standing there next to the altar! All smug and self-satisfied. So certain he'd win the title of Mr. Cool in his perfectly fitted best-man tux, polished leather lace-ups and crisp white shirt. Heck, he could even carry off wearing that silly dark-red bowtie. And with surprising flair.

So good looking. Nearly as loaded as that guy who'd founded Facebook. And the walking definition of "suave." Not that Bingley didn't know it, which made it all the more irritating.

Jane was pretty sure some singer in the Seventies had written a song about him called "You're So Vain." Just because Bingley hadn't been born then didn't mean it wasn't totally applicable.

She exhaled with a fierce puff, which she camouflaged by clearing her throat and smiling broadly when Beth sent her a concerned glance. Beth, looking relieved, smiled back and then turned her attention to her groom and the reverend. And they were off to the races.

In her head, Jane had made a list of all of the awkward moments she would have to politely endure this weekend before she would be free of Bingley for a while:

There had been the rehearsal dinner last night. *Check!* How she managed to sit at the same table with him for over two hours was a minor miracle. At least she got to catch up with Beth's parents—Charlotte and Lucas Bennet—who'd flown in for the wedding.

There was this morning's picture session with just the attendants and family members. *Check!* The photographer was a chatty dude who, thankfully, filled any silent moments with posing directions.

The ceremony itself. *Now in progress!*

Still to come were the remaining pictures of the bride, groom and wedding party all together. (She could only hope that the photographer hadn't run out of things to say.)

The reception. Although she'd have to dance with Bingley…ugh…she'd need a glass or two of wine beforehand, although that could be dangerous. Look at the trouble drinking had gotten her into at the engagement party?

And the morning-after breakfast. Hopefully, Bingley would be too tired to talk to her by then.

Certainly, for the sake of her best friend and her friend's new husband, she could fake her way through all of that, right?

Right.

When Reverend Elton presented the happy couple as "husband and wife," Will gave Beth an incredibly passionate kiss. The entire congregation erupted in cheers, and Jane sighed in happiness and, perhaps, just a touch of envy. Someday, maybe, her soul mate would find her, too. But, unlike how it'd been with Beth and Will, Jane doubted it would be a matter of a simple Love Match in her case.

In a different way, she'd been much more deceptive than her best friend had ever been. Beth had only lied about her name and a few other details on her online dating profile, but she'd always been, essentially, her true self. Jane's lies ran deeper and leaked into her everyday life. In public, she'd been careful to mask her true feelings about so many things behind a well-crafted wall of agreeableness and affability. People seemed to *like* her, but how could they possibly *know* her?

A few months ago, she'd been almost ready to open up to Bingley, but then she found out about his latest bet, and she realized how futile it all was. There wasn't a man on the planet that genuinely cared about getting to know her. Everyone wanted something, and if a guy didn't get it, he'd leave. She knew that firsthand.

Finally, the procession out of the church began and, this time, Jane had to walk back down the aisle with Bingley.

"Delightful ceremony," he pronounced loudly, insuring

that everyone nearby would hear, as he formally offered her his arm. But he looked at her as if he'd much rather promenade with a python.

"I agree," she said, smiling tightly and playing the part.

He cast an absolutely ecstatic grin at the friends and family in attendance as the two of them took their first steps toward the church's vestibule. "Only the receiving line and the final pictures," he hissed, his lips near her ear as if sharing a secret. "And then I can start getting drunk. I plan to be pretty buzzed before our *special* dance."

She leaned closer to him and hissed right back, "*So funny!* I was thinking *exactly* the same thing."

"Yeah? I remember the last time you got your hands on some champagne, Jane. Who are you gonna be making out with tonight?"

She gripped his arm perhaps a little more forcefully than necessary. "Not you."

He winced but didn't stop walking or faux grinning at the congregation. "Oh, I wasn't offering, sweetheart. I've already been burned once. I don't do second chances."

She gulped. To her ear, he sounded hurt, which both surprised her and pissed her off. He was acting like some innocent in the whole thing. Like he hadn't been trying to take advantage of her—one way or another. That he hadn't made a bet that involved her. Ha. She'd tear him apart limb by limb, this very second, in fact, if it wouldn't ruin her dress before the reception.

Beth and Will had stopped just up ahead of them and were getting ready to greet their guests in the receiving line. Before Jane pulled away from Bingley to dutifully take her place next to the bride, she gave the quote-unquote "best man" her parting shot. "I don't do second chances either," she informed him. "And, for the record, you might as well pay up Dustin and buy your own beer because there's no way you'll win your gamble with him. At least not with my help."

Jane had the satisfaction of seeing him freeze in his spot, a look of shock and confusion on his handsome face, as she turned her back to him.

Beth and Will, who hadn't heard the content of this conversation, nevertheless weren't completely oblivious to the weird vibe of tension whenever she and Bingley were nearby.

Her best friend kept glancing worriedly at her and, when there was a momentary breather between well-wishers, Beth asked, "Jane, is everything okay?"

Jane composed herself and tried to radiate tranquility. "Oh, yes. It's just…you know…an emotional day."

Beth squeezed her hand. "I know. Thank you. Thank you so, so much for being such a wonderful friend. I never could have been this happy without you there. You've always been so supportive."

And Jane knew that she would cheerfully deal with even Bingley and all of the discomfort of being around him in order not to disrupt the happiness of her sweet BFF.

Now that she'd told him off at last, he'd have to stay away from her, except when their attendant duties made interaction absolutely necessary. Seriously, how much more trouble could the guy cause in less than twenty-four hours, right?

Right.

**Learn more about Marilyn's books on her website:**
# www.marilynbrant.com

# ABOUT THE AUTHOR

Marilyn Brant has been told she writes with honesty, liveliness and wit (descriptors she's grown terribly fond of) about complex, intelligent women—like her friends—and their significant personal relationships. Although her favorite pursuits undoubtedly involve books, she proves she's not just a literary snob by confessing her lifelong fascination (read: obsession) with popular music, especially from the '70s and '80s, most flavors of ice cream, and a variety of sensuous body lotions/oils.

As a former teacher, library staff member, freelance magazine writer, and national book reviewer, Marilyn has spent much of her life lost in literature. She is the *New York Times* and *USA Today* bestselling and award-winning author of over twenty novels and novellas to date, and a lifetime member of the Jane Austen Society of North America. The Illinois Association of Teachers of English (IATE) selected her as their 2013 Author of the Year.

Her debut coming-of-age novel, *ACCORDING TO JANE* (Kensington, 2009), featuring the ghost of Jane Austen giving a young woman dating advice, won the Romance Writers of America's prestigious Golden Heart Award, the Aspen Gold, and the Booksellers' Best, and it was named one of the "Top 100 Romance Novels of All Time" by Buzzle.com. Her second novel, *FRIDAY MORNINGS AT NINE* (Kensington, 2010), was a Doubleday and Book-of-the-Month Club pick in women's fiction. *A SUMMER IN EUROPE* (Kensington, 2011) was featured in the Literary Guild and BOMC2, and it became a Top 20 Bestseller in Fiction and Literature for the Rhapsody Book Club. The Polish translation of the novel was released in June 2013.

She's also a #1 Kindle & #1 Nook bestseller, who

writes fun and flirty romantic comedies, like her stories in *THE SWEET TEMPTATIONS COLLECTION*, that involve sweet treats, unexpected love, and large doses of humor. *THE ROAD TO YOU*—a coming-of-age romantic mystery—was selected as one of the Top 20 Best Books of the Year (December 2013) by The Reading Frenzy. She also recently finished the "Mirabelle Harbor" romances. Look for the completed series: *TAKE A CHANCE ON ME, THE ONE THAT I WANT, YOU GIVE LOVE A BAD NAME, STRANGER ON THE SHORE, ONE NIGHT LOVE AFFAIR, COMING HOME,* and the bonus crossover novella, *GOING FOR IT.* And be sure to check out her short story, "When Life Imitates Art," in RWA's 2017 romantic anthology, *SECOND CHANCES.*

Marilyn currently lives in the Chicago suburbs with her family. When she isn't reading her friends' books or watching old movies, she's working on her next novel, eating chocolate indiscriminately, and hiding from the laundry.

Please visit her website: www.MarilynBrant.com.

If you enjoyed this novel by Marilyn Brant and would like to read more of her stories or be the first to find out about new book releases, special sales, and giveaways, be sure to visit her website (www.MarilynBrant.com) and sign up for her free newsletter.

Also, please consider leaving a review of this novel on your favorite book review site to let others know your thoughts on the story. Reviews help readers find great books!

www.ingramcontent.com/pod-product-compliance
Lightning Source LLC
Chambersburg PA
CBHW020401210626
46816CB00006BB/2072